Love Finds You

in

REVENGE
Ohio

Love Finds You

in

REVENGE
Ohio

BY LISA HARRIS

summerside
PRESS

Love Finds You in Revenge, Ohio
© 2009 by Lisa Harris

ISBN 978-1-934770-81-8

All scripture quotations are taken from the King James
Version of the Bible.

The town depicted in this book is a real place, but all
characters are fictional. Any resemblances to actual people
or events are purely coincidental.

Cover and Interior Design by Müllerhaus Publishing Group,
www.mullerhaus.net

Published by Summerside Press, Inc., 11024 Quebec Circle,
Bloomington, Minnesota 55438, www.summersidepress.com

Fall in love with Summerside.

Printed in the USA

Dedication

. . . .

To the One whose love for us is as high as the heavens are above
the earth, and who has removed our transgressions from
us as far as the east is from the west.

Acknowledgments

....

My wonderful crit buddies, Susan Page Davis, Darlene Franklin, Lynette Sowell, and Beth Goddard. I'd be lost without you.

Ellen Tarver, who's always willing to go the extra mile to make my story better.

And the incredible Summerside Press team, Rachel, Jason, and Susan, who are a joy to work with.

Special Thanks

·················

To Art and Kythrie and their precious three kids who spent
the day in Revenge, playing in the creek and roaming through
the cemetery so they could take photos of the area for my book.

"Bless the LORD, O my soul, and forget not all his benefits:
who forgiveth all thine iniquities; who healeth all thy diseases;
who redeemeth thy life from destruction; who crowneth thee
with lovingkindness and tender mercies; who satisfieth thy mouth
with good things; so that thy youth is renewed like the eagle's."

PSALM 103:2–5 KJV

WHILE THE QUAINT TOWN OF REVENGE IS LITTLE MORE
than a ghost town today, the former farming community is nestled
in southwestern Fairfield County where Clear Creek meets Middle
Fork Creek. Named after a competition between two shopkeepers, the
winner took his revenge and named the town…Revenge. The small
hamlet never had a booming population; for many years, the only major
business was the general store where local farmers could buy supplies.
At the time of my story, the Johnson Covered Bridge hadn't been built,
but today it's considered one of the country's historic bridges. Adding
to Revenge's image as a ghost town, rumor has it that a woman drowned
in Clear Creek during a thunderstorm and now haunts the bridge. While
I did take the liberty of adding to the small population for the sake of the
story, I hope you enjoy the flavor and history of the not-quite-forgotten
town of Revenge, Ohio.

Lisa Harris

Chapter One

....

Revenge, Ohio, 1884

The only thing worse than being a spinster is being a twice-jilted spinster. The notion struck Catherine Morgan like a spring tornado and brought with it a deluge of unwanted memories. It didn't matter that the implied words came from her well-meaning younger sister, Emily. Well-meaning or not, Catherine was tired of afternoons filled with tea and scones that consistently turned into an unrehearsed chorus of matchmaking schemes from one of her three sisters.

Corbin Hunter had been the first suitor to leave her with both a broken engagement and a broken heart. Technically, Robert Foster never proposed. Once he realized he'd be living under the same roof as all four of the Morgan sisters, he bolted. But she'd realized long ago that marrying either man would have been a mistake she'd have lived to regret. Any man unwilling to shoulder a parcel of responsibility in caring for her sisters wasn't worth the nest egg she'd hidden in the bottom of the sugar jar.

She bit into a sweet piece of molded chocolate to ease the sting and stared out across the tall prairie grasses framing the skyline to the west that eventually merged with the Appalachian forest to the east. A sticky breeze filtered across the wraparound porch of her sister's house and left her longing for the cooler days of springtime.

"I heard that the new sheriff is unattached." Emily poured herself another cup of iced tea from the cut glass pitcher made at her husband's shop. "And incredibly handsome."

Once again, Catherine ignored the implications and took a sip of her drink. She caught the smile on her sister's face that was as bright as it had been on her wedding day fourteen months ago. Catherine couldn't deny marriage had been good for her younger sister. As for herself, she'd long since given up on any expectations regarding her entry into the so-called blissful state of matrimony of which Emily constantly spoke. Not that Catherine felt she had any say in the matter. Last she looked, there were no eager suitors lining up outside her general store ready to profess their undying love to her.

She watched her sister absentmindedly reposition the ostrich plume that had fallen askew on her blue velvet hat. Porcelain skin, lightly blushed cheeks, dark lashes. Catherine didn't have to look into a mirror to know that her own complexion had one too many freckles, cheeks that were far too rosy, and a hat that…well… a sensible hat that only helped prove local gossip to be true.

Emily was the natural beauty of the family—the fashionable figure of the four Morgan sisters, with a husband who would do anything to please her, including his recent gamble at raising ostriches in order to supply his wife with an ample supply of feathers. Audrey, Emily's twin, was the creative one, and the youngest Morgan sister, Lily, was the adventurous sibling who longed for life outside their quaint Ohio town.

Catherine, on the other hand, had turned out to be the practical-minded, twice-jilted, oldest daughter who'd spent the last seven years holding the family together after the death of their mother. Not that almost twenty-five was old, she supposed, but a life that revolved around running the town of Revenge's general store left her with little time to pursue purely frivolous things. Such as securing a husband.

She ran her fingers across the plain brown taffeta of her dress and tried not to compare it to Emily's stylish sapphire colored gown. Her sister's brocade morning dress was everything hers wasn't. Added to that was the piercing reminder that Emily had been the one with the line of suitors outside the general store—until Grady O'Conner won her heart and hand in marriage and swept her away to his two-story home, nestled between wooded areas of Canadian hemlocks and oak trees and wide-open farmland on the outskirts of Revenge.

Catherine fiddled with the stitched edge of the white tea cloth in front of her. She couldn't remember the last time her appearance had turned a man's head. Somewhere during the course of raising her siblings, the soft ringlets that had once framed her heart-shaped face had been pulled into a tight bun for ease and her fancy dresses replaced with more practical versions.

All because of a promise made to her mother on her deathbed.

Ignoring the unwanted tears that laced her eyelashes, Catherine focused on the sprinkling of wildflowers dotting the landscape. Truth be told, it wasn't her mother's fault that Catherine preferred efficiency over strategies to catch a husband. Mother, with her fashionable, striped silk skirts and lavender perfume, had managed both.

Until Isaiah Morgan walked out on his wife and four daughters.

Catherine shifted in the padded porch chair. It was time for a new subject. "Did I tell you that I'm going to install a telephone switchboard at the store?"

"A telephone?" For the first time all afternoon, Emily's smile melted into a frown. "Why in the world would you want to do that?"

Catherine had already prepared her defense. "Think about when the baby comes. What if Grady is at the glass factory or out on the farm and you need the doctor?"

Emily waved her hand then placed it on her bulging stomach. "Grady's relying more and more on his employees and rarely leaves my side now. Do you actually think he'd leave me alone once the baby comes due?"

"If he has to go fetch the doctor, it will take twice the time. A telephone would save the trip into town."

"Fiddle." Emily snorted, her one unladylike habit. "I'm not the only critic who believes that the invention is nothing more than a craze that will disappear once the next fad comes along."

"Like ostrich feathers?"

"More like the Baldwin twin's stack of failed inventions."

Catherine couldn't help but laugh. Horace and Harold Baldwin had been a fixture in her store for as long as she could remember. When they weren't sparring over a game of chess beside the woodstove in the center of the store, they were busy inventing. But so far, their attempts to create the perfect liniment had only succeeded in producing a number of mysterious skin rashes.

"And as for my ostrich feathers," Emily continued. "At ten dollars apiece, I'd gamble on a dozen ostriches over the telephone any day." Her sister took a thin slice of caraway cake and set it on her plate. "You're far too serious, Catherine. Mark my words. The telephone will never become a practical necessity."

Catherine frowned. So it had been said, but she didn't believe it. And one simply couldn't compare Horace and Harold's Magic Tonic Water or Amazing Gum Turpentine Liniment to the modern communication miracle of the telephone. The hiss of a male ostrich jerked her attention to the nearby paddock. Popping a second bite-sized chocolate into her mouth—the one that was bound to add an extra inch to her slim figure—she ignored the mournful sound. Or at least tried to. Emily maintained that the mammoth birds were exceptionally docile creatures, but when it came to the eight-feet-tall and three-hundred-fifty-pound ostrich, Catherine had another opinion.

She saw a dozen intimidating birds with bulky bodies and pale, thin legs that ended in two toes. And lethal toes at that. The longest boasted a thick nail that served as a weapon when panicked. No. The heavy demand of a fashion rage would never have compelled her to invest in the wild birds. Black feathers and white plumes were simply not worth the monetary venture.

Her sister caught her gaze, the pale blue of her eyes sparkling in the late afternoon sun. "They're quite harmless, Catherine. I promise."

Three hundred fifty pounds of anything was never harmless.

Instead of arguing, Catherine simply reminded herself to be thankful for the sturdy wooden fence separating the porch of the main house and the herd. And, despite their ridiculous farming choice, Catherine couldn't argue with two important facts. Emily's husband was a decent, wealthy man who treated his wife well, and secondly, Catherine wasn't the one who had to live with Emily's experimental project that was bound to fail once winter arrived.

"I almost forgot." Emily clapped her hands and reached under her chair. "I have a present for you."

"A present?" Catherine caught sight of the neatly wrapped box with its red bow and quirked her left brow. "My birthday isn't until September."

"Exactly, and that hat will never make it that long."

"My hat?" Catherine touched the edge of the gray felt and felt a warm blush creep across her cheeks. She had no intention of admitting her inferior fashion choices. "There's nothing wrong with my hat."

"Perhaps not." Emily slid the lid off the box and pulled out a green velvet hat with three artistically placed ostrich plumes. "But look at this."

There was no denying that Emily had fabulous tastes when it came to clothes, a fact that suddenly made Catherine question why she'd always insisted that the store carry a sampling of the latest trends from the East but had, herself, always chosen the more sensible attire.

Emily handed her the stunning velvet accessory. "Try it on."

Catherine tugged on the silver hatpin at the base of her neck then set her gray cap on the table in front of her. She poked at one of the red berries that sat on top of it and frowned. Emily was right, of course. This hat didn't deserve to see the light of day.

In contrast, the green velvet shimmered in the afternoon sunlight. Even the dyed feathers matched the material perfectly. As she ran her hand across the fabric, she relished its smoothness. She placed it gingerly on her head.

"In the past two months, Audrey and I have sold a dozen of our hats. It's about time you had one of our originals." Emily smiled. "It looks beautiful on you."

Catherine glanced at her hazy reflection in one of the front window panes and laughed at the ridiculous comment. "You're the beautiful one. Remember?"

"All you need are a few new dresses to go with the hat, and you'll be the talk of the town."

Catherine's laugh stuck in her throat. "Who said I wanted to be the talk of the town?"

"You know what I mean." Emily floated around the table to adjust the hat. "You deserve more than ten-hour days at the general store and a pile of bookkeeping at night."

"I like bookkeeping." She was being obstinate and she knew it, but work had always come first. Just after her sisters.

"Catherine." Emily stepped back, her fists against her hips in protest. "It's what I've been trying to tell you for weeks. You need time off. Some fun."

Catherine reached for another sweet then pulled back her hand. Even chocolate couldn't compensate for the way she felt at the moment. Just because the chastisement might be legitimate didn't make it less painful to swallow. "I have my garden, fundraising projects for the church's mission society, and…"

She stopped mid-sentence. From Emily's expression, her sister wasn't impressed with her unending list of excuses. Maybe she was right. What would an updated wardrobe hurt? Or a bit more socializing at church functions and ladies teas, and less time worrying about the store and next month's orders.

Catherine sighed and tugged the hat an inch to the left. No. She knew Emily well enough to realize that her definition of fun translated into more than simply being more sociably inclined. It meant finding someone to court her, a short engagement, followed by a blissful marriage. She wasn't going to fall into the trap of even discussing suitors again.

A mournful roar came from the paddock. Catherine's temples began to pulse. "How does Grady put up with that?"

Emily slid back into her chair. "True love covers a multitude of sins."

Catherine couldn't help but smile. "I don't think the Good Book was referring to loving ostriches when that verse was written."

Emily's laughter flitted across the humid afternoon breeze. Love was blind, it seemed.

Sharing her husband's time with both a well-established glass factory and a dozen ostriches had never seemed to bother Emily. In fact, Catherine had been surprised at how involved her sister had become in the everyday workings of the experimental project even though it had been her idea. A project that further proved Grady's immense love for Emily in his agreeing to take a financial gamble on a herd of fair-weather birds not fit for the Ohio landscape. But whatever Catherine might think about the project, there was no denying Grady's eagerness to do anything to please his wife. Something Catherine had yet to experience when it came to men.

One of the farm boys approached them, stopping at the bottom of the porch stairs. He tipped his hat. "Sorry to disturb you, ma'am."

"That's all right, Tomas." Emily leaned forward in her chair. "What is it?"

"We've been cleaning out the paddocks and found eight new eggs. I was told you'd want to know."

Emily surprised Catherine by jumping up like an excited school child. Funny how the African bird had a mesmerizing effect on Emily, while Catherine, on the other hand, wanted to run the other way.

With her new hat in place, Catherine followed Emily and Tomas across the flat terrain, a good dozen steps behind. Her fears were irrational. She knew it. Grady had already assured her of the birds' docile temperament. To prove his point, he even rode one around the paddock until the brainless bird knocked him into the fence. Only once, he'd claimed, had he heard of an irate bird that had left a worker with a deep gash across his arm.

Catherine froze at the reminder. Once was all it took.

Emily stopped outside the gate, a look of anticipation written across her face. "Grady has come up with the most ingenious way to keep the eggs and young chicks warm, by adapting heating methods he uses at his glass shop."

They all knew that it was going to take a miracle for the young ostriches to survive Ohio's climate even with Grady's ingenious methods, but that fact obviously hadn't stopped Emily from convincing her husband to try.

Tomas entered the paddock and held up one of the eggs for Emily's inspection. Even from her position on the other end of the enclosure, Catherine was amazed at its size. The dull yellow egg was nearly six inches long.

A hissing sound broke through the relative quiet of the afternoon. A mere twenty feet from the farm boy, the male bird, left with the role of guarding the nest, stretched its head before shoving its wings upward. A glance at Tomas revealed that the boy wasn't paying attention to the bird. Was he new at the job, or simply taking for granted that the bird wouldn't harm him?

"Emily?" Catherine's voice cracked.

The ostrich took several paces backwards, his feathers ruffled. By the time Tomas noticed its movements, it was too late. The quick-moving bird ran forward then kicked, slicing Tomas across the shoulder. Blood oozed through his shirt. Emily screamed.

Catherine gathered her skirts and ran toward Emily, her heart pounding as she caught sight of the open gate beside her sister. The ostrich hissed again as it reached the opening. Emily had yet to move. Catherine quickened her pace but still wasn't close enough to intervene.

Someone shouted behind Emily. Catherine glanced up at the silhouette of a rider on horseback. The stranger jumped off the horse, his derby hat in his hand, and moved toward the ostrich. The bird jetted to the left, then back toward Emily. Catherine felt the air rush from her lungs, but she had no time to contemplate that the man standing between Emily and certain death was her once jilted beau—Corbin Hunter.

Chapter Two

. . . .

Catherine's pulse hammered in her throat. Six feet in front of her, Emily clung to the railing. The ostrich danced between her and Corbin as if trying to decide which of them would be the greater threat. The bird dodged to the right then stopped again. Catherine forced herself to remain still. Her fingernails bit into her palms. Another five seconds dragged out. Corbin walked slowly toward the ostrich and held out his hat. The bird hesitated, cocked his head, and then moved toward the hat.

Corbin continued to bridge the distance between him and the bird, while Catherine tried not to focus on Corbin's piercing gray eyes. Or his thick curly hair. Or the fact that he'd walked out on her all those years ago.

Catherine frowned. She had no idea why Corbin had returned to Revenge, but her heart told her it had nothing to do with her. The same way her heart once told her he was never coming back. Which was just as well as far as she was concerned.

Without a word, Corbin gripped the skin of the neck behind the bird's head and lowered it toward the ground. Tomas ripped off his bloodstained shirt and rushed to the other side of the ostrich.

"Are you all right?" Corbin spoke to the Tomas but kept his gaze on the ostrich.

"I'll live." Tomas started to slip the shirt over the bird's head, but it jerked backward.

Corbin gestured with his chin. "Grab the other wing. We've got to get him back into the paddock."

The men steadied the bird on each side then steered the bird toward the enclosure. A moan escaped the bird's throat. The creature jumped, yanking himself free from his captors. Emily screamed. Catherine held her breath and started praying as Tomas once again attempted to slip his shirt over the bird's head.

Another five seconds and it was over.

Catherine gulped a mouthful of air, rushed forward, and grasped Emily's arm. Her sister's normally rosy cheeks had paled to a pasty white. "Emily, are you all right?"

Emily's mouth opened, but no words came out.

"Emily?"

Her hands shook. "I…I think so."

Corbin latched the gate then turned toward Catherine as he set his hat back on his head. Beads of moisture dotted his tanned brow. "It's been a long time."

"Yes, it has." One more glance at his familiar face managed to confirm the unavoidable suspicions. Seven years had managed to completely erase all the feelings she'd once held for him. As they should have—because she was a different person today than at eighteen, when she'd been too young to understand the true meaning of sacrifice. She tightened her grip on her sister's arm and looked away. Right now her only concern was Emily. She had no time to stop and dwell on the complicated past that loomed between her and Corbin Hunter.

"Catherine, I…" Emily slipped toward the ground.

Catherine helped to hold her up, swaying under the extra weight.

Corbin caught Emily and lifted her into his arms.

"We've got to get her inside." Catherine raised the hem of her skirt and hurried toward the house. "Tomas, go find your mother. Have her bring some smelling salts and more hot tea, then make sure she takes care of your cut."

The heels of Catherine's high-buttoned shoes crunched against the pebbled ground as she hurried up the drive. The sun had already begun to dip toward the western skyline, casting gray shadows against a row of hemlock trees, while the rollicking yodel of a wren punctuated the late afternoon air.

Stumbling over a stone, Catherine glanced back at Emily's motionless body in Corbin's arms. If anything happened to her or the baby...

Two minutes later they had Emily settled on the sofa. Catherine waved the smelling salts beneath Emily's nose until her eyelids flickered open. "Are you all right?"

Emily struggled to get up.

Catherine pressed her hand against her shoulder. "Don't get up. Not yet. Just take some deep breaths."

"I...I couldn't breathe, then...then everything went black." Her sister sank against the rose-printed fabric of the sofa. "Last time I fainted was at a church picnic when Willie Barton stuck a bullfrog in my lunch box."

Color began to fill Emily's plump cheeks, and Catherine let out a sigh of relief. At least she hadn't lost her sense of humor.

Milena entered the room with a teapot and plate of cakes and set them on the parlor table beside them. Catherine poured a cup for Emily then made one for herself, thankful for something to do with her hands. It didn't matter that the room was stuffy or the tea scalding hot. She needed something to calm her nerves. That attacking ostrich belonged on some open African veldt. Not in Revenge, Ohio.

Corbin stood not three feet away, dangling his black hat between his fingers like a schoolboy forced to face the headmaster for unruly behavior. Catherine stopped the smirk that threatened to erupt across her lips. At least he was as uncomfortable in her presence as she was in his.

She nodded toward a mahogany armchair. "You can sit down. Milena makes the best cake in the county."

"Thank you." He folded his tall frame into the chair and sat back against the upholstered cushion.

She'd forgotten certain details over the years. The hairline scar above his left brow. The deep timbre of his voice. How his presence overtook the room... All things she had no desire to remember.

"Is there anything else I can do, Miss Morgan?" Milena asked.

"Yes." Catherine hesitated before shifting her gaze from Corbin to Milena's round figure. "Have you had time to see to Tomas's shoulder?"

"The gash is long, but not deep, ma'am. He'll be fine." Milena's brow creased. "I've always warned him that those birds would end up hurting someone someday."

Emily pressed her hand against her heart. "They're normally so docile. We've never had trouble from them before."

"She's right." Corbin spoke for the first time. "Ostriches, for the most part, are quiet and content creatures, but they can be a bit nervous. I have a feeling that when Tomas showed you ladies that egg, nature took over and the male was simply trying to defend his nest."

Catherine took a sip of her tea, burning the tip of her tongue. The pain, though, was overshadowed by her surprise. The Corbin she knew had been more at home behind a stack of books than a flock of oversize birds. "You sound as if you know a thing or two about ostriches."

His grin left a familiar dimple on his right cheek. "A few years back I worked on a couple ranches down in Texas—one where they raised ostriches—and managed to pick up a few things. Even rode as a drag rider in a cattle drive once."

Catherine had wondered from time to time what he was doing, imagining him as a banker or a doctor. The Corbin she'd known had always preferred schooling over farming and outdoor chores. She studied him now and tried to imagine him breathing dust for days on end and dealing with stray cattle. Apparently, he'd decided to trade in his more polished attire for denim blue jeans, white button-up shirt, and a shadowed jawline that gave him a rugged look.

Tomas stepped into the doorway wearing a clean shirt. "I must apologize, Mrs. O'Conner. All this was my fault. I never should have tried to impress you. The other workers told me you like the ostriches, and I thought…well…I thought wrong."

Emily shook her head, her hands wrapped around her cup. "What's done is done. Thankfully the bird is back in the paddock and no one was seriously injured."

Catherine wasn't willing to dismiss the incident without a few choice words of caution. "Next time, the outcome might not be quite so fortunate."

"I realize that, ma'am."

Footsteps pounded up the steps, and Grady O'Conner burst through the front door. "I heard there was an accident—"

"Everything's fine, Grady." Emily rose to greet her husband, tottered for a moment on the edge of the sofa, and then plopped back against the cushions. "I was out near the paddock and one of the ostriches got loose."

"Emily!" Grady rushed to his wife and knelt beside her. Though he was ten years older than Emily, it had been clear from the moment they met that she had lost her heart to the red-headed Irishman. And her sentiments had been just as quickly reciprocated. "You could have been killed."

"Tomas was cut on his shoulder, but Milena said it's not serious. It was this man who saved me, Mister—" Emily raked her silk fan in front of her face. "I'm sorry. In all the commotion I never got your name."

"Mr. Hunter. Corbin Hunter."

"Corbin Hunter. I remember you now." Emily grasped her husband's hand. "It's been so long, I didn't recognize you. If I remember correctly, you and Catherine—"

"It has been a long time." Realizing the direction her sister was headed, Catherine jumped into the conversation, determined to evade any flood of inquiries regarding their relationship. "I'm sure you don't remember much, Emily, as you were quite young when he moved away."

"Still, we owe you our deepest thanks, Mr. Hunter." Emily's husband took off his hat then reached out to shake Corbin's hand. "Name's Grady O'Conner. I was told that if you hadn't shown up when you did, my wife could have been seriously injured. I don't know how to thank you."

"There's no need. I'm simply glad I could help."

Tomas had vanished, but Milena still hovered in the doorway. "I am sorry for my son's actions, Mr. O'Conner."

"I will speak to the boy later." Grady tossed his hat onto an empty chair and melted into the settee beside Emily. "For now, I just want to ensure that my wife is going to be all right. Has one of the workers sent for the doctor?"

"I'm fine, Grady." Emily tried to sit forward again, but Grady stopped her.

"I intend to make sure, darling."

"It was nothing more than a fright that made my heart race—"

"Milena? Have someone fetch Dr. Morrilton." Grady obviously wasn't convinced. "I want him out here as soon as possible."

Milena nodded as she slipped from the room.

Emily's lower lip jutted out. "Catherine, please talk some sense into this man. He's prone to treat me like an invalid instead of a joyful mother-to-be."

Catherine set her half-empty teacup back on the tray and shook her head. "I learned many years ago never to interfere in the business of a married couple."

"A complete evasion of the subject, Catherine." Emily tugged on her husband's forearm. "I really am fine."

"Now, Emily, enough. We're neglecting our guest." He squeezed his wife's hand. "You've yet to tell us why you stopped by, Mr. Hunter."

Catherine leaned forward and caught the lemony scent of the cake. Any other afternoon she would have enjoyed another sampling of Milena's cooking, but today she was anxious to hear Corbin's response. She had a list of questions herself. The first one being what had brought Corbin Hunter back to Revenge?

Corbin stiffened in his chair. "I was on my way into town, but thought I'd stop by to see a friend who used to own this property. Lawrence Lowery."

Catherine caught Corbin's gaze. "Things have changed since you left. Mr. Lowery died four years ago."

* * *

Corbin stared into Catherine's pale blue eyes that had, years ago, set his heart to racing. But as much as he regretted what happened between them way back then, he hadn't come back for her. Once, he'd planned to stay in Revenge, marry Catherine, and live out his days working at the general store. But life had pushed him in another direction and now too much time had passed between the moment he'd left and today.

He swallowed the lump of pain and focused instead on the memory of his old friend. "I'm sorry to hear Mr. Lowery passed away. He was a good man."

"Yes, he was," Mr. O'Conner said. "Came down with a case of cholera. We lost several from town and the surrounding area during that time."

Corbin expected to find the small town changed. Revenge was still no larger than most of the small towns dotting the Ohio landscape, but that didn't take away the sting of reality. He'd been back a mere thirty minutes and already discovered Lawrence Lowery had passed away—and the woman Corbin had once given his heart to no longer looked at him with longing in her eyes.

He let out a slow breath. Not that he'd expected Catherine Morgan to have pined for him. More than likely she had a husband and a passel of children by now, which was perfectly fine by him.

Corbin pressed his hands against his thighs and stood. "I'd best be going if I'm to make my appointment in town."

"How long will you be staying in Revenge?" Mr. O'Conner asked.

"Only temporarily." Corbin hesitated at revealing the truth, but the whole town would know by noon tomorrow. "I was called to fill in for Sheriff Lansing until he recovers from his accident."

"So you're our new sheriff." The color had returned to Emily's cheeks. It was hard to believe that the Emily Morgan he remembered with pigtails and freckles had become a wife and expectant mother.

"As I said, just temporarily." He rotated the brim of his hat between his fingers, trying to gauge Catherine's reaction.

Mr. O'Conner slipped his arm around his wife's shoulder. "I'm sure you've heard of the gang robbing banks through the surrounding counties."

"That's partly why I'm here." Corbin stood, ready to leave. "The governor wants to make sure each town is adequately prepared. We will catch them."

Mrs. O'Conner leaned against her husband. "Mr. Hunter, before you leave, you must agree to join us here tomorrow night at seven. We're celebrating the birthday of our sister Audrey's fiancé, Harrison Tucker."

The name shot through Corbin like a bullet from a Colt .45.

"Harrison Tucker?"

"You sound as if you know him," Mr. O'Conner said.

Corbin swallowed hard. He'd heard of him all right. If his informant was correct, Harrison Tucker was the man who had murdered his father.

Chapter Three

....

Catherine locked the front door of the general store then flipped the CLOSED sign, thankful Mrs. McBride had finally left. That woman was impossible. After sorting through the store's entire stock of notions, she had the nerve to leave, saying she would find what she wanted the next time she was in Lancaster. Which meant Catherine would have to spend her afternoon reorganizing the woman's handiwork.

Halfway toward the back of the store, Catherine stopped to run her hand across the smooth olive green fabric of one of the dresses she had for sale. She'd learned quickly that keeping a limited stock of fashionable attire and fine ladies' accessories paid off. Even those who couldn't afford the lavish designs still often chose to shop at Morgan's General Store over Ed Harper's Dry Goods & Grocer just so they could take a peek at the latest fashions from back East. In the end, they more often than not walked out the front door with a parcel of sundry items, which suited Catherine just fine.

She rubbed the silk between her fingers. The design was stunning with its princess lines and slimming panels. She'd already sold a similar one to Priscilla Masters, who no doubt would flaunt her recent purchase at the church meeting come Sunday.

Catherine frowned and reminded herself that storing up treasures in heaven was far more valuable than a closet full of the latest fashions, even if the divine cache didn't come with long suede gloves and silk stockings. Besides, since when did she start worrying about things as shallow as evening dresses and dinner costumes?

Since Corbin Hunter walked back into town.

Catherine's sigh depleted her lungs of air at the thought of him seeing her without a husband, or even a viable suitor. Not that there was an ounce of shame in the fact that she'd never married. Better to have stayed single than to have married the wrong man. And besides, for all she knew, Corbin had a wife and children back home— wherever that was.

Brushing the material with the back of her hand, she let out an unladylike *humph*. Tonight was Harrison's birthday party and the beige garment she'd pulled from the wooden wardrobe earlier today suddenly seemed as exciting as P.T. Barnum's traveling circus without its extraordinary exhibitions. Of course, by tomorrow morning no one would remember what she'd worn to the party. Instead, they would return home with stomachs full of the hors d'oeuvres Milena had spent the past week preparing. A fancy dress from back East paired with a dozen fashionable ostrich feathers could never smooth over her and Corbin's turbulent past.

She hesitated before leaving the storefront, her lips pursed. Emily was right. Her tastes were old-fashioned and outdated. Didn't being a spinster prove it?

"You should wear that dress tonight. It would look perfect with your new hat."

Catherine spun around. Her youngest sister Lily stood in the back doorway with a lopsided grin on her round face. Lily Morgan's dark brown eyes sparkled in the reflection of the dipping sun that flooded through the store windows. At seventeen, Catherine's youngest sister yearned to see the world beyond the small town of Revenge. So far,

family, and perhaps John Guild, her current beau, had stopped her
from leaving. For now, anyway.

Catherine turned away from the dress. "I couldn't justify such
an extravagance for myself. Besides, it's far too fancy for a simple
birthday party." She cleared her throat, ready for a change of subject.
Two sisters reminding her of her status in life in as many days were
enough. "Is John coming to pick you up for the party?"

A pink blush drifted across her little sister's high cheekbones.
"He'll be here at half past six in his buggy. You're welcome to ride
with us if you'd like."

"I would, thank you."

Catherine turned back to the dress and studied the detail in the
oriental lace. In truth, it was exquisite. She lifted layers of fabric on
the skirt then watched them flutter back into place. The dress was
her size; the color perfect. With a few wisps of hair framing her face,
she could soften her normally severe style. Corbin would be forced
to take note that not only was she a successful businesswoman but a
charming and fashionable lady as well. Not that it truly mattered what
he thought.

She bit her lower lip and strutted away from the dress. Nor did
it matter that Corbin would be at the party tonight. All his presence
would manage to do was dredge up old memories she'd prefer to
forget. He'd once whispered his undying love for her beneath the
flowering passion vine in the garden. A month later, he'd left her heart
to dry up like the purple blooms at the end of summer. No. That part
of her life was over. Obviously God had other plans in store for her
when He took their mama and left her with three younger siblings
in her care, leaving no time for dreams of marriage and a family.

Not that she blamed God. At least not most of the time.

Hurrying into her bedroom, she shoved aside any remains of self-pity and pulled the practical dress up from the bed. She held it up against her chest and let the skirt fall stiffly to her feet. The green velvet hat Emily had made for her lay cockeyed on her dressing table. The color would be enough to add a touch of festivity to the dull dress for tonight's party.

But instead of pulling on the dress, she paused to study her reflection in the beveled mirror. Rosy cheeks, with a sprinkling of freckles, looked back at her. She glanced at the wardrobe out of the corner of her eye. Her choice of what to wear was limited, a fact she'd never seriously stopped to consider before. It had made life simple. Five practical dresses for working in the store, and two with simple ribbon trim for church meetings and special occasions. She'd never needed more.

Her eyes squeezed shut. She could picture the green silk dress with ecru oriental lace at the bottom of each sleeve. What was she hoping for? The unlikely possibility that Corbin would apologize for walking out on her when she had needed him most?

She swallowed hard. The whole idea was ridiculous. But still… she tossed the dress onto the bed. Her neck pulsed. Maybe Emily was right. Maybe she did deserve more than working at the store from dawn until dusk, serving customers who didn't think twice about taking their business to a bigger city or buying from a mail-order catalog. She scurried toward the storefront, her head held high. Her decision had nothing to do with the return of a former suitor.

Catherine Morgan was about to become the talk of the town.

* * *

Corbin crinkled the folded paper inside his pocket. He stood in the corner of Grady and Emily O'Conner's parlor, studying the profile of the man whose features resembled the sketch on the wanted poster he held. Harrison Tucker. It had to be him. A despicable con man who was nothing more than a bank robber and murderer, whose stories of the life in the Alaskan gold fields had been noted from New York to Kentucky to be taller than Ohio's tallgrass prairies.

A surge of hatred ripped through his chest. As much as he longed to drag the man to the hanging post himself, he knew he couldn't let emotions take over the dynamics of his job. He first had to prove this, indeed, was the man wanted in half a dozen states.

Tucker's smooth voice held his audience's attention with stories of Joe Juneau's dramatic luck in finding gold in Alaska's treacherous terrain. Even his slight limp seemed to simply add to the persona the man had created. Corbin rolled the paper into a tight wad and licked his lips. The more he listened to Harrison Tucker the more convinced he was that his suspicions were correct. Catherine's future brother-in-law might be charming to the ladies, but Corbin was certain there was nothing behind his honey-coated words.

Harrison, dressed in an immaculately tailored shirt and jacket, paused for emphasis, adding gestures as he animated his voice then leaned toward his audience.

Emily O'Conner walked toward Corbin, distracting him with a plate full of rich-smelling food in one hand and a glass of lemonade in the other. With motherhood around the corner, her face glowed.

"I won't have it said that one of my honored guests went home hungry."

Corbin took the offered plate and smiled. "You won't hear me complaining. Thank you, Mrs. O'Conner."

"I'm the one who should be thanking you again, Mr. Hunter, for your daring rescue yesterday. I now have a greater respect for the ostrich—and for you, of course."

"I was simply grateful I was there, Mrs. O'Conner."

Corbin's mouth watered as he bit into a slice of savory pie. Harrison's voice continued to rise and fall in dramatic measure. One of the women raised her finger to her lips in revulsion at the mention of a brutal fight over five dollars in gold that had left one man dead and another maimed for life.

Mrs. O'Conner nodded toward the narrator. "Harrison's quite the storyteller."

"Not too violent for the ladies?"

Mrs. O'Conner's full lips widened into a grin. "Ah. You don't give us enough credit, Mr. Hunter. Dime novels were a forbidden entity growing up, so Harrison Tucker's stories of Juneau and the quest for gold keep the women sitting on the edges of their settee. We love every minute of it." Her blue eyes sparkled. "As you can imagine, it didn't take long for him to weave his way into the hearts of not only the town folks, but in particular, the heart of my twin sister, Audrey."

He worked to keep his emotions in check. "I have to admit that even I was enjoying the tale while waiting for—"

"Catherine?"

"Catherine? N–no." Corbin floundered with his words, surprised at the woman's forwardness. Seeing Catherine again was inevitable, but he certainly hadn't been waiting for her. "Though I assume she's coming?"

"Of course." Mrs. O'Conner glanced toward the door. "I expect her to arrive any minute."

"With her husband, I assume." He took a sip of the ice-cold drink. "I didn't really get a chance to talk with her yesterday, and it's been so long since I've seen her."

"Husband?" Mrs. O'Conner shook her head. "I assumed you knew. Catherine never married."

Corbin gulped down the news along with the lemonade, hoping Mrs. O'Conner didn't catch his startled reaction. He had once loved Catherine. How could such a striking woman fail to capture the heart of another suitor after all these years?

Because you walked out on her and broke her heart.

The unwelcome notion shook him to his very foundation, because Catherine had been as much to blame for the termination of their engagement as he had been. And he certainly wasn't responsible for any unhappiness she had accumulated over the years. He struggled to grasp hold of his errant thoughts. No. Such thinking was arrogant and egotistical. After all this time, he had no doubts that Catherine Morgan had completely forgotten him and their intentions to marry.

He glanced at Mrs. O'Conner, who appeared to want a response from him. "I'm sorry. I'm just…surprised. I assumed she'd be married with a passel of children lined up behind her."

"After our mother died, she took care of us. I suppose I've always felt a bit guilty over the fact that she's poured all her energy into the three of us, but Catherine was always stubborn. Maybe all that will change soon, though. With Audrey's nuptials close at hand, Lily will soon follow. Then maybe Catherine will feel free to pursue her own dreams."

The massive front wooden door swung open, stopping their conversation. A handsome young couple walked through the front door, followed by Catherine. Corbin felt his breath catch. The hair on the back of his neck stood up. Yesterday the changes he'd noted in her had been evident. He expected her to have aged, but the years that had separated them had been further emphasized by her homely dress and the way she'd pulled her hair into a severe bun. Somewhere over the years, she'd lost the smooth curls that had framed her face, as well as the carefree smile she'd once reserved for him.

Tonight, though, Catherine Morgan seemed transformed back to the girl he remembered. Not only was her dress fashionable, a softness had returned to her face beneath a fringe of bangs. Her gaze met his, and his heart trembled. Her long lashes fluttered shut for an instant, and he couldn't read her expression. Regret? Affection? No, certainly none of those things, but he hated the fact that he could no longer tell.

He took a step back toward the ceiling-high stone fireplace that lay dormant because of the warm summer air and tried to stop the guilt—and resentment—from resurfacing as she glided toward him. Maybe he shouldn't have left Revenge when Catherine had needed him most, but what other choice had there been?

Corbin took in a raspy breath and forced himself to remember why he'd returned to Revenge. He would find out the truth about Harrison Tucker even if it meant hurting the woman he once loved. There was simply too much at stake.

* * *

Catherine caught Corbin Hunter's gaze and raised her chin. The past few years had erased the boyish features and added not only broader shoulders, but also an air of confidence. She glanced down at the silky olive green fabric and decided Emily had a valid point. There was something about wearing a new dress and new hat that amplified her level of confidence.

Her smile widened. "It's good to see you again, Mr. Hunter."

"It's good to see you again as well, Miss Morgan." He licked his lips and balanced a plate of food in one hand, lemonade in the other. "You look…lovely tonight."

Emily studied her new outfit. "Catherine, your dress is stunning. You know I had my eye on it."

"It is beautiful, isn't it? I simply couldn't resist it." Catherine's laugher filled the room as she turned back to Corbin. "Did Emily introduce you to some of the guests? I'm assuming you haven't met Mr. Tucker yet."

"Not yet." Corbin shook his head. "He seems to be quite the storyteller."

Catherine glanced at the small crowd. Audrey stood beside her fiancé, her eyes wide with interest as he told a tale she'd more than likely heard a dozen times already.

Corbin cleared his throat. "If you will excuse me. I believe I'll go speak to your husband, Mrs. O'Conner."

"Please. I'm sure he'd enjoy talking with you."

Catherine opened her mouth, but nothing came out. Surely he wouldn't just leave her after barely more than a passing conversation. After all, they had once been engaged. She deserved more than the brush-off he was giving her.

He smiled at her. "Until we meet again, ladies."

Catherine stared in disbelief. Of all the nerve…Corbin Hunter gave her a parting nod then walked away.

Chapter Four

....

Corbin felt Catherine's piercing gaze bore into the back of his head as he strode across the room to where Mr. O'Conner stood. Once he'd dreamed about the day Catherine would become his wife, but seven years had apparently been enough time to snuff out any lingering desires he'd once held toward her. He might have even once memorized the subtle smile that reached her eyes, the shade of her honey-colored hair, and even the familiar tilt of her determined chin. They were all traits that had—at one time—affected him more than he cared to admit. But no more. Especially in light of their last conversation...and the events of the day he left Revenge.

Still unable to stop himself, he turned slightly and caught the confusion registered in her eyes. He shouldn't have been so abrupt. But while the last thing he wanted to do was offend her, Catherine wasn't a part of his plan in returning to Revenge. And if his presence was going to be a problem, his only option was to avoid her.

As one of the few bachelors in his last hometown, he was used to the single women vying for his attention while the older ladies worked on their matchmaking skills. He, on the other hand, had ignored their schemes and buried himself in his work. Of course, no one had yet to capture his attention the way Catherine once had. Which was fine as far as he was concerned. He was certainly better off without the likes of Catherine Morgan in his life.

He pushed away the lingering scent of her perfume, and the

memories it brought with it, and approached O'Conner. Even if he
had once loved Catherine—as much as a young man with no true
experience in the world could love a woman—there was no need to
prolong the awkwardness between them. Once he finished his job,
he planned to leave this town for good.

Corbin shook his host's outstretched hand.

The corners of O'Conner's lips formed a half-smile. "Don't let her
fool you, Mr. Hunter."

"Excuse me." Corbin couldn't help but take another quick look
at Catherine.

Mr. O'Conner nodded in the direction of his wife and sister-in-
law, but Corbin quickly turned back to the older man, pretending he
didn't notice the inconspicuous stares behind the fluttering of dark
lashes. "I don't remember the last time I saw Emily's sister so gussied
up. New dress, new hat…"

"New hat?" Corbin shook his head. "I don't understand."

O'Conner leaned against the carved mantelpiece. "Normally,
Catherine spends most of her time behind the counter of her store,
dealing with customers and bookkeeping. Can't say that I've ever
noticed her taking time for such feminine wiles. Unlike my wife, all
Catherine seems to need is a handful of practical dresses for her work
and Sunday meetings." His smile broadened. "At least until tonight."

"Tonight?" Corbin lowered his voice to just above a whisper.
"Are you implying she did all this for…for me?"

O'Conner chuckled. "The way I figure it, an old beau shows up
in town that Catherine never quite got over. Now, I'm not sure if the
idea was hers alone or if her three meddlesome sisters had something
to do with it, but somewhere during the past twenty-four hours, she

decided to make quite a transformation. If you were to ask me, she's actually quite lovely."

Corbin felt the heat rise along the back of his neck despite the cool breeze from the open window. Lovely, charming, intelligent… But this was Catherine. Lovely or not, he'd already learned his lesson.

O'Conner nudged him with his elbow. "Don't worry. My wife didn't give any details of your past relationship with Catherine, but—"

"Good." Corbin cringed at his own abruptness, but he couldn't help it. Small towns meant inflated rumors, something he intended to squelch before they even started. His past with Catherine was not a subject he wanted resurrected. For both their sakes. "It was a long time ago. People change."

"You're right, and I didn't mean to offend you."

"No. I'm the one who's sorry. It's just that…"

Corbin bit his tongue. Despite his own words of caution, it was all he could do to stop his curiosity from asking the barrage of questions that plagued him regarding Catherine. Why hadn't she married? Because she'd never really gotten over him? Or had she forgotten the day he left Revenge, leaving a piece of his heart behind?

Of course she'd put him behind her. O'Conner might be right in the fact that Catherine spent most of her time running her store, but there was nothing wrong with a woman who was also a capable business owner. From what he could see, she'd done quite well. And most importantly, she had forgotten him and any thoughts of their relationship years ago. Which of course she should have. There were women who didn't need a husband and family for fulfillment. Catherine was obviously one of them.

Corbin cleared his throat and turned back to O'Conner. "The truth is, my reasons to return to Revenge had nothing to do with Miss Morgan."

"I suppose I assumed she was at least part of the reason for your return."

Corbin frowned. "Yesterday you mentioned the gang that's robbing banks through the surrounding counties. I specifically asked the governor to be involved in the attempt to capture the men and take them into custody."

"Sounds rather personal."

"It is." Corbin's jaw tensed. "And my new job as sheriff of this town gives me the perfect opportunity to track down what the authorities are now calling the Masked Gang."

The rustling of ladies' skirts swished behind them as Mrs. O'Conner and Catherine moved to listen to yet another one of Harrison Tucker's stories. Her laugh rang out across the room, a bit more boisterous than he remembered. Of course, he really didn't know her anymore.

He focused his attention back on his host. "Mr. O'Conner, I've been gone so long, there are quite a few new faces for me. I was wondering if you could tell me about your guests."

"Certainly. Where would you like to start?"

His gaze swept past Catherine to the dark-haired man who held her attention. "How about Harrison Tucker."

* * *

Corbin Hunter was no different than her father, the man who walked out on her mother. And just like her father, Corbin had made it perfectly clear that he no longer harbored any feelings toward her. Nor remorse over walking out on her. Which was fine with her.

Catherine took another small bite of Milena's cheesecake, a treat she normally savored. Tonight it was as hard to swallow as another one of Harrison's stories. Despite the fact that she was quite certain Audrey's charming fiancé was spinning yet another tall tale of adventure in the Alaskan gold mines, she'd managed to smile and laugh with the other women at the appropriate pauses as if his story was the most amusing thing she'd heard of since steerable roller skates. She'd much rather be sitting in the backroom of her store finishing up the monthly accounts. At least figures didn't lie. Nor did they walk out on her in the middle of a conversation.

She glanced down and frowned at her new dress, with its ecru oriental lace that had depleted a good portion of her savings. Her sisters had been completely out of line to encourage her to believe she could actually turn the head of a possible suitor because she happened to be fashionably attired. Watching Corbin...Mr. Hunter... interact with Emily's husband and the other guests tonight might make her wonder—if only for a brief moment—what would have happened if things had turned out differently. If he'd never left Revenge. But too much time had passed for second chances. She'd accepted that fact years ago.

Catherine took another small bite of the cake from the glass dessert plate. Who said she needed a man in her life anyway? Being a spinster— even one who'd been twice jilted—was no cause to be ashamed. She'd taken what life had handed her, raised her sisters on her own, and turned a once floundering business into a success. She had her family, her church work, and Morgan's General Store. Life was good. Something many people only dreamed about. She took another veiled peek across the room at Corbin, who had been joined by two of the local farmers. No, memories of Sunday afternoon walks, church picnics, the day he proposed were better left kept where she'd buried them years ago.

She glanced across the room at Philip Rutherford and smiled. Now there was a man who knew how to treat a woman. While he'd never asked permission to court her, he'd implied his interest on several occasions. Perhaps it was time to consider the possibility.

"Catherine?"

Catherine startled at Lily's voice.

"Are you all right?" Lily rested her hand on Catherine's forearm. "You've been quiet tonight."

"Of course. I just…"

Just what? She looked down at the empty plate she now held. Emily's living room was almost empty as well. Apparently, while she was lost in a past she'd intended to forget, she'd missed Harrison's latest narrative, and the departure of the majority of the guests.

"What time is it?"

"Just past nine," Lily told her. "Are you ready to leave? John went to get the buggy."

"Already? Yes, I…" Catherine set the plate down on the table Emily had decorated with fresh flowers and candles, the wicks now burnt down to short nubs. "I didn't realize it was so late."

"The sheriff's ride left early, so I offered him a ride back into town. I hope that's all right with you." Lily grabbed Catherine by the hand and pulled her toward the padded bench where they had laid their shawls and gloves. "If I didn't already have my heart set on John, I might just be having second thoughts."

"Really, Lily, you should be ashamed of yourself. For one, Mr. Hunter—"

"Sheriff Hunter."

"Sheriff Hunter is far too old for you, and two, you know nothing about him other than the fact that he's—"

"Handsome, intelligent, and witty?" Lily grinned. "Exactly my point. I'm surprised he's not working in some big city like Boston or New York. He's bound to be bored to death in this town."

"Really, Lily." Her sister's habit of finishing other people's sentences could be quite exasperating.

Lily leaned forward as she slid on her gloves. "Don't tell me you haven't seen the way he looked at you all night from across the room."

"Looked at me? If I didn't know better, I'd think you were trying to play matchmaker, a game I thought I'd made perfectly clear I wasn't going to play."

"And why not?" Audrey appeared out of nowhere beside Catherine, her eyes bright with a hint of mischief. "There's nothing wrong with helping to fan a few dimming sparks of romance along, now is there? With a little encouragement from your side, I can guarantee that Sheriff Hunter will come calling on the prettiest storekeeper in town. I know a man who's interested when I see it."

"Audrey!" More than likely his expression was due to indigestion. Milena's food always was a bit too rich for some people.

Lily nodded knowingly to Audrey. "And if you ask me, the sheriff wasn't the only one who couldn't keep his eyes from straying across the room tonight. Catherine seemed to spend the entire evening daydreaming."

Audrey nodded.

"Lily…Audrey! Why I certainly did no such thing."

"Really?" Audrey asked. "So you're telling me that even after all these years, you have no feelings whatsoever for the man who once stole your heart."

Before ripping it in two.

"None, whatsoever." Catherine's jaw tensed and she made her hand into a fist. "I'll aim a sockdolager at his upper lip before ever agreeing to let him court me again."

"Why Catherine Morgan." Audrey swung her shawl across her shoulders and shook her head. "I do believe you protest far too much. And besides that, you ought to be ashamed of yourself for talking that way about a perfectly fine gentleman."

The room suddenly became far too hot and stuffy. Catherine glanced across the large living room. Emily was saying good-bye to the last of her guests, and thankfully, there was no sign of Corbin.

Catherine grabbed her lace shawl from the table. "Sheriff Hunter might be a fine—and handsome—gentleman. And we might have once held…feelings for each other. But none of that holds true anymore."

"It's all perfectly clear to me." Audrey linked her arm with Catherine's. "You still hold a burning flame for him, but you're too stubborn to admit it."

"Why I never…"

Catherine pulled away from her sister and waltzed out the front door without even stopping to tell Emily thank you. She'd apologize later for her rudeness, but the last thing she'd ever do was admit that Audrey was right.

Because she wasn't.

Her sisters knew nothing about what had transpired between them the last time she'd seen Corbin Hunter, nor the fact that her injured pride would never allow her to let a man like him back into her life.

Catherine fled toward the buggy while trying to hold back the stream of tears threatening to spill. Seeing Corbin again had dashed—for a second time—every hope and dream she'd carried as a young girl. Plans of marriage, children, and protection had vanished with the early morning mist the day he'd left. And she'd been thrust into mothering her sisters while Corbin had gone on with life without her.

She stopped short at the edge of the buggy. Her lips parted. He stood there, hands in his pockets, head cocked to the side, looking just as uncomfortable as she felt. But despite what her sisters claimed, she knew that Corbin no longer harbored a spark of interest in the town spinster.

"Mr. Hunter," she began, "I hope you enjoyed the party."

"I did, thank you." Corbin shifted his weight. "And I hope you don't mind sharing the buggy with me. Your sister was rather insistent that it wasn't a problem. I hitched a ride here with the Parkers, but they had to leave early."

"So she said." Catherine prayed she'd be able to tame her tongue, as the Good Book required, the next time she saw Lily, but at the moment she wasn't sure who she desired most to give a tongue-lashing to—Corbin Hunter, for daring to walk back into her life and turn her orderly world upside down, or her interfering sisters for trying to make her believe that they could pick up where they left off.

"Are you cold?" he asked. "I could give you my jacket."

Catherine's gaze dropped to the ground. She tried counting pebbles beneath the light of the full moon as a distraction from his gray eyes, which seemed to penetrate all the way through her. "I'm quite warm actually, Mr. Hunter. Thank you."

The deep laugh that followed sounded forced. "Do you really think that such formalities are necessary between us? We were, at one time…engaged to be married. And if I'm to be living here again, even though temporarily, it seems as if we can at least be cordial toward each other without feeling so uncomfortable."

Soft laughter distracted Catherine momentarily. John had returned inside and was now escorting Lily to the buggy. They strolled arm-in-arm, the way Corbin once escorted her to various social events. She remembered clearly the whispered words, stolen touches…

Catherine's face flushed. "I agree, as we are now older and wiser, we should be able to live in the same town without a wall of awkwardness between us. But as for formalities…Mr. Hunter…yes, I believe they are necessary."

She turned away from him again, wishing her words hadn't come out as cold as they had. That hadn't been her intent. Far from it. But she had every intention of guarding her heart, something she couldn't well do if she were to do something as intimate as call him by his first name.

* * *

Corbin felt his lungs press against the walls of his chest. He reprimanded himself for letting the woman sitting beside him affect

him, but a buried sea of resentment flooded through him in fresh
surges. He'd planned to spend the evening gathering information,
primarily on Hamilton Tucker, and instead he'd become distracted
with—he glanced over at Catherine with her fancy hat and silk dress—
with her. The problem was that there were far more serious issues at
hand. If Mr. Tucker was the man Corbin thought he was, it was only a
matter of time until he'd be able to apprehend him. O'Conner had given
him little useful information other than the fact that Harrison was
new to town and that he'd quickly woven his way into the hearts of the
town—especially the heart of Audrey Morgan. Within three months
of his arrival, he'd asked for Audrey's hand in marriage, and no one
seemed to question that they might not really know who the man was.

Which left Corbin facing the undeniable reality that if his
instincts were true, Audrey's heart would be broken. Something he
knew Catherine would never forgive him for. But he also knew that
it was something he couldn't avoid. Duty had to come first. That had
been something Catherine herself had taught him.

He watched her from the corner of his eye and had to smile
despite the awkwardness of the situation. She looked as if she were
heading to an execution, not simply driving home from a party on
a lovely summer evening. She stared straight ahead, shoulders taut,
hands clasped in front of her. Had the night he'd left Revenge affected
her that much? He might not be able to forget that night, but surely
it was possible for them to live in the same town without continual
skirmishing between them.

He cleared his throat, determined to break the silence between
them that hung heavier than the approaching storm clouds. "I was
surprised to hear that you never married."

He saw her eyes widen in the silvery glow of the moon and instantly regretted his words. Apparently he wasn't any more sensitive to a woman's needs than he had been all those years ago.

He combed his fingers through his hair. "I'm sorry…it's certainly none of my business."

"No, it's not." Her fingers tightened against the wad of fabric they clutched in her lap. "Though I suppose, unlike my sisters, I've never found the one person I wanted to share my life with."

Corbin felt the well-placed jab prick his heart.

"What of you?" she continued. "Isn't there a wife and family waiting for you to return when you're finished with this job?"

"I, too, have yet to find that one person." Not that he'd been consciously looking. He'd spent his life dodging the calculated plans of matchmakers and had eaten enough homemade pies and cakes— from both eligible young women and widows whose goal it was to trap him into the confines of matrimony—to feed an army.

He cleared his throat. "All I've got waiting for me back home is a dog named Badger."

The rest of the trip toward town was silent except for John and Lily's continued whispers from the front of the buggy that only seemed to add to the awkwardness in the back seat. Finally, Morgan's General Store came into view, bringing with it an inaudible sigh of relief to Corbin's lips.

Except that there was one more thing he needed to say to her. "I'm not sure how to say this, but I've always wanted to apologize for that day. The situation was—"

Her hand brushed his sleeve, sending a flood of memories through him, despite the pleading in her eyes. "Please, don't. Sometimes the past is better off forgotten."

He nodded. If she didn't want to talk about it, that was fine with him. Besides, he'd already discovered she was right. He jumped to the ground to help her down. She took his hand but avoided his gaze as she alighted from the vehicle, stumbling on the last step.

She quickly found her balance. "Good night, Mr. Hunter."

"Good night, Miss Morgan." He watched her walk away, his resolve to forget the past strengthened. The next time he encountered her, he'd be a perfect gentleman. Because he hadn't returned home for Catherine Morgan. He'd come here for one reason and one reason only. Revenge.

Chapter Five

Catherine stood inside the darkened store, took a deep breath, and filled her senses with the rich aroma of coffee and molasses. With her hands at her sides, she clutched the smooth fabric of the new dress. Part of her longed to recapture the look Corbin's eyes had held when he'd first seen her tonight—if only to relive the satisfaction it had brought. She'd seen the admiration briefly reflected in his gaze, until he'd turned around and walked away.

Which meant that the other part of her wanted to set the frivolous dress back on the store rack and retrieve the portion of her nest egg she'd foolishly squandered. She would do it, if it weren't for the fact that Mrs. McBride and the other ladies who'd attended tonight's party would notice its reappearance.

Moonlight spilled into the front of the store, reminding her she'd forgotten to pull down the shade that covered the front window. Stopping before the windowpanes, she stared down the deserted boardwalk. The store faced the brick facade of the hotel across the street that offered five rooms and some of Mrs. Peck's homemade food for a decent price. Beside it sat the doctor's office, then the sheriff's...

The sheriff's office.

Her stomach lurched as a light illuminated its front window. The silhouette of a figure stood within its wooden frame, broad shoulders, tall build... It was Corbin. He was talking to someone she could barely make out in the background. She watched the animated conversation progress until Corbin spun around to face the window. She jerked back her hand and let the shade fall into place, hoping he hadn't seen her.

Securing a wisp of hair that had escaped her chignon, Catherine hurried to the back room of the store and lit the brass oil lamp on her desk. She had no desire to resurrect the past, but it was proving to be difficult when every time she turned around he was there. She pulled out the store's accounting ledger. She had plenty of things to do besides reminisce about her life with Corbin Hunter. There was filling out next month's stock order, ensuring that the store's accounting was up to date, organizing the recent shipment of flour, sugar, and penny candies. As far as she was concerned, her past relationship with Corbin...Mr. Hunter...was a closed book.

Sliding into her chair, she picked up her pencil, brushed off the open page of the ledger, and went to work. Business would be significantly better if she lived in a larger town like Lancaster, but she still managed to do well for herself. After years of working, duties like settling the accounts and ordering stock had become routine and helped to clear her mind.

The door connecting the house and the store opened behind her, causing the lamp's flame to flicker in the draft. Catherine looked up from the ledger. "Lily? I thought you'd gone to bed."

"I wanted to talk to you first." She pulled her dressing gown closer around her and sat down beside Catherine on an empty wooden chair. "I...I came to apologize."

"To apologize? For what?"

"For inviting the sheriff to ride home with us. I saw how uncomfortable you were. I should have been more sensitive to your feelings instead of trying to get involved in something that clearly isn't my affair."

"You don't need to apologize." Catherine shook her head and started doodling with the pencil she held, a habit she'd picked up years ago...before Corbin. "I simply wasn't prepared for his return. I'm sure you don't remember as you were too young, but Mr. Hunter and I were once engaged. Then Momma died, and I had the three of you to raise." Catherine started doodling again, pressing down on the pencil. "When Corbin showed up, he arrived with memories I'd prefer not to dredge up." The lead snapped.

"I know."

Catherine sat back. "You know?"

"About the engagement, I mean. And that he walked out on you."

Catherine had hoped it had been too long ago for her sisters to remember the details of that time. Apparently she'd been wrong. "How?"

Lily's dark brows arched. "I didn't think it was a secret. Everyone in town knows."

"Everyone?"

"Well, maybe not everyone."

Catherine closed her eyes. Who was she fooling? Of course everyone knew. People didn't forget things like that. "So that's what they whisper about me as I walk down the street."

Lily gripped Catherine's hand. "No. You've got it all wrong. And even if it were true, you're the one who always taught me that who we are doesn't depend on what people think about us. Or our profession. Or whether or not we might have a husband."

If only it were that simple. Catherine pulled her hand away and shut the ledger, no longer interested in the distraction. It seemed

that she simply couldn't escape Corbin Hunter's reach. She grasped
the handle of the lantern and headed into the small, three-bedroom
house she'd lived in her entire life. "I know what they call me. That
they see me as the town spinster."

Lily followed right behind her. "Everyone in this town looks up
to you and respects you. We all do, and anything we did tonight, any
'match making,' as you call it, was simply an effort to make sure that
you're happy."

"Did you ever stop to consider that maybe I am happy?"
Catherine trotted up the narrow stairway to the second floor, trying
to decide if her own words were true. Of course they were. She was
extremely happy. "And why shouldn't I be happy? All my sisters are
either married or soon to be married. The store is doing well enough
for me to put aside a small nest egg each month, and—"

"Tell me about him." Lily grasped Catherine's arm at the threshold
of her bedroom.

Catherine swallowed the lump in her throat, wishing she could
push her sister away along with the memories.

"Why did he leave?"

Catherine frowned. Lily's curiosity had always managed to get
her into trouble, and apparently, tonight was no different. Catherine
set the lantern down on the oak dresser and picked up her brush. Her
hair tumbled halfway down her back as she let it down. "I thought
you just apologized for interfering."

"I did, but I saw something pass between the two of you when he
first saw you across the room. I can't help but wonder if it happened
once, why it couldn't happen again."

"Life's not that simple." Catherine sat down on the thick quilt that her mother had stitched together from scraps of the girls' clothes and continued brushing her hair. "You don't always get second chances with love."

"I don't believe that." Lily plopped down beside her and drew her legs against her chest. The girl simply wouldn't give up.

But as much as Catherine wanted to believe in dime-novel endings when it came to love, she'd seen firsthand that those storybook endings didn't happen in real life. She'd seen it in her momma's eyes the day Isaiah Morgan had left, and again the day Momma had died without the presence of her husband at her side. Which made Catherine all the more determined to forget any past she'd once had with Corbin Hunter. She knew from experience that a man like him came with a peck of trouble.

Catherine fiddled with a strand of her hair. Jumping into those memories was as unpleasant as jumping into Clear Creek during wintertime. "I remember talking to Momma about him and telling her how tall and handsome he was. He came one Sunday afternoon to ask Daddy if he could court me."

Lily's eyes glowed in the lamplight. "That's so romantic."

"He told me it was my eyes that had first captured him. He couldn't decide if they were green or blue, so he decided he wanted to find out. The following fall, he took me aside at one of the church picnics and asked me to marry him."

Lily pressed her lips together as if suppressing the flow of questions that was about to spout.

"Then, everything changed." Catherine crossed the worn rose-garland carpet and set the brush on the dresser beside her mother's hand-carved jewelry box. "Father left for Alaska. I had to take more responsibility in the store, which meant there was much less time for Corbin. When Momma got sick, everything changed overnight. Being the oldest, I had to take care of Momma and the three of you. And then…like I said. Everything changed between us."

"I'm sorry. I never realized you lost Corbin because of us."

Lily's gaze swept the floor as if pulled down by the weight of guilt. But Catherine had not, nor would she ever, blame her sisters for what had happened.

Instead, she forced the remaining fragments of resolve into her voice and moved to lift up her sister's chin until Lily looked at her. "I never regretted my decision to take care of you. You, Audrey, and Emily are my family. Nothing comes between us."

Not even Corbin Hunter.

Lily shook her head. "It just doesn't seem fair."

"No one ever promised me life would always be fair. And besides, I've still got you, don't I?"

"I suppose, though I don't know that I'd be so forgiving if I was forced to give up my one true love."

"You're far too romantic, Lily." Catherine shot her sister a half smile to mask the familiar jab of pain. "Save the fairytale endings for your stack of dime novels and get to bed. We have a busy day tomorrow with the new town telephone system coming."

* * *

Emily had been right about the townspeople's resistance when it came to the installation of the new town telephone, but Catherine hadn't expected Emily to be the most outspoken of any of them. Or for

Grady to be their first subscriber to the service. It was insurance well worth it, he told Catherine when he had his telephone installed in the house, to ensure that they were able to call the doctor when the time for the baby came. Emily, though, still wasn't convinced of the necessity.

By the following week, some of the outlying farmers, as well as a number of businessmen in town, had been the next in line to pay the monthly subscription fee. But there were still plenty of people convinced that the telephone was nothing more than a passing fad that didn't need anyone's time or monetary investment, and most of them were quick to let her know their opinion.

Catherine worked to straighten several bolts of material Erma Potter had looked at while Lily sat in the adjoining room in her newly found job as the town telephone operator. Knowing how Lily spent half her time daydreaming of John Guild and life beyond Revenge, Catherine hoped the switchboard was what she needed to keep herself busy. Horace and Harold sat in their chairs in the center of the store, their inventions forgotten for the moment as they indulged in a lively game of chess.

The front door jingled, and Mrs. McBride bustled in. "I understand you received several new bolts of fabric."

"I've just got them set out, Mrs. McBride." Catherine slid into her selling tactics. "Mrs. Potter just bought four yards of the purple. It's gorgeous, isn't it?"

The older woman fingered the edge of the fabric and frowned. "The quality of fabric seems to deteriorate more every season."

Catherine shook her head at the expected response. "This is all the way from back East, Mrs. McBride. The best you can buy."

"I find that hard to believe." The woman's frown deepened, emphasizing the lines around her mouth. "Why, even the store in Lancaster has better quality than this."

Catherine worked to hold her tongue. While Mrs. McBride exasperated her, she was also one of her best customers, so there was no profit in arguing with the woman. Besides, no matter what she said, Mrs. McBride would contradict her.

"Feel free to look all you want, Mrs. McBride. I'll be at the counter if you decide you need anything."

Catherine headed toward the front of the store then stopped at the sound of Lily's voice.

"I'm sorry to interrupt, Mrs. Garrett," Lily was saying. "I just heard Erma Potter leave the store a couple minutes ago. If you hurry, you might be able to catch her before she heads home."

Catherine retreated to the back of the room, folded her arms across her chest, and leaned against the doorframe, wondering if restraining Lily's inquisitive nature was possible. In the week the switchboard had been up and running, Lily's enthusiasm over her job had only managed to increase. Especially when she knew each subscriber by name and was frequently called upon for morning wake-up calls, recipes, or simply a long chat.

"Lily."

Lily held up her hand and motioned for Catherine to wait.

"Lily." Catherine wrestled the headset from Lily's hand and held it up. "This is a telephone switchboard, not a women's quilting bee."

"I was simply trying to save Mrs. Garrett a trip all the way out to the Potter farm when Mrs. Potter is still in town. She was just in, wasn't she?"

"That is beside the point. You're listening in on other people's conversations. How do you justify that?"

"I—"

"We are already facing a sizable amount of resistance, and if people feel as if someone is listening in on everything they say, well, it simply isn't professional."

"People like the personal touch."

Catherine blew out a quick breath. "And I'm tempted to treat you like the city operators who aren't even allowed to use the necessity without permission."

Lily shook her head. "That's ridiculous."

"The man who installed our switchboard told me that after only three weeks, the telephone has become a solid institution in Golden, Colorado, much like it's becoming across the country. Do you think this is going to happen here if we continue to act like a backward, small town?"

"We're not in the city." Lily grabbed the headset out of Catherine's hands and connected a call. "This is Revenge, where people like a bit of personal service. Which is exactly what I'm giving them."

"Lily."

"Wait a minute." Lily held a finger to her lips. "I've heard these two men talking before."

"What's so strange about that?"

"They're talking in some sort of code."

"Maybe they're speaking in code because someone is listening."

The front bell rang, giving Catherine an excuse to leave before she lost her temper. She swept into the store and marched halfway to the counter before she looked to see who had entered. It was Corbin.

She let out a somber sigh then looked down at her dress. When she'd put the outfit on this morning, the brown flecks in the fabric seemed fine, but now the color suddenly looked plain and dowdy. So much for keeping up appearances. She took a deep breath and touched the fringes of her hair to make sure they were still in place. Maybe if she'd prayed a bit harder, Sheriff Lansing would have been miraculously healed by now, and Revenge wouldn't need a temporary sheriff.

"Miss Morgan?"

She forced a smile. "Good morning, Sheriff."

She'd been right. Sheriff definitely sounded less intimate than... Corbin. She busied herself behind the counter like she had a million things to organize, even though she'd finished long before the store had even opened.

He shoved his hands into his pockets and let his gaze rake the floor. Apparently his return was proving to be just as awkward for him as it was for her.

"How do you like being back in Revenge?" she finally asked.

"I've been able to catch up on a few old friends."

"Really?"

"Had lunch with Philip and Beatrice Smith and saw their new son."

Catherine nodded. "He's number five."

"I hear the Marshalls have seven."

"Eight."

Corbin's eyes widened. "Wow. How do they keep up with eight?"

Catherine stifled a laugh. "I don't know, though I'm certain I don't care to find out. Not that I wouldn't like children...someday... but eight..."

She felt a blush cross her cheeks at the too-intimate line of conversation. Why couldn't she just stick to impersonal topics like coffee and sugar?

He leaned against the counter and popped a lemon drop into his mouth, a habit she remembered from years ago. "I heard you have a telephone."

"A telephone?" Catherine worked to make the switch. "Yes. I felt it was about time the service was available to the people of Revenge."

"It's an intriguing concept. I think progress—in most areas— is necessary."

She couldn't read his expression. "But not in this case?"

"I didn't say that." He tapped his fingers against the wooden counter. "It must be nice that you don't have the rivalry some of the larger towns have with more than one telephone system."

"I already have eight subscribers."

"Quite an accomplishment, I would say, after only a week."

"It's a much-needed service in my opinion. Of course, I've yet to convince Emily of that. She sees it as some newfangled fad that won't last."

"I'd say it's already too late for that. There are hundreds of telephones across the state, so I'd say you made a wise business decision in getting this town involved."

Catherine smiled at the compliment and felt her cheeks blush.

Corbin cleared his throat. "I'm here, in fact, because I need to make a phone call."

"Oh?"

"And I was also thinking that the sheriff's office probably should have a phone installed. In case of an emergency, you know."

"I think that's an excellent idea." She pointed to the wooden box where customers who didn't have their own phone could make outgoing calls for a small fee. "Who would you like to call? For now we are only hooked up to those with telephones in town, Lancaster, and a few other nearby towns."

"The sheriff in Lancaster, please. It will save me time if I don't have to ride out there."

While Corbin talked on the phone, Catherine busied herself with Mrs. McBride's purchase of five yards of the new sky blue cotton. Apparently the quality of the fabric wasn't that bad after all.

"Catherine?" Lily stood in the doorway. "A call just came through for you. I'll finish up for you in here if you'd like."

Catherine glanced over at Corbin, who was still talking on the public phone. "Thanks."

She sat down in the back room at the switchboard, hoping it was Emily deciding to take advantage of her own phone. "Hello?"

"Miss Morgan?"

"Yes." Catherine searched her mind for the name that went with the familiar voice, but came up blank.

"This is Samuel Peterson. I'm not sure if you remember me or not, but I used to be a close friend of your parents."

"Mr. Peterson, yes, I remember you. What can I do for you?"

"I wish I could talk to you in person, but when I found out you had a phone in your town, I decided that this was the quickest way to contact you."

"Is something wrong?"

"Yes. It's your father."

"My father? I…I never expected to hear anything from him

again." Catherine fiddled with the long cord of the telephone and wondered if having a phone system in town was a good idea after all. It seemed as if all it had caused was trouble. "What happened, Mr. Peterson?"

"I'm sorry to have to be the one to inform you, but your father's dead."

Chapter Six

....

Catherine couldn't remember the last time she and her three sisters had gathered around the dinner table with their mother's fancy lace tablecloth and the Blue Willow patterned china dishes she'd brought to Ohio from back East after her marriage. Tonight there were no husbands, fiancés, or courting gentlemen—only the four sisters. And for Catherine, the additional roomful of memories that whispered in the background.

Because their father, Isaiah Morgan, was dead.

She took a bite of the fried chicken she'd prepared along with sweet corn from their garden and buttery mashed potatoes, but the rich food tasted drier than a spoonful of sand. She had yet to say the words out loud, but she knew she was going to have to, eventually. Her sisters had to know the truth.

"The dinner is wonderful, Catherine," Lily bubbled as she scooped a second mound of potatoes onto her plate. "But I can't imagine what the occasion is for you to cook a feast like this in the middle of the week. Why, it isn't even a holiday."

Catherine forced a smile and decided to put off the inevitable. "Does there have to be an occasion for the four of us to get together?"

Audrey helped herself to another biscuit and smeared on a thick layer of homemade butter. "It is kind of fun, isn't it? An entire evening sitting around the table like we used to before Grady and Harrison came into the picture."

"And don't forget John Guild." Emily shot a knowing glance at Lily. "I'm still waiting to hear the announcement of a wedding in the future for the two of you."

Lily's cheeks flushed, and she ducked her head to avoid the attention of her sisters. "It's far too early for our relationship to have progressed to the stage of matrimony."

"But you are hoping it does, aren't you?" Emily prodded.

Lily's broad smile answered the question as the three girls continued chatting about courting, beaus, and weddings. Catherine shoved the fleeting picture of her own family from her mind. Courting and weddings were something she'd likely never experience in this lifetime, a fact she'd long ago accepted.

Instead, she ate in silence, wishing she could forget the real reason she'd invited them all here. She wanted to be wrong about the man her father had been, but that wasn't a fact to be argued. She'd been there the day he caught gold fever from reports that beckoned all able-bodied men to pack up and head for the mines and a guaranteed fortune. She'd been there the day he'd announced to their mother he was leaving. Then afterward, she was the one who'd read the letters he'd sent along with a few dollars and vain promises that he'd found a spot that would make them rich. Promises that he'd return to Revenge as soon as he made his fortune. But he never had. And except for an occasional letter, there had been no communication. Not even when Sarah Morgan died, leaving the four sisters on their own.

Catherine looked up and realized that her sisters were staring at her.

"Do you agree, Catherine?" Lily asked.

Catherine shook her head. "Agree with what?"

"You haven't been listening to a word we've been saying, have you?" Emily said.

Audrey leaned forward with an odd expression on her face. "We've been discussing Corbin Hunter's bathing habits."

Catherine nearly choked on her mashed potatoes. "Bathing habits? Why, I—"

"He came in two days this past week for lemon drops and a bar of soap." Lily cut her off before she could put a stop to the improper thread of conversation. "And on the third day he bought two bars of soap. No man needs that many bars of soap."

Catherine swallowed a sip of water in an attempt to compose herself. The implications—at least to her sisters—were all too clear. "I'm sure you must be mistaken."

"You didn't notice?" Lily asked.

"Or didn't want to notice," Emily added.

"Neither." Catherine frowned. "It is certainly not any of our business how many bars of soap Mr. Hunter buys—or any of the customers for that matter—and I'm not going to discuss—"

"The fact that he's quite handsome?" Emily asked.

"Or that you've started wearing your hair softer around your face and your Sunday best to the store on weekdays?" Lily added.

Catherine wiped the edges of her mouth with her napkin then pushed back her plate. She certainly hadn't gathered her sisters together to discuss the personal habits of Corbin Hunter, whether or not he was handsome, or even what she decided to wear this morning. And she was only fooling herself if she thought she could put off the inevitable any longer. "I think it's time we laid the subject of Mr. Hunter and his, er, private routines aside, because while I don't have anything to celebrate tonight, I do have something to tell you."

"And you're telling us it doesn't have anything to do with you and the newly acquired sheriff?" Apparently Lily wasn't finished.

"It has nothing to do at all with Mr. Hunter. It's about Father." Any lingering thoughts of matchmaking vanished as Catherine's patience snapped. "I…I received a telephone call this afternoon from an old friend of father's."

"And he had news?" Emily's eyes brightened as she squeezed Audrey's hand beside her. "It's been so long, but I knew he'd come back one day. I just knew—"

"He's dead, Emily."

Emily's gasp made Catherine regret her words the moment they slipped unguarded from her mouth. Lily's face paled, as did Audrey's. She'd invited them to dinner so she could tell them in private and had wanted to ease into the discussion. Instead, she'd dropped the news on them like a weighted millstone.

"There has to be some sort of mistake." Emily's hand pressed against her stomach, as she looked to her sisters for confirmation that what Catherine said wasn't true. "He told us he's coming back. He has a grandchild coming. I even wrote him a letter last month… just in case."

"It's been eight years, Emily." Catherine's voice rose a notch as she attempted to downplay the emotion in her voice. She'd spent that time holding onto hope that she'd been wrong, but Isaiah Morgan's death had confirmed the inevitable. "I know you've all waited for his return, but you didn't really think he was ever coming back, did you?"

"Yes." Tears welled in the corner of Audrey's eyes. "He promised."

Catherine twisted the cloth napkin between her fingers. "Just like he promised he'd strike it rich? Or promised to build us a big house? What about the things that really mattered? Like being there when Momma died? Or when the four of us were left alone to care for each other and run the family store?"

Catherine winced at the harshness in her voice, but she'd lost the softness in her mannerisms years ago. And besides, what other way was there to dispel the bitter truth that their father had broken every promise he'd ever made? She should have told them the entire truth before it came to this.

"He's really dead?" Audrey's fork clanked against her plate as it dropped against the table. "How?"

"He died in a mining accident several weeks ago. Mr. Peterson promised that he would try to find out more details, but beyond that I don't know...I'm sorry."

Emily pushed back her plate. "I remember how he used to go hunting every Christmas in order to bring us back a turkey."

Audrey rested her chin in her hands. "And buy us penny candy when he went to Lancaster."

"And peppermint sticks," Lily added. "They still make me think of him."

Catherine pressed her hands against the edge of the table. Memories of toys, candy, and Christmas dinners had been buried in her mind beneath his bouts of drinking, loss of temper, and the fact that their mother had died because of their father. Catherine shoved back her chair and excused herself from the table, wishing she could erase what she knew about Isaiah Morgan.

In the kitchen, she leaned against the counter and took a deep breath, trying to calm the guilt and regret that warred within her.

Guilt for not telling her sisters the truth about their father sooner. Regret for what the truth would do to them now. Today reminded her too much of the day their mother had died. She'd sat them all down in the parlor on Momma's fancy settee to tell them that she'd drawn her last breath during the night. It didn't seem any fairer now than it had then.

"You're lucky, you know?"

Catherine looked up at Lily, who'd entered the kitchen with a stack of half-filled plates in her hands. Apparently dinner was over. "Why do you say that?"

"Because you remember Momma and Papa. I have fuzzy memories of Papa bringing me peppermint sticks and Momma singing me to sleep at night, but I want to remember what it was like to sit down and eat Sunday dinner together, picnics at Clear Creek, hayrides in the fall, and all the other things you've told us about them."

"Remembering isn't always good, Lily." Why couldn't they understand it could be a curse? "Right now, the only thing I can remember is the day Isaiah Morgan walked out this very door and never came back."

Lily set the plates on the counter and shook her head. "But it wasn't his fault. Surely even you know that. He was only trying to provide for his family."

"Provide for his family?" How could they have missed the truth that Isaiah had never planned to return? "In eight years he never sent more than a few dollars to provide for us. Instead, he caught gold fever and left us to chase after some foolish dream of finding his fortune. You would have thought that when his wife died, he'd return to look after his family, but even that couldn't entice him away from the gold mines."

Tears sprang up in Lily's eyes. "Maybe he didn't know about Momma."

"He knew. I sent him a telegram. I have letters from him. They're filled with his empty promises and excuses for not returning. His death doesn't change the fact that he never planned to return."

Emily stopped in the doorway behind Lily, her arms wrapped around her thickened waist. "Why didn't you tell us years ago about this? Why now?"

Anger that had been brewing for years rose up and gushed out uncontrollably. "Because I didn't want you to know that our father was nothing more than a greedy, gold-digging scoundrel who left his wife to die and his children to survive on their own."

Emily reacted as if she'd been slapped.

"I'm sorry." Catherine's hand flew to her mouth, wishing she could take back the flood of emotion that had just erupted. But it was too late.

Emily blinked away a flow of tears. "You have no right to talk about Father that way. Whatever he did, it was because he loved us. All of us. And just because he never struck gold doesn't make him any less of a father."

"A father? Can't you see that he was never a father to us? If he hadn't died, he'd still be looking for gold. He had the fever, Emily. Gold fever. And it cost him everything he had."

Tears spilled down Lily's cheeks as well. "You're only saying these things because you think you lost Corbin because of him, but don't blame what you lost on Father. It's not his fault."

Catherine grabbed her coat from the hook on the back door and bolted outside. Her own tears that had remained unshed began to flow. She'd spent her entire life protecting her sisters from the reality of who Isaiah Morgan really was. Never one harsh word against him. Never any indication that he'd simply neglected coming home because of the lure of the gold. His excuses had been plentiful, and because of them, she'd long ago accepted that he wasn't returning. She somehow expected her sisters to have given up hope that the man would return. Apparently she'd been wrong.

Instead, they'd held on to her reassurances that one day he'd return and they'd be a family again. And now, in one foolish moment, she'd destroyed their perception of their father forever.

* * *

Corbin's long strides led him toward the outskirts of town. The telegraph he'd just received had put him one step closer to the proof he needed to arrest Harrison Tucker. But while he longed to watch his father's murderer pay for what he'd done, he also knew that the apprehension of Tucker would mean breaking another piece of Catherine's heart. Something that shouldn't matter to him, but it did.

He strode down the endless dirt road and studied the familiar terrain, hoping the serenity around him would help calm the turmoil he felt. He'd missed it here. Even with all the bittersweet memories that had become continual reminders of why he'd left, a part of him regretted not staying and setting down roots here. Thick oak and hickory forests stood tall in the distance, interspersed with giant hemlocks and bushy ferns. Farms scattered across rolling countryside. He'd hunted with his father here for turkeys and deer, and fished in the summer for fat brown trout out of Clear Creek that his mother used to fry up for supper. He might not yet have seen thirty years, but it all seemed like a lifetime ago.

A drop of rain splashed off the tip of his nose. The sky had darkened to the east, but from the looks of the clouds above him, he didn't expect much of a downpour. He strode toward the town cemetery, wishing his mother were here with him instead of buried beneath the rich Ohio soil. She'd always been an unending source of advice and wisdom, and there were a dozen questions he wanted to ask her today.

A moment later, the heavens unleashed a torrent above him. He'd been wrong about the rain. Dashing toward the shelter of a stand of trees, he hurried beneath the heavy, open boughs then stopped short. Catherine huddled against one of the thick trunks.

"Miss Morgan."

"Sheriff. I…" Her eyes widened. "I didn't realize anyone else was out here."

"Anyone who's smart isn't." He chuckled, more from nerves than the humor of the situation, and then tugged his hat down farther onto his head. "I didn't mean to startle you. I was out walking and didn't expect the downpour."

"Me neither."

She pressed against the trunk of the tree and lowered her head. She'd been crying and tears streaked her rosy cheeks.

He fought the urge to tip her chin back with his thumb so he could look into her cloudy eyes. "Is everything all right?"

"Of course." She brushed her hands across her face before she shoved them into her coat pockets. "Why wouldn't it be?"

She wasn't a good liar. Something was obviously wrong.

He folded his arms across his chest. "Let's see. You're standing in the middle of a cemetery during a downpour and your eyes are red and swollen."

She opened her mouth then shut it again before saying anything. Her hesitation surprised him. If there was one thing he remembered about Catherine, it was that she never lacked for something to say. Nor did she typically hesitate to say what was on her mind.

He glanced beyond the cemetery fence to a green field sprinkled with black-eyed Susans and wild rhododendrons. The rain fell at a steady pace, dousing any hopes of escape that either of them might hold. Unless the rain dissipated as suddenly as it had started, they were both stuck together for the moment.

"My mother's buried here," he began, needing to break down the curtain of silence hanging between them.

"And mine as well. I used to come out here every afternoon to talk to her. I missed her so much after she died, though there was little time to mourn. I had Emily, Audrey, and Lily to take care of and the store to manage. And today...I just miss her."

"I know how much it hurts to lose someone." He leaned beside her against the rough bark. He wasn't going to tell her about his father. Not now, anyway. "I don't know that I ever had the chance to tell you, but you did an amazing job raising your sisters."

"Whatever good I did, I just destroyed in the course of one meal."

He studied her defeated expression. "What do you mean?"

Her shoulders slumped. "I found out yesterday that my father is dead."

"Dead?" The tall, broad-shouldered stature of Isaiah Morgan filled Corbin's memory. He'd stayed up an entire night trying to find enough courage to ask permission to court Catherine that summer. The fact that Catherine's stern father said yes had left him flabbergasted. He never had understood exactly why the man had decided to let him marry his eldest, but back then he'd been cocky enough to believe that he was the only one for Catherine. That was before everything changed between them.

"There was an accident in one of the mines. I don't have any details other than the fact that they found his body along with those of two other miners." Catherine stared at the ground. "After eight years of hoping he'd return…"

Corbin shoved his hands into his jeans pockets. "I'm sorry, Catherine. I know how hard this must be on you and your sisters."

"The only problem is that they remember Christmases, handmade dolls, and penny candy. All I remember is that I had to take care of the store and raise my sisters because he was too selfish or stubborn, or both, to come home."

"Gold fever's done worse to a person. Murder, theft, even suicide…there's no end to the problems it brings, nor the reality that few come home with their pockets lined with the gold they went after in the first place."

"So we can just blame it on the gold, then? This fever, as they so conveniently call it, sounds more like a fatal case of cholera than the vice of gambling."

"I'm not excusing at all what he did. I'm only saying that gold will do that to a man. Many a good husband and father have been destroyed because of it."

"Even that doesn't give me any right to say what I did."

She fingered the folds of her navy blue dress. Simple...practical... Perhaps Grady O'Conner had been right after all. Gone was the girl from his past that he'd caught a glimpse of the other night. Today, she seemed to carry on her shoulders the problems of the world. And from what he'd just heard, she felt as if she did.

"I'm sure your sisters will forgive you. Give them time to absorb what has happened. In the end, they're going to remember what you've done for them since the day your father left. Not a father who never came back to take care of them."

Catherine shook her head. "You didn't see the pain in Audrey's eyes or the anger in Emily's expression. They don't remember him the way I do, and even if I were to tell them the entire truth about who Isaiah Morgan really was, that wouldn't change how they see him. It would only make them resent me for it."

"Do you resent the past eight years, and what you had to do to care for them?"

Their gazes locked for a moment. She'd given up far more than most would ever realize, and he knew it.

"No." She shook her head. "I did what I knew was right."

"And they know that. Just give them time." Corbin glanced up at the sky that had cleared above them. "Come on. The rain's stopped and it's going to be dark soon. I'll walk you home."

He offered his arm as they started back down the lane, surprised when she took it. If he closed his eyes he could almost erase the past few years. Almost. But a glance down at her reminded him that they'd both changed from the innocent couple they'd been when he first had come courting. And nothing could erase what had happened between them. He'd been right to leave Revenge all those years ago, and as soon as he'd found his man, he wouldn't hesitate to leave again.

"I never had a chance to ask you if you enjoyed Mr. Tucker's birthday party last week."

"The party?" He looked down at her again, the question drawing him from his place in the past to the present. "Yes. I particularly enjoyed meeting some of the new people in town, though of course most of them probably aren't new. I have to keep reminding myself that I'm the newcomer." He mulled over his next words and decided to follow the opening she'd just thrown his way. "I have been curious, though. What exactly does Mr. Tucker do for a living?"

"I'd say the man has done a bit of everything from peddler to prospector. A few months ago his grandfather died and willed him a piece of land outside town, so he decided to try his hand at farming."

"Grady told me he was up in Alaska before that."

"You've heard his stories, of course." Catherine laughed. "He manages to keep everyone's attention with his gift for storytelling, even though we all know that most of the details have been greatly embellished."

Corbin stopped. The blurred colors of a rainbow framed the corner of the western skyline.

"It's beautiful, isn't it?" Catherine said.

"Yes, but…"

She looked up at him. "What is it?"

Corbin debated whether or not he should continue. Her nervous mannerisms when he was around had all but vanished for the moment, but he knew that what he was about to say would erase any unspoken truce that had come between them.

"You know I'm investigating the rash of bank robberies that have spread across the state."

"I heard you mention it to Grady. They killed a man last year, didn't they?"

"They've killed five people." *Including my father.* His jaw clenched. A shadow crossed her face. "What is it?"

"They robbed the bank in Lancaster yesterday." He started walking again, wishing he could bury the consuming bitterness growing inside him.

"Was anyone hurt?"

"One of the gang members was shot. I headed out there to join the posse, but we lost the trail pretty early on. It was as if they vanished into thin air. But it's only a matter of time until they strike again, and the next time, we might not be so lucky."

Catherine looked up at him, her eyes filled with concern. "These robberies, they seem...personal. Why?"

"Because whenever a life is taken because of greed, it becomes personal." There was more to his involvement in the case, but for now, that explanation would have to do. Memories of his father were wrapped in a thick layer of pain and bitterness. He'd died for a handful of bank notes that the robbers more than likely spent on booze and women.

Corbin's anger spiked. Catherine might see Harrison as her future brother-in-law, but his take on the man was completely different. Harrison had waltzed into a town with nothing more than an easy fortune on his mind as he weaseled his way into the Morgan home. And Audrey—along with all the Morgan girls— was naïve enough to believe that his tall stories of Alaska were as innocent as a realistic look at life out West. How was he supposed to convince her that Harrison might not be the perfect husband-to-be he claimed?

"There is one other thing about the robberies you need to know, Catherine," he began. "I don't know how to tell you this other than simply coming out and saying it. I have reason to believe that Audrey's fiancé might be involved in the recent bank robberies."

"Harrison?" Catherine stopped short on the edge of town where the outlying forests faded into the whitewashed storefronts and houses. "I don't understand."

"For the past few months I've been tracing his movements, and there is no record of him applying for a stake of gold anywhere in the Alaska territory."

"Alaska's a frontier that sweeps thousands of miles, and because your source doesn't place him there, then he's lying? I thought you were more intelligent than that, Corbin Hunter." Catherine quickened her pace toward town. "The thought that Harrison could be a bank robber or a murderer for that matter is ridiculous."

"Not if I'm right. His real name is William Marker. He's a bank robber, a con man...and a womanizer."

Catherine stopped and crossed her arms. She obviously wasn't buying into his reasoning. "I don't believe you."

"Like your sisters don't believe you about your father?"

"That's not fair."

"Why not? I've been tracking this gang for months, and I'm finally closing in on them. And I'm going to make sure they pay for what they've done."

"What led you to Harrison?"

They started walking again, but at a slower pace. "I have a source named Brad Sanders. He's a Pinkerton agent who's following the case. He's the one who originally told me that he believed Harrison Tucker is the leader of the Masked Gang, and that he'd recently arrived in Revenge. He just didn't have enough solid evidence to prove it."

"So you used your connections to get the job here so you could catch Harrison."

"That was part of it. Mr. Sanders and I met about a month ago and swapped information. He'd followed up on a tip regarding Harrison and found that parts of his story didn't check out. Including the fact that there is no record of him applying for a stake of gold anywhere in the Alaska Territory. The timing of his arrival in Revenge also corresponded closely with new territory the gang took over."

"What was Mr. Sanders's original tip that Harrison was involved in this?"

Corbin paused, not sure he was ready to confess the one main weakness of his case. "It was an unidentified source, but everything they said checked out."

"Which means you have nothing. There still isn't enough proof in anything you've told me to convince me that you're after the right man."

"All you have to do is look at Harrison. He knows how to work his way into a town and win the hearts of the entire population in a blink of an eye."

"Since when is that a crime?"

Corbin watched her expression and knew exactly what she was thinking. The man who'd swept into town like a fresh summer breeze was nothing more than a farm boy who'd managed not only to inherit

his grandfather's land, but who'd happened to steal the heart of her
sister. And if Corbin was honest with himself, he wanted her
to be right. But there were too many facts stacked up against
the man that he couldn't ignore.

"Let me ask you a few questions." He cleared his throat,
determined to convince her that there was at least a possibility
that Harrison wasn't who he said he was. "Where did Harrison
live before Revenge?"

Catherine shook her head.

"Catherine..."

"I don't know."

"What about his family?"

"He...I'm sure he said that he's an only child. His parents are
dead. His grandfather was his last living relative."

"And what of his grandfather? What proof did he bring with
him when he claimed the land?"

Catherine shook her head. "The land claims office obviously
didn't have any problem with his claim. But the bottom line is that
Audrey loves him and—"

"And you're going to let her love for him override anything
I might say? If I'm right, this man could end up doing more than
simply breaking your sister's heart. The man's a murderer."

"No!" She flung her hands toward him.

Corbin grabbed her wrists and held them against his chest.
Whether Catherine liked it or not, he would find a way to prove
Harrison's guilt. "I know you don't want your sister hurt, but if it's
true, then we have to stop him."

"I won't let you hurt her. Not the way you hurt me."

"The way I hurt you?" Both of them fell silent. He dropped her hands and let his arms fall to his sides. Resentment bared its ugly head. She stood in front of him, looking as vulnerable as she had the first day he'd come calling on her all those years ago, but he knew the truth.

"Since we're speaking the truth, why don't you remind me what really happened that night I left. I was there. And if I remember correctly, it wasn't about me walking out on you."

She turned away from him, but he grasped her arm and pulled her back.

"It's time both of us face what happened that night," he continued.

"Why? So you can break my heart again?"

"I never meant to break your heart, but I was eighteen years old and didn't know how to deal with the situation."

Catherine broke free from his grip. "And I had no choice but to deal with the situation."

Chapter Seven

By the time Catherine slipped through the back door of the store, her heart still pounding over her encounter with Corbin, the sky had begun to clear, allowing the sun to drop over the edge of the horizon and cover the surrounding farmlands and wooded areas in the yellow glow of twilight. Grady's buggy was gone from out front, which meant that Emily had already returned home, a fact that didn't surprise her. Grady would never allow her sister to travel alone after dark in her condition.

Catherine closed the door behind her then waited for her eyes to adjust to the fading light in the kitchen. If only she could shut out the prevailing guilt that rose within her like the humidity of the Ohio evening. Meeting Corbin had only added to her turmoil. Thankfully, the house was quiet. Emily's absence was just as well. After what happened this evening, she wasn't ready to face any of them again.

Especially after Corbin's disturbing accusations regarding Harrison. His words still stunned her, but she knew the town's new sheriff well enough to realize he would never point fingers if he didn't believe his suspicions were true. But if his instincts were correct, fate had just played another trick on all of them. Losing their father, no matter what he'd done the past eight years, had devastated her sisters. She'd seen that in their eyes. Losing the man Audrey planned to spend the rest of her life with would be yet another devastating blow.

Yet, while her head might be forced to consider the possibility of Harrison's involvement in the recent robberies, her heart struggled to believe it could be true. Harrison hadn't lived in this town long, but surely she was a good enough judge of character to know the difference between a young man in love and a criminal. And just because a person could spin a good story and engage an audience in the telling, that certainly didn't make him a murderer. Even Corbin had to have something more substantial on the man before he arrested him.

She started to shed her wet coat then stopped midway when she heard someone coming down the stairs. Audrey entered the room carrying a lantern.

"Catherine?" Audrey set the light on the counter before planting her hands on her hips. "I was about to send the sheriff after you. Where have you been? You're absolutely drenched."

Catherine looked down at her rumpled clothes then pushed a stray strand of hair from her eyes. The last thing she was ready to confess was that she'd been with Corbin. As the town spinster, there was bound to be enough talk over his return and their past relationship. She wasn't going to add any fuel that might fan that fire, even to her sister.

"I went for a walk to clear my head and got caught in the rain," Catherine began.

Audrey grabbed at the sleeve of her wet coat. "If you don't hurry and change into something warm, you'll catch your death of cold."

"I'm perfectly fine and not even a bit chilled."

"All the same, you need to change. I'll take care of these wet things."

Catherine obeyed and peeled off her soaked dress before laying it on top of her coat. "I see that Emily went home."

"Grady drove her."

"And Lily?"

"She fell asleep upstairs not too long after you stormed out."

Another wave of guilt pressed through her. Even in the flickering lantern light, it was obvious that Audrey's eyes were red from crying. She knew Corbin was right, and they'd eventually forgive her for what she'd done, but the pain was still too raw at the moment, even if her actions had only been to protect them.

"I know you're upset, Audrey, but you have to believe that I never meant to hurt any of you. I am sorry."

Audrey's silence seemed to fill the house, and not knowing what else to say, Catherine started up the stairs, shivering beneath the thin fabric of her undergarments.

"You were wrong, you know."

Catherine turned to face Audrey, who still stood at the bottom of the stairs. "I was wrong to tell you the truth?"

"No." Audrey mounted the stairs, stopping halfway. "You were wrong to tell us the truth after all these years of making us believe he would return."

Nights of restless dreams and unanswered prayers returned to haunt Catherine. The picture she'd painted of her father throughout the years had been one lined with false hopes and expectations that had never materialized. But in spite of that, part of her had grasped onto that very same hope she'd offered her sisters—the hope that one day Isaiah Morgan would appear on their doorstep with that pot of gold he'd searched for—and even more importantly, that he would once again take up the role of father he'd laid aside when he left for Alaska.

But obviously her attempts to help her sisters had only managed to create a wedge between them in the end.

"Don't you think I, too, hoped he'd return? No matter what he'd done?" Catherine swallowed hard. "No matter how he treated Momma, he was still our father. Every night I prayed that he'd find what he was looking for and come home, because I knew you needed him."

"Even later on, when you knew he was never returning?"

"It was never that simple."

Catherine sank down onto the edge of the top stair, wishing she had easy answers to Audrey's questions. But as many times as she'd attempted to prepare herself for this day, every answer she'd thought of evaded her. The fact was that while she had prayed for Isaiah Morgan's return for her sisters' sakes, she held little love for the man she'd once called Father.

"I was eighteen years old when Momma died. Father was gone. I had the shop to run and the three of you…I did the best I could, Audrey. And back then I wanted to believe his letters and promises. Especially if it was the one thread of hope left to tie the four of us together."

"And later? After the months and years passed?"

Catherine fiddled with the perfectly stitched hem of her white cotton chemise. "I finally realized that no matter how hard I prayed, or how many times I asked him in my letters, he wasn't coming back."

"Then why didn't you just tell us the truth?" Audrey sat down beside her on the top stair.

Catherine gnawed on the side of her cheek. "I suppose it was because for a long time I believed he really would return. And then later I was afraid that saying what I felt out loud would simply make it all the more real for me. I knew how much you longed for him to return. That you held memories of a father who loved you, and that Emily longed for him to see her child. And maybe part of me, even after all these years, still held onto the slight hope that those things would happen. That he'd show up for Christmas dinner this year and hold his first grandbaby. I wanted that, Audrey. I wanted it for you."

Audrey grasped the heart locket she wore around her neck and dropped her gaze. "I guess I never thought about it that way."

"I heard you at the dinner table tonight. You remember all the good things."

"And you?"

"A good father doesn't leave his family and never return. Not even Mother's death brought him back home."

Audrey's frown deepened. "But knowing he's dead makes everything so final. Especially when I always believed he'd come back one day."

Catherine eased up from the stairway. In a way, their father's death came as a relief. If nothing else, the truth would eventually bring closure. No longer would they be caught up in a tangle of dreams that reality had turned into dashed hopes.

"Your locket's beautiful," Catherine said, changing the subject as she made her way to her bedroom. Healing and forgiveness wouldn't come overnight for her sisters, but for the first time she could believe that it would come. "I don't remember seeing it before."

A smile flickered in the depths of Audrey's eyes as she looked down at the gold heart in the lantern light. "Harrison went to Lancaster yesterday and bought it. He stopped by to give it to me this afternoon."

"He was in Lancaster?"

The bank in Lancaster had been robbed yesterday.

A shiver swept over Catherine as Corbin's words replayed in her mind. *He's a bank robber...a con man...and a womanizer...* No. She choked back the words of caution she was tempted to speak. Now was not the time, because this was nothing more than a coincidence. She'd seen the way Harrison looked at Audrey. There was no doubt in her mind that Harrison was nothing more than a young man in love.

"Catherine?" Audrey set the lantern down on the dresser in Catherine's room before turning back to her sister. "You've caught a chill."

"No, I'm fine. Really. I suppose just the combination of all that's happened today..." Catherine searched for the right words. She may not believe that Corbin was after the right person, but she still had to know more. "Why was Harrison in Lancaster?"

"He needed a few supplies for the farm. He's building on to the barn to hold a larger crop come winter."

"He seems to have taken to farming." Corbin's earlier concerns continued to ripple through her, and she realized that no matter how badly she wanted to believe in Harrison's innocence, she also couldn't let her sister marry him if there was any chance that he wasn't the man he claimed to be. Even if it meant telling Audrey the truth and breaking her sister's heart again. But not yet. So far, Corbin's accusations were nothing more than a pile of coincidences.

Catherine proceeded cautiously. If there ended up being no truth to Corbin's claims, she wasn't going to spoil Audrey's wedding. Nothing would be said to Audrey unless the proof Corbin came up with was indisputable. "I heard that the bank in Lancaster was robbed yesterday afternoon."

Audrey's face paled in the lamplight. "That makes how many times? Five? Six?"

"Six, I believe."

"Was anyone hurt?"

"I don't think so." Catherine measured her words. "I wonder if Harrison saw anything?"

"I don't know. He didn't mention anything. Perhaps it happened after he left."

"Or perhaps he simply didn't want to scare you."

Audrey's hand rested against her chest. "What if he had been there and something happened to him, Catherine? I don't think I could bear to lose anyone else I love. Not after Father."

Catherine gave her sister a reassuring hug while trying to swallow her own fears. "Harrison's fine, so there's nothing to worry about."

"You're right, of course."

Catherine told her sister good night, praying that she wouldn't end up being the one to dash her sister's dreams.

* * *

Catherine paced the boardwalk in front of the sheriff's office a dozen times the next morning before finding the courage to walk inside and face the town's newly appointed lawman. She'd stayed up half the night trying to find the elusive answers to Corbin's suspicions, but as much as she longed for him to be wrong, she couldn't deny that his accusations could be true. If he were right, she certainly had no intention of allowing Audrey to marry the man. Gathering up her courage, she turned the door handle and stepped into the small office.

Corbin sat behind his desk with a coffee cup in his hand and a frown on his face. The bare room boasted of little more than a wood desk, chairs, and a handful of wanted posters tacked on a wooden board. Nothing had changed since Sheriff Lansing's departure, including the pile of dime novels on the shelf and the prevailing smell of burnt coffee that filled the room.

"Sheriff?"

Corbin looked up from the paper he was filling out, not bothering to mask his surprise at seeing her. "Miss Morgan. How are you?"

"Dry." She shot him a half smile, hating how his presence stirred up memories she preferred to forget. She felt the back of her chignon to ensure her hair was still in place. Not that it mattered. She wasn't here for personal matters.

She clutched her handbag with her gloved fingers and eyed the door. "If you're too busy right now, I could come back later…"

"No. Of course not." He stood awkwardly and nodded at an empty chair. "I can't offer much more than a wobbly chair and a cup of bad coffee."

"The chair's fine." She perched on the edge of the wooden seat, wishing she could shake the air of suspicion that settled between them every time they were together. Surely he'd been right the other night when he'd said they were both wiser. Which meant that their turbulent past shouldn't affect them today. Or so she'd hoped. Pride reared its ugly head and made forgetting the past, even with all the years between them, impossible. She started to stand. This was definitely a mistake. "I shouldn't have come."

"But you did, so sit down."

She obeyed without another word. All she had to do now was

to say what she came to tell him and leave. Any personal feelings she felt—or had felt—didn't matter anymore. "I talked to Audrey last night after I returned home."

"Has she forgiven you?"

"I think so. For the most part anyway. But that's not why I came to see you. She said something about Harrison that...well...that I felt you should know."

Corbin leaned forward.

"I'm still not convinced that Harrison is the hardened criminal you've made him out to be, but..."

"But..." Corbin prodded.

Catherine squirmed in the chair. "She told me Harrison was in Lancaster day before yesterday."

Corbin's brows arched. "Audrey told you that?"

"Yes. She said he had some business for the farm to take care of, which isn't anything out of the ordinary. He always seems to be going here and there for supplies."

"What kind of supplies?"

"He's adding on to the barn. It's not unusual for him to go out of town for a day or two to pick up things for the construction."

Corbin tapped his fingers against the desk, complacent in his expression. "I had heard that he's making a number of improvements on his farm. Have any idea how he's able to pay for it?"

"We all assumed it was from his grandfather's estate. Norman Tucker didn't have a fortune by any means, but most of us believe he had a bit of a nest egg under his mattress. Apparently, we were right."

Corbin reached up and ripped one of the wanted ads from the wall then slid it across the table at her. "This is William Marker.

Wanted in four states and twice that many counties just here in Ohio. One of the witnesses from a previous robbery gave the details of this sketch before he died from a gunshot wound."

Catherine studied the pencil drawing then shook her head. "This man could be anyone. The town blacksmith, wheelwright…why, even the circuit rider Mr. Landon."

Corbin jabbed at the bottom of the poster. "Read the description, Catherine. Harrison has the same build, average height, dark hair color.… Even you have to admit that the resemblance is startling."

"But it's still not enough, and you know it."

Corbin crossed the room and pulled a dime novel from the shelf. "You've heard Harrison's stories of Alaska and the Wild West."

"Of course."

"Stories where he claims he saved a dozen men from a collapsed mine shaft, or when he—"

"What's your point, Sheriff?"

"Everyone in town, I suppose, knows how Sheriff Lansing was a sucker for the adventures of a dime novel. He's probably read every one written, or at least will die trying." Corbin pointed to the dusty shelf. "I couldn't sleep the other night and picked up one of these dusty covers and started reading. Now, I'm not well read when it comes to these fictional stories, but halfway through this gold-miner account in Alaska, I started to wonder. There was the odd story combined with details about the countryside, the towns, and even specific events. And some of them were details I heard Harrison recount the other night at his birthday party."

Catherine squirmed in her chair. "That's not proof that Harrison is a murderer."

"It proves he might not be who he says he is. And with a bit more evidence, like placing him in Lancaster the day the bank was robbed, the time is coming when I'm going to have to arrest him."

Catherine's stomach knotted. If Audrey knew she was here, she more than likely would never speak to her again, but while she still didn't believe Harrison capable of murder, she was beginning to wonder if Corbin might be right about the man not being all he claimed to be. But no matter how convincing Corbin's evidence, part of her wanted to justify her future brother-in-law's actions. "All you've proven to me so far is that Harrison might have a habit of exaggerating the facts."

"Exaggerating?"

"The fact that he was in Lancaster could very likely be nothing more than a coincidence, and you know it. And the same thing goes for these dime novels. He probably reads them to embellish his own experiences."

"Maybe, but you know I'm onto something, Catherine." Corbin rested his hands against the desk and leaned forward. "And I will find out who's behind these robberies. It's just a matter of time until I've gathered enough evidence to bring the entire gang in."

Catherine matched his intense stare. Corbin Hunter was no less stubborn than he'd been all those years ago. "I have no doubt that you will, but before you go and break Audrey's heart, I need you to promise me that you won't arrest Harrison until you have solid evidence that he's your man."

"Of course not."

"Because the fact that he reads dime novels or happened to be in Lancaster doesn't prove anything. If that were true, you'd have to arrest every person who happened to be in Lancaster at the time of the robbery."

"I understand what you're saying, but I thought you came to me because you want to know the truth."

"I came to you because I felt it my duty, as a citizen of this town, to tell you what I know."

"And I appreciate it."

"But you also need to remember that just because the man can tell a good story doesn't mean you can hang him."

"Catherine…" Corbin rested his arms against the table and leaned forward. "You know I would never do anything to intentionally hurt your family, but I will find out the truth. And when I do, I personally will make sure the guilty party hangs."

Catherine shoved the wanted poster across the table. "Why does it matter to you what happens after he's arrested?"

His jaw tensed. "Five murders. Isn't that enough?"

She dipped her chin, hating the situation Corbin had unwittingly drawn her into. Because of some ridiculous need to prove to him she'd made something of herself, his arrival had her worrying more about what dress to wear and how to style her hair than the numerous business decisions she needed to make every day. But not coming to Corbin was taking a chance that Harrison really was a murderer and her sister was stepping into something they might all regret the rest of their lives. No matter how much she hated the situation, it was a chance she couldn't take.

Corbin stood to tack the poster back on the wall. "I need you to do something for me. You're around Harrison. I need to know about anything that might point to who he really is."

Catherine rose to leave. Half a night of worry had put her in this position. She already felt as if she were betraying her sister. "I don't know if I can do that, Corbin. Audrey's my sister."

"You want to know the truth as much as I do, or you wouldn't be here right now, would you? If I'm right, Audrey could end up marrying a criminal, and I know that's not what you want."

"Of course not, but…"

"You don't have to do anything. Just listen and observe any discrepancies in his stories. Any trips out of town. Anything that seems suspicious."

"I'll watch him, but don't you dare break my sister's heart unless you can prove without a shadow of a doubt that you're right. And if you find proof that Harrison is involved, come to me first. I'll be the one to tell Audrey."

"Okay."

She looked up and caught his gaze. "Promise me, Corbin."

He nodded his head. "I promise."

Chapter Eight

Corbin stepped into Morgan's General Store, praying he'd find
Catherine before one of her sisters noticed him. Finding time to
speak with her in private wasn't going to be easy, but he had promised
he'd tell her if there were any developments in the case. If he were
lucky, Lily would be running the switchboard while Catherine dealt
with the customers.

He glanced quickly around the orderly mercantile, thankful there
didn't seem to be any other customers at the moment. He'd slept little
the past three nights after his conversation with Catherine. It might
have broken down part of the barrier between them, but in the end
simply seemed to have left them both feeling exposed.

Still, he needed to speak to her in private, and the last thing he
needed was someone like Mrs. McBride seeing them together and
making things worse with a spoonful of the rumors she loved to
spread. Not only did he not want anyone overhearing what he had to
say, he knew Catherine wouldn't appreciate further gossip regarding
the two of them.

It continued to amaze him how long some people's memories
were. No less than half a dozen middle-aged women had pulled him
aside at church to ask him when he was going to marry Catherine.
Apparently they'd forgotten how much time had passed between his
proposal and today. Nor did they know the truth behind what had
happened the day he'd left Revenge.

Lily appeared at the front counter before he could vanish behind a display of men's ready-made shirts. "Good morning, Sheriff Hunter. You're up early."

Corbin cleared his throat, suddenly regretting his decision to drop by. He should have waited for a better opportunity. Not that his reasons for coming were personal. Besides the news he carried, he also felt the need to apologize. He regretted bringing up the subject of Harrison Tucker with Catherine, especially since he still lacked the solid evidence he needed to arrest the man. And knowing she'd just found out about the death of her father, his behavior had been insensitive and heartless.

Lily didn't seem to notice his solemn expression. "What can I help you find today? A bar of soap, perhaps?"

"A bar of soap…" Corbin bit his tongue at her question. She didn't have to say anything for him to know what she was thinking. But just because he'd bought three, maybe four, bars in the past week didn't mean anything other than the fact that he liked to stay clean. It certainly had nothing to do with Catherine.

"No soap today. Just a pound of…" Corbin searched the nearest barrel for something… "A quart of pickles, please."

"A quart of pickles?" Lily's eyes widened.

"And five cents' worth of licorice." Corbin winced. Like that would make things better.

"I thought you liked lemon drops."

"I do." Why did it suddenly feel as if his life were an open ledger?

Lily began ringing up his order. "I never cared much for licorice myself, though Catherine loves it."

He hesitated. "I'd forgotten about her sweet tooth."

Liar.

Corbin pressed his lips together. He simply needed a peace offering, and the fact that he'd always brought Catherine a pocketful of penny candy whenever he'd come calling had nothing to do with it. At least Lily would have been too young to remember that. Catherine had loved anything sweet, but her favorite had been licorice. And he'd been happy to keep her in a supply of the treat.

"She's out back if you'd like to speak with her." Lily handed him his purchase, and he fished for the proper amount of change in his pocket before setting it on the counter.

"Thank you, but I'll just take my licorice and…pickles…and get back to work." He turned to leave.

"She's working her garden, something she tends to do when she's upset."

Corbin turned back around and planted his heels against the hardwood floor, irritated once again by his insensitivity. "I know the past couple days have been difficult, and I meant to express my condolences. I heard about your father's passing and know how hard this must be for all four of you."

Her cheery expression faded. "Thank you. It was a shock to all of us, though I was young when he left. Thankfully, I have a few good memories."

"I'm sure you do. And if you will, please express my sentiments to your sisters as well, in case I don't see them in the next few days."

"Of course. Thank you, Sheriff."

The bell jingled behind him as Corbin rushed out of the store and almost bumped into Mrs. McBride. Tipping his hat in greeting, he hurried down the boardwalk, stashed the pickles behind a wooden bench outside Johnnie Kirkland's barbershop, and then shoved the sack of licorice into his jacket pocket. For a moment, he was tempted to simply forget the original errand, but as he turned the corner, a glimpse of Catherine behind the store made him hesitate.

She knelt among a row of roses in the small garden plot nestled just beyond the back of the store. Beyond the colorful array of flowers lay a thriving vegetable garden, much of it ready for harvest. The wind blew loose fringes of hair around her face and framed her serious expression. He leaned against the whitewashed wall of the store and watched her work. Seeing her almost made him forget the reason he was here, and for a moment, Harrison, Isaiah Morgan, even his own father's death faded into the background. He could almost believe he was eighteen again and coming to call on the girl he intended to marry.

The look on her face intensified, and he wondered what she was thinking about. Her father? Harrison Tucker? Their past relationship?

No. That last thought was ridiculous. He took a couple steps toward her then stopped again. His heart wanted to turn back and forget everything between them—something he thought he'd done years ago. The truth was, ignoring the issue wouldn't make it disappear. And besides, he could control his past feelings for her, because that's simply where they were going to stay. In the past.

* * *

Catherine jammed the narrow spade into the ground and tugged out another weed. With all that had happened over the past few days, she'd neglected her garden. The vegetable patch, already laden with

beans, corn, potatoes, and peas, needed to be weeded and some
of the flowers cut back. And the garden wasn't the only thing that
had been neglected. So had her normal talks with her Heavenly
Father. The last thirty minutes of praying had started to remedy that,
and while it might not have changed her situation, it was already
helping her spirit by putting things into perspective.

She scooted down a few inches to another rose bush and breathed
in the sweet scent of the red bloom. Out of respect for her father,
she'd refrained from saying anything else negative about him, but the
tension from that first night—when her words had flowed untamed—
still loomed between her and her sisters.

To make up for her impulsive words, she'd worked hard on
the memorial they were planning for him. But how did one plan
a funeral for a man none of them had seen for almost a decade?
Or without a body to place in the grave beside her mother? With
far more questions than answers, she'd slipped out of the house early
this morning to work in her garden and pray for answers—answers
that still seemed as elusive as her father's pot of gold.

Catherine stopped midway through her continual prayer and
looked up. Corbin's shadow hovered over her. "Miss Morgan?"

"Sheriff?" She flipped up the brim of her straw hat. "Good morning."

"Your garden's doing well. I'm quite impressed."

"Thank you." She jumped up from the soft soil then brushed the
specks of dirt from the front of her apron, immediately self-conscious
of her untidy appearance. The last person she'd expected to see
this morning was Corbin. She picked up the wooden basket full of
potatoes to give her hands something to do, wondering if she should
excuse herself and escape to the house.

"Please, don't stop working on my account." He smiled down at her, bringing out the dimple in his right cheek. "Lily told me you would be out here."

She set the potatoes on the small, wrought iron table beside the back door then began picking up her tools and dropping them into the other basket she'd brought out. "I need to get back to tending to the store, but things were quiet this morning, and I needed a few minutes just to think and pray." She waved her hand toward the garden. "And as you can see, I've neglected the garden the past few days."

"I can hardly blame you for needing some quiet. I know how difficult all of this has been for you." He pulled something from his pocket and handed it to her.

Her eyes widened at the gift. "Licorice?"

"It's your favorite, isn't it?"

"Yes, I'm just surprised you remembered." Not that she'd forgotten how he loved lemon drops, that his favorite meal was roast beef with potatoes and pumpkin pie for dessert, or that he loved peaches on homemade ice cream and lemonade in the summer—all things she should have forgotten years ago. She resolutely shoved aside the handful of memories. "Thank you."

He cleared his throat. "I heard you're planning to hold a service for your father."

"I might not have agreed with how he spent the end of his life, but he deserves that. Especially since I can't even give him a decent burial."

"I'm sure everyone will understand."

Catherine clenched the sack of licorice between her fingers. "Pastor Landon promised to say a few things for those who attend.

There are some of the old-timers around who were friends with him years ago who will appreciate the gesture."

"I'm sure they will."

"That's not the real reason you're here, though, is it?" Catherine's stomach felt queasy. She dreaded news about Harrison, but from Corbin's solemn expression, she knew that whatever he'd come to tell her wasn't good news.

"I came for two reasons. The first to apologize."

"To apologize?" His confession caught her off guard. "I don't understand."

Corbin combed his fingers through his hair, looking as uncomfortable as when he'd seen her the first time out at Emily's ranch. "I realize that I probably never should have brought up the subject of Mr. Tucker. Especially when I've yet to receive the solid proof I need. All I've managed to do is dump an extra burden on you, which is something you don't deserve. I have to admit that I could be wrong. You were right that his being in Lancaster, for example, could be nothing more than a coincidence."

Catherine dropped her gaze. "You don't have to apologize. As much as I hate to consider that he could be a criminal, the last thing I want is for Audrey to marry the wrong man."

"I felt that with the news of your father, the last thing you needed right now was another problem."

"I agree, but that won't make the problem disappear." Catherine put the last garden tool into the basket before setting it beside the potatoes. "You said there were two things you needed to speak to me about."

Corbin nodded. "In examining the last half-dozen shootings, we've picked up on an interesting common thread."

"What's that?"

"The leader of the gang uses .69 French Dragoon bullets. To put it simply, they have a triangular base instead of the typical round base, and they're stamped with an M. For Marker, I'm guessing."

"Are they rare?"

"They were used primarily in the War between the States."

"So what does it mean?"

Corbin shrugged a shoulder. "I don't know. Maybe nothing more than his attempt to be unique."

"His trademark." Catherine squeezed her eyes shut for a moment, wishing she could open them again and all of this would disappear. Audrey's best dress lay out on the settee in the living room, ready for its final touches of lace. The invitations had been sent out, and the food for the reception planned.

But it wasn't simply the fact that the wedding might have to be canceled. It was that Audrey might lose the man she loved. Something Catherine didn't want to happen. Because it was something she understood all too well. And all she could do was to try and prove Harrison's innocence.

"Let me talk to Harrison," she began. "I'm sure he has a perfectly good explanation. And more than likely it's nothing more than the fact that the man can spin a good tale, even if much of what he says is an exaggeration of the facts."

Corbin shook his head then reached out and grasped her arm. "You can't confront him. If he is one of the gang members, he's not going to let you walk away once he knows you have knowledge of his secret. We've got to keep this quiet for now."

Catherine raised her chin. "Then what would you have me do?

Despite my father's funeral, Audrey's determined to go ahead and get married. And with the wedding just over two weeks away, you haven't given me anything more than a handful of suspicious rumors, none of which are enough for me to call off the wedding."

"This isn't my fault, Catherine."

She stopped, knowing he was right. "I just wish this would all disappear."

"And I promise I'll do everything to find out the truth. Just don't do anything. Not yet." He tipped his hat and took a step backward.

Catherine watched Corbin walk away before heading back to the store, wondering if he'd be able to keep his promise. And how long she could be silent.

Chapter Nine

....

Late morning brought with it nothing to ease Catherine's growing
sense of restlessness. She ran her fingers across the store's polished
pine counter, stopping when a square nail head bit into the edge
of her thumb. She checked the rough spot on the wooden counter,
which her father had planed with his own hands. She'd turned fifteen
the day her parents had opened Morgan's General Store, completely
stocked with everything from barrels of pickles, molasses, and
vinegar, to bushel baskets of dried legumes.

But neither the responsibility of running the general store, nor
her mother's fervent pleas, had been enough to tame her father's
heart. He'd first caught gold fever when he was nothing more than a
young man of seventeen looking for adventure and his fortune. Idaho
in the early 1860s had given him both—or at least the adventure.

Catherine began straightening the jars of penny candy that
eight-year-old Gregory Allen had disturbed on his last visit into
town. According to her mother, Isaiah Morgan had returned with
more stories than gold, but by that time it was too late. Gold fever
was in his blood. He managed to ignore the rumors of a stampede
to Cassiar, British Columbia, in '71 and Sitka in the same year, but
a deep-seated desire kept the yearning alive. When prospectors
began heading into Alaska again in the mid-seventies, the thought
of another possible strike had taken him away from Revenge. And
this time he never returned.

Isaiah Morgan had made it clear that he placed a higher value on his thirst for gold than his own family, something she'd long ago been forced to accept. Thankfully, keeping track of her three sisters and running the store hadn't allowed her to dwell on the loss of her father.

She set the last candy jar in place and realized that the unwanted memories from her past weren't the only source of her disquiet. Corbin's unexpected visit this morning had left her restless…and guilty. Guilty because she knew there might not be anything she could do to stop her sister's heart from getting broken.

Beads of perspiration formed at the back of her neck as she moved to the front of the store and glanced out the clear windowpanes framing the door. Dark clouds billowed in the distance against the afternoon sky's pale blue canvas, signaling the possibility of more rain that would bring relief to both the earth and the farmers.

She studied her dusty view of the town. Except for an occasional buggy or horse and rider, the streets were empty. Apparently, she wasn't the only one suffering from the abnormally hot weather. Her one customer all afternoon had bought half a pound of sugar. Hardly justification to keep the store open. She'd far rather be resting outside in the shade, drinking lemonade, or chatting on Emily's front porch. Anywhere but sitting behind a stuffy counter waiting for customers to arrive.

The back door to the store flew open then slammed against the wall. Catherine jumped as Audrey burst through the entrance carrying a large, leather hatbox.

Catherine pressed her hand against her heart. "I do declare, you've got to learn to make a quieter entrance."

"Sorry." Audrey dropped the box onto the counter in front of Catherine. "I want to know what you think."

Before Catherine could respond, Audrey pulled out a tall cadet blue velvet hat with three golden ostrich feathers peering over the left side.

Catherine's eyes widened. Women's fashions had become far too elaborate in her opinion. "I...I can see that you're putting Emily's ostrich farm to good use."

"And..."

She attempted a smile. "I love the blue you chose. It will definitely stand out."

Audrey frowned. "But..."

Catherine wrinkled her nose at her sister's prodding. "It's a bit gaudy?"

"Gaudy?" Audrey grabbed Catherine by the hand and pulled her from behind the counter. "Styles are changing, Catherine. You've got to stay up with them."

Catherine protested as Audrey set the hat on her head then spun her toward the full-length beveled mirror in the corner of the store.

"The typical straw hat is a thing of the past," Audrey insisted. "In all the big cities back East, women are flaunting masses of plumes, flowers, and feathers with pride."

Catherine planted her hands on her hips. "Before you know it, these hats will include the very bird itself."

"Something that's already being done. I could show you pictures where an entire bird is mounted on wires and springs so its head and wings can move about." Audrey clicked her tongue in excitement. "They stuff robins, bluebirds—"

"Enough." Catherine held up her hand. At least Audrey hadn't added an entire bird to this hat, though she had obviously spent far too much time reading copies of *Harper's Bazaar*. The residents of Revenge—including herself—had managed just fine with simple straw hats and bonnets for as long as she could remember. "So simplicity has now been replaced with velvet, silk, lace, and…and stuffed birds?"

Audrey laughed. "And higher crowns. Much, much higher."

Catherine studied her reflection. Any higher and the hat would be scraping the store's ceiling. "I had thought my new dress was enough of a statement to get the town talking. Surely you don't expect me to wear this as well?"

"This isn't for you. Mrs. Middleton special ordered two of them. One for herself and one for her daughter back East, with specific directions that it have that added flare that will catch everyone's eye."

Catherine pulled off the hat and handed it back to her sister. "That it certainly will. What's the occasion?"

"She's going back East for several months to attend the birth of her first grandchild."

"So the fame of my millinery sisters continues to spread. Next thing we know, they'll be featuring your hats in Macy's Department Store in New York City." While she might not have the bold tastes of her sisters when it came to fashion, she couldn't deny the surge of pride over their growing business. "As long, of course, as it doesn't take you and Harrison away from Revenge."

Audrey's smile faded as she slid the hat back into the box and avoided Catherine's gaze. Catherine tried to gauge the sudden change in her sister's behavior. Did Audrey, like Lily, yearn to escape the rural confines of Revenge?

Catherine tapped her fingers against the counter, still uncertain as to what she'd just stumbled upon. "You and Harrison aren't thinking about moving away, are you?"

Audrey dropped the lid and snapped it shut. "Moving? No. Harrison decided he wants to stick with farming for the long haul."

"Then what's wrong?"

"Nothing, I hope." Audrey pulled two pieces of licorice from the glass jar and handed one to Catherine.

"Whatever you're brooding over doesn't sound like nothing."

Audrey finally looked up at Catherine, her expression still serious. "I've been debating whether or not I should speak to you about something."

"You're not having second thoughts about getting married, are you?"

"Of course not. It's just that...despite what happened between you and the sheriff in the past, I've seen the two of you talking together several times in the past couple weeks."

Catherine bit off a piece of the licorice. "I thought you said this had something to do with Harrison?"

"It does." Audrey dropped her hands against the counter. "I need to know if the sheriff has talked to you about him."

Catherine's guard stiffened. "What exactly do you mean?"

"He paid Harrison a visit this week."

Catherine felt her temper flare. Why had Corbin failed to mention during their short talk this morning that he'd been out to the Tucker farm? She struggled to find a reasonable explanation to give Audrey. "Corbin mentioned he wanted to get to know some of the newcomers in town."

"This wasn't, shall we call it, a neighborly visit," Audrey continued.

"What exactly did he say?"

"As ridiculous as it sounds, I believe he thinks Harrison is somehow involved in the rash of bank robberies that have been taking place across the state."

Catherine's chin dipped.

"Catherine." Tears welled in the corners of Audrey's eyes. "I need to know the truth. Has the sheriff spoken to you about Harrison?"

Catherine hesitated. "While it's true that Corbin returned to Revenge to fill in for Sheriff Lansing, he's also here to investigate the Masked Gang."

Audrey's face paled as she took a step back. "Then I don't understand. We all know Harrison has nothing to do with the rash of bank robberies."

Catherine pulled another licorice from the jar. The last thing she wanted was for Audrey to overreact. There was still a good chance that nothing would come from Corbin's investigation of Harrison. How could it when the man was innocent? "The sheriff is just doing his job."

"Harassing innocent people?"

"Audrey, that's not fair."

"What isn't fair is that Harrison is being looked at as a suspect in a murder investigation."

Catherine wanted to believe that all her reassurances were correct and none of this could be true. Because while Harrison's stories might seem somewhat unbelievable at times, no one thought him to be a murderer. Catherine stared at the leather hatbox. But if that were true, then why did the doubts insist on mingling with her continued stance for his innocence? Corbin might not have solid proof, but neither was she completely able to dismiss his concerns. Not if her sister's future happiness was at stake.

"What if Harrison isn't who he says he is?" The words slipped out before Catherine had a chance to fully weigh them. She grasped Audrey's hand. "I'm sorry. I didn't mean—"

"Catherine?" Audrey's face paled. "Then why did you say it? Surely you don't believe it."

"Because…" Catherine pressed her lips together. "Because as happy as I am for you and your relationship with Harrison, the sheriff has found some discrepancies in his stories."

"Discrepancies?" Audrey shook her head. "I don't understand."

"They're just small things, but when added together they become a bit more significant."

"Like what?"

Catherine preferred to shield her sister from what was happening, but keeping things from her would only make things worse in the end. "Like the fact that there is no record of Harrison staking a claim in Alaska."

"That's ridiculous. You know as well as I do that he staked a claim."

"That's what he says—"

Audrey jerked her hand away. "So you've decided to side with the sheriff?"

"Of course I'm not siding with him. I've spent my life protecting you. The bottom line is that I believe Harrison is innocent."

"But if the sheriff believes Harrison is involved with the robberies…"

Catherine shook her head and bridged the gap between her and her sister. "He just needs time to find out the truth. Harrison is innocent, because we both know that Harrison would never hurt anyone. These men have robbed and murdered…Harrison would never do any of those things."

"But you just said…"

"I'm sorry about what I just said." Catherine pressed back a loose strand of hair from Audrey's cheek. Didn't she know how much she loved her? That she'd do anything she could to protect her? "Listen to me. We both know that if the sheriff had any real evidence that Harrison is involved, he'd be sitting in a jail cell right now. Corbin's just doing his job."

"I don't know."

"Listen to me, Audrey. Do you love Harrison?"

"Of course."

"And he loves you. We both know that Harrison had nothing to do with the robberies, but let the sheriff do his job."

"It's just that I had thought…hoped…that his visit was simply routine." Audrey began to sob. "I could understand if he were going around and asking people if they'd seen anything suspicious, but this was different."

"Then let's start there." Surely action on her part was better than waiting for Corbin to come up with the truth. "I want you to tell me exactly what the sheriff wanted to know."

Audrey leaned back against the counter. "The sheriff knew that Harrison had been in Lancaster the day of the robbery and started asking him questions about that day specifically. Then he wanted to know what Harrison did before moving here. It was the same questions, over and over."

"He's fishing for information because he doesn't have anything concrete."

"But if he ends up believing his suspicions, he'll arrest Harrison. We're supposed to get married in two weeks."

"I know."

"What am I supposed to do?"

"For now, I just want you to trust me. I'm going to figure out a way to take care of this. Because any evidence the sheriff's gathered hasn't been enough to arrest him. We've got some time."

"Harrison didn't do this." Audrey's chest heaved. "He's not a bank robber…or a murderer."

"Breathe, Audrey."

"If I lose Harrison…"

"Breathe, honey." Catherine gathered her sister in her arms.

"You've got to help me prove he didn't do this. Please, Catherine."

* * *

Twenty minutes later, Audrey left and the store was quiet again. Corbin might not want her to get involved, but it was already far too late for that. Catherine sat down at the telephone and made the connection.

"Mr. Peterson? This is Catherine Morgan."

"Catherine, it's good to hear from you, but I'm afraid I don't have any further information regarding your father."

"I didn't expect you to know anything yet. It's…it's something else. I need your help, Mr. Peterson."

"Of course. You know I'll do anything I can for you girls."

Samuel Peterson had connections throughout the state of Ohio that rivaled any Pinkerton agent. Some things she knew never to ask about. But that wasn't going to stop her from digging until she found the truth. "I need you to find out everything you can about someone's background."

"Give me their name and I'll see what I can do."

"The man's name is Harrison Tucker."

Chapter Ten

....

Catherine stepped into the kitchen and started yanking out the pins that secured her hat. No doubt, Pastor London's sermon to the congregation this morning had been yet another well-spoken address, but she hadn't caught more than its bare essence. Instead, she'd found her mind deliberating on the problem pertaining to Harrison. Audrey had sat beside her stiff as a washing board, her mind obviously on unspiritual matters as well.

Clutching the freed pins between her fingers, she shot up a short prayer that God would forgive her for not only failing to pay better attention to the pastor's words, but also for her inability to protect her sister. Not only did the poor girl have to mourn her father's unexpected passing, but she was contemplating the possibility of a future without Harrison as well.

Revenge's new sheriff seemed to be the only party unconcerned by the turn of events. Dressed in a white button-down shirt with a navy and gray checked lapel vest, he'd sat on the far side of the church singing "It Is Well with My Soul" with the rest of the congregation like he didn't have a care in the world, while she'd tried not to blame him for the trouble he'd brought with him to Revenge. She stomped her foot against the hard floor. How that man exasperated her!

The faint smell of cigars teased her senses. Strange, considering most of the men she was acquainted with didn't smoke. The back door opened, and Lily slipped into the kitchen behind her. Catherine reached for the last pin and made a conscious effort to rein in her befuddled thoughts. Lily didn't need to know that their family problems now entangled matters beyond the death of their father. Especially if Harrison was proven innocent, as Catherine believed he would be. Lily already had enough to deal with.

"I thought you were headed to Emily's for lunch." Catherine set her hat and the pile of pins on the counter.

"Emily's out of salt and asked if I'd bring her some." Lily grabbed a small package from an open shelf then paused. "Are you sure you don't want to come with us? Milena's making fried chicken and mashed potatoes for Sunday dinner this week."

Catherine rubbed the back of her neck. "Tell Emily I appreciate the invitation, but I have a headache. And besides, I could use a quiet afternoon to catch up on some accounting."

Lily frowned at Catherine's feeble excuses, but both were true. Sunday afternoon lunch at the O'Conner farm might be tradition, but so were the never-ending inquiries on her prospective marital status, something Catherine would prefer to skip today, considering her current mindset. And the corners of her temples did pound, though not from the bookkeeping waiting for her in the other room.

"Accounting on the Lord's day?" Lily folded her hands across her chest, obviously not impressed. "You should have been listening to Pastor Landon's sermon today. I believe he emphasized how today is a day of rest."

"I was listening." Sort of. "He spoke of casting our burdens on our Heavenly Father so we can find rest for our souls, not about taking time off from our work."

Casting her burdens on anyone else had always been a challenge, let alone giving them to God.

Catherine gnawed on her bottom lip. *I'm trying, God, really. But I'm the one who has to finish planning tomorrow's memorial service and find a way to prove Harrison's innocence.*

Lily shook her head. "Maybe he wasn't specifically speaking of a day off from your work, but I'm sure the idea was implied. Besides, even if the Good Lord didn't exactly use those words, it's still a good idea. How many times do we have to tell you that you work too much?"

Catherine grabbed a dishcloth and began wiping down the already clean counter space. "I'm fine, Lily. I promise."

Lily made no move to leave. "I know you're worried about Audrey. She told me about the sheriff coming around and questioning Harrison. Surely he doesn't actually think Harrison is involved with the Masked Gang?"

Catherine rubbed harder. So much for keeping secrets. "I don't believe there is anything to worry about. He's just being thorough in his investigation."

"How thorough?"

"There is evidence suggesting his involvement, but apparently none of it is enough for an arrest, or Corbin would have had him locked behind bars days ago."

"Mrs. McBride's gossip certainly isn't helping."

Catherine stopped and stood up straight. "What did she say?"

"That it's scandalous for Audrey to go ahead with the wedding when Father has just died."

"Surely even she can understand that things would be different if he'd been around the past few years and then died, but he's not even been a part of our lives. Why should Audrey have to wait to be married because of him?"

"Mrs. McBride said—"

"Perhaps you need to spend less time listening to gossip and more time listening to Pastor Landon's sermons." She stopped. Why was it that her mouth was always getting in the way of her good intentions?

"Catherine—"

"I'm sorry." Catherine dropped the cloth into the kitchen sink then rested both hands against the counter. "Tell me, what are we going to do if Harrison is guilty? Audrey's just lost Father and now Harrison."

"Audrey's stronger then you think, Catherine. We all are. You raised all of us to deal with what life brings us. Both the good and the bad." Lily cocked her head. "But you're the one I'm worried about. You've spent your entire life making sure we're all right. And yes, I know we continually nag you about finding a husband, but it's only because we care. We want you to be happy."

"I'm all right. Really." Catherine weighed her words. "Besides, even though everyone assumes it does, having a husband doesn't equal happiness."

Lily didn't look convinced. "I suppose."

"And you're right about Mrs. McBride, too. Why let her high opinion of etiquette stand in the way of Audrey's happiness?"

Or Corbin's worthless pile of evidence.

Catherine sucked in a breath. "We'll get through Father's service tomorrow, and then we have a wedding to finish planning. And neither the sheriff's quest nor Mrs. McBride's feelings on propriety are going to diminish Audrey's wedding day."

Lily's smile widened. "So you'll come to lunch?"

Catherine laughed. "No, but go and have a good time. I'll be fine."

Catherine closed her eyes and reveled in the quiet as Lily slipped out the back door. As much as she loved her sisters, she really did need an afternoon to herself. No customers. No fiancés and beaus. Only...

Cigar smoke.

She wrinkled her nose then went back to her current problem regarding Harrison. One thing continued to niggle at her despite her words of assurance to both Audrey and Lily. What if Corbin was right and Harrison was guilty? She needed to find out the truth, but she certainly had no training in the ways of a lawman. She pinched the bridge of her nose to stifle a sneeze then started for the parlor. A glass sat at the end of the counter.

Strange. She hadn't noticed it before, but she'd cleaned up the kitchen after breakfast this morning and washed and dried all the dishes. Lily had left for church with John after her and had obviously left out the glass. Which was typical of Lily, who never remembered to pick up anything. If the girl was to marry, she was going to have to learn a few more things about running a household.

Catherine continued into the parlor and stopped short. The smell of cigars hung heavy in the air. Her mother's glass curio cabinet stood open. A rose-patterned plate had been knocked over and now lay cracked. A glass pitcher, porcelain figurines, and photo frames, once sitting on the shelves, lay scattered about the floor. Papers and correspondence from the desk lay in a pile beside them. A sick feeling washed over her. This was not Lily simply forgetting to put a few things away. Someone had been in the house.

Or possibly someone was still in the house?

She stood in the middle of the parlor, listening for signs of an intruder, but all that she heard was the faint tick-tock of her mother's clock that still hung on its place above the fireplace mantel. Catherine felt her chest constrict. Most of the things in the house were of sentimental value, which made her wonder why anyone would even want to break in.

Catherine grabbed her father's gun from the top of the curio cabinet and climbed the stairs, searching through the bedrooms one at a time. The tooled-leather box filled with her mother's silverware and the gold earrings Audrey kept on her dresser were all in place.

Catherine stopped in the doorway of her room and tried to make sense of what she was seeing. This was Revenge, Ohio, not the Wild West where gunfights were a daily occurrence. There were always a couple of the local boys who had a nose for trouble, but for the most part, crimes constituted nothing more than the stealing of a couple of chickens from one of the nearby farms.

She sat down on the edge of her bed. The pounding in her temples increased. A pair of stockings hung from the corner of her dresser. Pulling open the drawer, she stuffed the undergarment back in. Someone had methodically gone through the house, searching for something. But why?

Her mother's music box lay cracked on the floor. Catherine fell to her knees beside the wooden box and gently twisted the key. Warped strains of a melody filled the air.

She needed to see Corbin.

Catherine winced at knowing that the first person to come
to mind when there might be a problem was Corbin. Of course, she
did have good reason. He was the sheriff, and this had to be reported,
even if he was the last person she wanted to see at the moment. She
couldn't take any chances. Shoving aside any remaining personal
feelings, she hurried toward the sheriff's office.

* * *

Corbin poured himself a cup of coffee, took a sip, and then set it
down to wait for it to cool a couple degrees. Pastor Landon's words
had tumbled through his mind all morning, reminding him of how
long it had been since he'd truly cast his burdens on his Savior.

A hard thing to do when he was looking for revenge—something
he wasn't sure he was willing to let go of. Which made him a
hypocrite. Hadn't he sat in the meeting hall this very morning and
sung "It Is Well with My Soul" while a wall of hatred toward one man
surrounded him?

Arresting William Marker wasn't the only distraction in his life.
He'd known from the moment he took on the job of sheriff that facing
Catherine was going to be far more difficult than catching any band
of criminals.

And he'd been right.

She'd greeted him this morning with nothing more than a nod
of her head and a polite "good morning." So much for his attempts
to apologize. Even his peace offering had done little to improve
their relationship. Not that he was trying to win her back, but he did
understand how she felt. In the past week, she'd lost her father and

faced serious doubts about whether or not her future brother-in-law was who he said he was.

It was a loss he knew far too well.

He combed his fingers through his hair then picked up his coffee again. It still tasted bad, but at least it wasn't going to burn his tongue. He'd contacted no less than half a dozen sources trying to connect Harrison to someone who'd fought on the Confederate side. Who was he kidding? The way his luck was running, the Masked Gang would be headed for the state line before he made any progress.

With his coffee back on the table, Corbin pulled out a sheet of paper and his ink pen. There had to be a logical way to look at the situation. He knew he was missing something. He dipped his pen into the inkwell and began writing down a list of the evidence against Harrison.

The man had a secret, he was certain about that, but a secret didn't necessarily equal a life of crime. Had he become so intent on settling the score because of his father's death that he'd stretched facts and circumstances in order to find a man to blame for the death of his father? He tapped the pen against the paper and watched the patch of black ink spread across the page. No. He couldn't let emotion determine his action. As an officer of the law, he had a sworn duty to uphold justice.

Which was why he'd paid a visit to Harrison's farm. If the man were innocent, Corbin had hoped to find something that would exonerate him, but his probing had accomplished little. Either the man was a first-rate liar, or he was innocent. But the questions still remained. If Harrison Tucker wasn't the leader, then who was? Because whether he liked it or not, every lead he had pointed to the fact that Tucker was involved.

Even if the clues he had were purely circumstantial. He started another list. The gang wore black masks, while the leader, purported to be William Marker, had a white star stitched on the back of his. Marker also used triangular-based bullets, but it wasn't as if they were going to catch the man on the type of bullet he used. No. He needed proof. Undeniable proof.

Which meant he was going to have to find a way to be a step ahead of the gang and catch them in action. But how he was going to do that, he had no idea.

Corbin looked up as Catherine stepped through the door of the sheriff's office for the second time in a week. He tried to swallow the feelings of resentment her presence always brought with her. Then he reminded himself that he wasn't here to deal with emotions from the past. Not when there were lives at stake.

And his father's life to revenge.

He forced a smile. "Miss Morgan, what a pleasant surprise."

"It is, I suppose." She peered up at him from beneath a pair of long, dark lashes. "A surprise I mean."

His chair creaked under him as he sat back and crossed his arms. She still wore her Sunday-meeting dress, a pale blue fabric that made her eyes shine. Even he couldn't deny that truth. "You look lovely today."

He closed his mouth. What had gotten into him? The last thing he needed to do at this point was entangle the present with emotions from the past, because he had no plans of stopping until his father's murderer was hanged. Even if it meant having to hurt Catherine a second time.

"I spoke with Audrey." Catherine's smile disappeared. "She said that you went out to Harrison's place asking him questions about the robberies."

Corbin knew he had to proceed carefully. The last thing he wanted was for her to believe that he was no longer on her side. "Part of my job is questioning people."

"Questioning them, maybe. But not treating them as criminals."

"I did no such thing, and you know it."

She smacked her palms against his desk. "What I do know is that you have a handful of worthless clues that point to Harrison. Unless you've found something that proves he's a murderer beyond a shadow of a doubt, I want you to leave him alone."

"Just because Mr. Tucker is marrying your sister is no reason for me to look the other way." Corbin shook his head, struck with her stubbornness. She wanted the truth to equal what she wanted to believe. "Is this why you came by? To criticize my investigation methods?"

"I'm not interested in your methods, only in the welfare of my sister."

"You always did put their welfare above everything else."

Corbin regretted the sharp sting of his words, but he wasn't going to allow her to compromise his investigation.

"I didn't come here to argue with you." Her fingers tapped against the wooden desk. "There is something else. The real reason I stopped by."

He saw a look of fear cross her face, a rare expression for the Catherine Morgan he knew. She'd always been good at controlling her emotions. Which perhaps wasn't a fair assessment on his part. He'd once fallen in love with a girl who could laugh and cry at the beauty of a sunset in the same breath. And he'd been the one who brought that out in her—or so she'd once told him.

"What is it?"

"Someone broke into our house during this morning's church service."

Her words caught him by surprise. Up until this point, he'd been thankful for the relatively few instances of crime he'd had to deal with in Revenge. It had allowed him to focus his time on the real reason he was here. "You're certain?"

"Of course I'm certain. Though I have to say it was an odd collection of things taken, most with little value."

"Like what?"

"A couple of inexpensive figurines, a picture frame, and some jewelry."

"What about the store?"

Her shoulders pressed back, and her chin rose. The Catherine he knew had returned, hiding any remaining emotion under the surface. Restrained and in control. "Both doors were locked and nothing was touched that I could see."

"Seems odd that a would-be burglar would steal an assortment of worthless objects from your house and leave the store alone."

"I thought the same thing. Except for a few sentimental things I have in the house, the store holds much greater value. Everyone in town knows that." Catherine fingered the edge of the desk.

"You're going to need to keep your doors locked at night, and I'll keep a watch on the place for you." Corbin hesitated. The last thing he needed was further involvement with her.

"I would appreciate that." Catherine rose from her chair. "But I'm sure it was a one-time thing."

Was she trying to convince herself, or him?

"Perhaps." Corbin grabbed his hat and gun. It still wasn't a good enough explanation for him. Thieves didn't break in for a handful of bric-a-brac. "I think it would be best if I were to come out and see for myself."

Five minutes later, Corbin was standing in the very room where he'd asked Isaiah Morgan for Catherine's hand in marriage. He hadn't expected the memory to assault him the way it did, but seeing her standing in front of him in her fancy dress that brought out the color of her eyes, looking pretty and vulnerable, was almost enough to make him forget about the real reason he'd returned to Revenge. This had been a mistake.

He wiped the back of his neck, suddenly needing a way of escape. "I'd like you to make a complete list of all the things that are missing for my personal records."

"I can have the list for you tonight."

"Tomorrow will be fine, though I'm afraid that the chances of recovering the lost items are slim." He tried to read her expression, needing to know if she felt as vulnerable as he did at the moment. Had her presence always made him this defenseless?

"I understand, though I still can't see what someone would want with most of the items they took."

He took a few mental notes of the downstairs parlor. It appeared to him more like someone was searching for something rather than out to rob the house. But what? "Where else were things taken?"

"A few things from upstairs."

He should look.

Corbin followed her up the stairs toward the bedrooms. He stood in the doorway of her bedroom, remembering how once he'd planned to make this their home together—their room. Inside he was met again with further signs of the destruction left behind by the robbers.

Who would do something like this? If the thief had been looking for some fast cash, they'd have helped themselves to the silver.

"This doesn't make sense. Taking the inventory from your store or stealing the cash box would feed a thief's quest to make a quick dollar, but why your bedroom? Why rummage through papers in a desk?"

Because it was personal. Whoever did this was looking for something specific. Not just a stash of money or valuable jewelry.

He cleared his throat, unable to stop the surge of worry that coursed through him. No matter what their past relationship might have been, his job had suddenly become even more personal.

"Maybe you should stay at the O'Conners' for the next few days. At least until I can figure out who did this."

"Don't you think you're overreacting? For all we know the intruder was Mr. Fields because I wouldn't extend his credit yesterday."

Corbin shook his head. "This isn't someone making a statement over a bushel of wheat or a pound of sugar."

Catherine headed back down the stairs. "I can't leave and you know it."

"But—"

"I can't shut down the store. I'd lose too much business, something I can't afford to do."

She turned around at the bottom of the stairs and looked up at him. "And besides, I live across the street from the sheriff, and from what I hear, he's not someone you want to mess with."

He couldn't help but match her faint smile. "No, he's not."

"Then I don't have anything to worry about. Right?"

He wanted to assure her such was the case, but that was something he couldn't do. And there was more besides. There was something about being here, in her house…alone.

He shouldn't be here. He brushed past her and headed toward the back door.

"Audrey's wedding is less than two weeks away." Her voice stopped him in the middle of the kitchen. "I need answers."

What else could he do? He didn't have answers.

A knock on the back door rescued him from responding.

Corbin pulled his gun from his holster. "Are you expecting anyone?"

Catherine shook her head.

"Go ahead and open it, but I'll be right behind you."

More than likely, whoever had trashed her house was long gone, but he wasn't going to take any chances. Catherine opened the door then gasped.

Isaiah Morgan stood on the back porch.

Chapter Eleven

....

Catherine felt the air whoosh from her lungs. She grasped the counter to steady her legs as they threatened to buckle beneath her. What she saw couldn't be real. Isaiah Morgan was dead. She blinked her eyes, but the bearded man who resembled the father she remembered still stood there.

"Catherine." He smiled, cocked his head, and then pulled her into his arms. "You're all grown up."

Catherine breathed in the strong scent of lye and pulled away. She studied his bearded face. The years had darkened his skin and added a thick line of wrinkles around his eyes. He'd aged at least two decades in the past eight years.

She sucked in a breath and tried to make sense of what was happening. Tomorrow they were planning to hold a memorial service for Isaiah Morgan and post a grave marker beside their mother. Her sisters would weep through the ceremony, and she'd try to forget how he'd vanished from their lives, and what her life would have been like today if he'd stayed. She bit her top lip and shook her head. It didn't matter. He might have finally returned to Revenge, but that didn't mean she was ready to welcome him back with open arms.

"Mr. Peterson told me you were dead."

"Isn't the first time an old codger like me was proclaimed dead ahead of his time." The half smile was back. "Thought it was time to come back, what with my first grandbaby on its way."

Catherine fought the swell of anger that rose within her. Surely he didn't think he had the right to simply waltz back into their lives and pick up the role of father, let alone grandfather. In her eyes, he'd lost that right the day he chose to chase a fortune over caring for his wife and four daughters.

Catherine blinked. "He called me and told me that they'd found your body in a mining accident."

His jaw twitched. "Which was all an unfortunate mistake, because as you can see, I'm not dead."

Her legs melted beneath her. Corbin grasped her shoulders from behind to hold her steady. For the first time since he'd returned, she was thankful for his presence.

"Besides, if I was dead, would I be starving?" Her father patted his stomach. "I know it's been a long time, and I've a lot to make up for, but I'm here. Surely that ought to count for something."

Like her mother's picture stereopticon, memories flashed before her and filled her mind with dozens of images. She pushed them aside. She'd made allowances for her sisters' sake to remember her father in a good light, but that didn't mean she was going to welcome him into her house.

Catherine sucked in a lungful of air. "I'm sorry, but I don't think—"

Corbin squeezed her elbow. "Why don't you come inside, Mr. Morgan. We'll find something for you to eat, and then you can explain the...the false reporting of your death. And I'm sure the rest of your daughters will be anxious to see you."

Catherine reined in her turbulent emotions. Corbin was right. The least she could do was offer the man something to eat before she sent him back to where he'd come from. She would be perfectly

content for him to battle the gold mines the rest of his life and leave
her and her sisters alone. But that was something she'd have to sort
out later tonight in the privacy of her room.

She turned to Corbin and motioned to the cabinet. "I've got
bread, homemade apple butter, and some leftover roast."

Corbin pulled her into the kitchen to allow her father to enter.
"Catherine, if you'll take your father into the sitting room, I'll get
him something to eat."

Isaiah nodded. "I'd appreciate that, young man."

Catherine brushed through the kitchen toward the sitting
room. The years had passed and with them all hope of her father's
return. The unexpected announcement of his death had squelched
any lingering possibilities of their ever being a family again. Guilt
sprang its ugly head, but she, for one, was perfectly happy to forget
the man.

Catherine sat down on the settee while her father walked around
the room. The floral tapestry sofa with its matching walnut armchairs,
her mother's slant-front desk, the corner whatnot filled with her
mother's bric-a-brac... Except for the mess left behind by the thieves,
little had changed in this room since her death. She bit back the
crushing words poised to spring from her lips. These were things
he had no right to any longer. And then there were the questions.
Like why he'd walked out on them, and then believed he could simply
show up at the back door like nothing happened.

Her father turned to face her. "What happened in here? It looks
like a—"

"A break-in." She finished his sentence, something Lily would
have done if she were here.

"A break-in?" He crossed the room in a couple broad steps. "Were you hurt?"

"No." Catherine brushed the question aside. "More than likely it was some of the boys in town. It's not important."

Isaiah sat up straight. "I can't say that I agree."

"Nor I." Corbin entered the room and placed a plate of food on her mother's embroidered cloth that lay across the table.

Catherine searched for her manners. "I'm sorry. You remember Corbin?"

"Of course." The twinkle was back in her father's eye as he pulled out a chair and sat down in front of the tray. "The handsome young man who captured my daughter's heart."

Who had once captured her heart.

All that had been lost with the selfishness of one man. The walls closed in on her again. Catherine squeezed her eyes shut, wondering how her quiet, ordered life had managed to spin out of control in the past couple of weeks.

"I always figured he'd be good for you." Her father continued, before taking a bite. "I remember the day he stood before me in this very room—"

"No." Catherine fidgeted on the edge of the settee and shook her head. Corbin stood across the room looking just as uncomfortable. "No, we never married...I thought I wrote you."

Her father shook his head.

Corbin cleared his throat. "I'm the sheriff now, here on official business."

"The break-in," her father repeated.

"There are a few things missing or broken, but that's not

important right now. I need to understand something." Catherine rose from her seat to address him. She clenched her hands at her sides. "You sit here like only a couple days have passed since we saw you last, not a lifetime. You left me to care for my sisters and watch my mother die, and now you expect to simply waltz back into our lives like nothing's happened." Her voice broke as it rose in volume. "I'm the one who had to make sure the store was taken care of, that your daughters attended school and married decent men."

Isaiah Morgan dropped his fork onto his plate. "I realize it was hard for you, but I thought—"

"Whatever you thought, you thought wrong. Can't you see that we're not the same family we were when you decided to leave?" She clasped her hands together. "You're not welcome here."

Corbin brushed his hand against her shoulder. "Catherine."

All the anger, frustration, and bitterness poured from her lips. "Don't expect me to calm down. Did you ever stop to realize what I've given up to keep this family together? To keep the store running so I can provide food and clothing? Or what your desertion did to Emily, Audrey, and Lily?"

"I truly am sorry, Catherine." Isaiah stood up, forgetting his food. "You've got to understand that I never meant to hurt you. I love you. All of you. That's why I'm back. I gave up drinking, made my peace with God, and now I need to make things right with my family. I realized finally that I was looking for the wrong thing. That pot of gold was always in front of me, but I couldn't ever find it. My own pot of gold was sitting right here back in Revenge, and I almost lost it."

Catherine forced herself to breathe slowly. "You didn't almost lose it. You did lose it."

Corbin reached for her elbow and led her toward the kitchen. "Will you excuse us for a moment, sir?"

"Of course." He slumped back down on the chair as Corbin pulled her into the kitchen.

"You're not thinking straight," he began.

She avoided his gaze. "I'm thinking perfectly straight."

"I'd give anything for my father to walk through that door right now and tell me that he loves me."

"Your father didn't walk out on you."

"No, but that doesn't mean you shouldn't give him a second chance."

She looked up at him, furious at his stance. "You're on his side?"

"I'm not on anyone's side. I know you've been hurt, but the fact is that you're father isn't dead. He's sitting in the other room, waiting for you to decide whether or not he can be the father he should have from the beginning. Doesn't he deserve a second chance?"

She took a step back from him. No. Things would never be the same again. Why couldn't he see that? "Tell me how to get past what he did to my mother, to my sisters, and to me. He let my mother die. And he never came back when he knew we were alone."

"But what if he's telling the truth? Maybe he has changed. Besides, sending him away won't do anything to change the past."

"I lost you because of him. Doesn't that mean anything to you? Don't you have any regrets that you and I aren't sitting in the parlor right now, married, with a family?"

"Your father is not the reason you lost me."

Catherine reached up and slapped Corbin across the face. The instant her fingers burned against his face from the impulsive action, she jerked her hand back.

"I'm sorry. I never meant to…" She glanced up at him, her eyes burning with unshed tears. All the anger, hate, and brokenness she'd carried for years bubbled to the surface of her emotions. How had it come to this?

"You told me that sometimes the past is better off forgotten," he began.

Her chest heaved. "I don't know if I can forget this time."

Blinking back the tears, Catherine ran past Corbin up the staircase toward her room. Tears poured out as Catherine wept for all she had lost. And for the father who had long ago become a stranger.

* * *

Catherine searched for normalcy in the bewildering scene before her. Her sisters sat scattered throughout the room, swapping stories faster than a spring tornado—with her father. In spite of the hours that had passed since his arrival, her heart still stung with fresh grief. Corbin might have been right in his desire to forget the past, but any true measure of forgiveness—if it came at all—would take time.

Forgiveness, though, apparently wasn't an issue in the minds of her sisters. Laughter filled the room, but instead of joining in with the lively banter, Catherine stood in the corner, wishing there were a way to melt into the heavy fabric of the curtains and disappear. Her sisters had rejoiced in the news that not only was their father alive, but he was here in town.

Grady tightened his arm around Emily, forcing old regrets to the surface, including the part of her that wished Corbin had stayed. Because for a few moments, with her own world floundering, he'd

taken on the supportive role she'd once longed for—until she'd
foolishly pushed him away. She forced her lungs full of air then
breathed out slowly. The truth was, Corbin was gone, and she was the
one who had to decide how she would deal with her father and with
three sisters who somehow didn't seem to have any apprehensions
about forgetting the past and simply letting Isaiah Morgan step back
into their lives like he'd never left.

She watched as her father leaned forward in the upholstered
chair—the same chair he used to retire to after a day of working
in the shop. Another memory surfaced. This one of sitting on the
staircase late at night, peeking around the corner into the sitting
room as Mother brought Father a cup of coffee before picking up
a needle and thread to work on her quilt. It was one of their nightly
rituals. One of the good ones she managed to dredge up.

Lily's laughter snapped Catherine back to the present. Her
younger sister reached up and tugged on the corner of their
father's beard.

Catherine pressed her hands against the small of her back. As
angry as she felt over his desertion, there was still a small part of her
that longed to embrace him back into their family. Even she could
remember the days before he made that fated decision to head west
after the tempting lure of gold struck. And if she were honest with
herself, perhaps his good days had outweighed his drinking bouts.
Like when he'd found time to play in the snow with her on a cold
winter day, or spend a hot summer afternoon fishing in Clear Creek,
or teaching her how to hit a target with one of his rifles.

Had she chosen to forget those moments because it lessened the
pain of what she'd lost?

The truth was, Isaiah Morgan could be a decent father until liquor passed his lips, but that truth had been lost over the years. And even the scene before her wasn't enough to make her forget the whole truth. There was still one issue Catherine couldn't erase no matter how much she wanted to. She knew the other side of the man who had the entire room riveted to his pocketful of stories that managed to rival Harrison's own vivid accounts of gold fever. And no matter how much she wanted to forget, she couldn't.

Because there had been other nights when she'd sat on that same staircase, praying fervently that God would listen to a young girl's cries. Isaiah Morgan might have been the perfect gentleman sober, but drunk was a different story. His voice had risen to her upstairs room, drawing her down the staircase in fear that his sharp words would do more than simply cut at her mother's heart.

And that was why, no matter what anyone else said or thought, she couldn't welcome him back into her house like nothing had happened.

"Catherine, come join us." Audrey patted the plush chair beside her. "These stories of Father's almost outshine Harrison's."

A lump swelled in Catherine's throat as she fumbled for an excuse. "I need to go and check on supper."

She rushed from the room, thankful she had something to keep her busy.

Audrey was right behind her. "Do we have any more lemonade?"

"There's a second pitcher on the counter."

Audrey tugged on Catherine's arm. "You need to come and sit with us. Dinner will cook without your standing over it. We're planning a welcome-home party, and we need your input."

Catherine handed Audrey the pitcher, then stopped. "A party?"

"I know it seems a bit odd considering we were just planning to hold a memorial service for him, but what better way to let everyone know that Isaiah Morgan is back in town? We can have it out on Emily's farm—"

"I don't know, Audrey." Catherine moved to pull the lid off the stew that simmered on the stove and began stirring. "There is so much to do at the store, and—"

"You don't have time, or you don't want to make the time?"

Catherine bit back a tainted response. "You must understand that this isn't easy for me."

"No matter how long he was gone, I never stopped praying for him to return. He is our father. Nothing can change that."

He was a father who'd never learned how to fill his role.

"Catherine." Isaiah appeared in the doorway. "I think I've done enough storytelling for now. What do you want to ask me? We might as well get it all out in the open now."

"Okay." Catherine folded her arms across her chest. Her sisters gathered around him, seeming content to let her play the role of villain alone. "Why did you wait so long to come back?"

Stories of the Alaskan frontier slipped away and in their place remained a marked silence. At least he seemed man enough to face the truth.

"Catherine…" Emily's hand rested on the child within her.

Catherine wasn't finished with her questions. "Where were you when Lily broke her arm falling out of the old oak tree out back, or when Emily had the measles, or most importantly, when our mother died?"

"Catherine—"

"No. It's okay." He motioned them all back into the parlor then slumped against the back of the settee. "Catherine has every right to ask...and the right to know the answers. You all do, in fact. And I knew I couldn't simply return without facing the past. I spent the past several hundred miles asking myself those very same questions."

"What do you mean?" Lily asked.

"Questions like why didn't I come back years ago?" His mouth drew in tighter. "The first few months I was gone were horrible. I was always hungry, cold, and I missed all of you terribly. Especially your mother. For no matter what you think, Catherine, no matter how many times we fought, I did love her."

He rubbed his chin. "Once in Alaska, I knew that my chances to strike it rich were next to none, but I managed to find just enough gold dust to keep me hungry for more. I convinced myself that my big find was just around the corner. All I needed was another day...another week...and I'd have the fortune I promised you. I wanted to build all of you girls a new house, enlarge the store, perhaps buy land outside town."

"None of that took the place of growing up with a father." Catherine cut in.

"I know."

"And when Mother died?" Catherine held her gaze steady. "Didn't that make any difference at all?"

"I didn't know how I could return when I had nothing. I had enough for a bed at night and a couple of meals during the day, but that was it. I...I didn't want you to know that I'd failed."

"You're right about having nothing," she countered. "No gold, no money...and no family."

He moved to stand in front of her. "No matter what you feel about me, Catherine, that was the part that hurt the most. I've wasted the past eight years feeling too ashamed to come home. Something happens to a man who's been proclaimed dead when he's really very much alive. It's like I was given a second chance, and I realized that it was time I returned to Revenge…and to my family. Something I should have done years ago." He grasped Catherine's hands. "I know I don't deserve your forgiveness. All I can hope for is that someday, you might grant it to me anyway."

Chapter Twelve

....

Catherine dug harder into the soft soil at the base of a tomato plant, hoping the physical work would alleviate some of the anger that had taken root around her heart. She'd attended enough church services to know God's command about forgiving your neighbor, but what about her father? Surely God understood that forgiveness wasn't something she could simply dole out, like slices of Mrs. McBride's apple pie at a church picnic. It was a question she'd wrestled with the entire night.

She moved on to the next plant and continued digging and pulling out the weeds. Her father's arrival two days ago had turned the memorial service they'd planned into a welcome-home party... and had left her full of questions and suspicions. While she tried to understand her sisters' exuberant welcome, they had yet to grasp her hesitation in letting him back into their lives. And she'd seen from the looks on their faces that they wanted her to grant their father the forgiveness he'd begged for. But she hadn't been able to voice the words that could never come from her heart.

A shadow crossed behind her, blocking the early morning sun. Catherine glanced up at the figure looming over her. Isaiah Morgan stood beside her.

"Your garden's beautiful. Looks as if you're going to have a nice crop come harvest time, and the flowers...you definitely have your mother's touch."

"Thank you." Catherine continued working.

He rubbed his chin with his fingers, a longtime habit she remembered from her childhood. So he was just as nervous as she was. "I just thought we could talk awhile?"

Catherine pushed the soil back into place. "I'm not sure that there's anything to talk about."

"Just for a few minutes. I promise." He turned toward the sun that was just reaching the tops of the oaks behind the store property. "I can't seem to get enough sunshine after all the frigid winters I've lived through."

Catherine adjusted her straw hat to block the light then handed him the basket sitting beside her. While she had purposely avoided a personal encounter with her father since his arrival, perhaps it was time to make an effort. "I was planning to pick some raspberries while Audrey watches the store this morning. You could help me if you'd like."

He took the offered basket and followed her. "I remember watching you and your mother working in the garden. You always had a knack for living things—that and numbers. We all know you got both of those gifts from your mother."

"They are things I enjoy."

Catherine quickened her pace, unsure of what he wanted from her. How did one pick up a conversation left forgotten for such a long time? She didn't know him any more than he knew her. And any thoughts of wanting things to be as they had been were marred by the fact that eight years now stood between them, and no excuse he could come up with would erase that. They stopped at the long row of vines laden with juicy red fruit that lined the back boundary of the property. Catherine popped one of the berries into her mouth then started filling the basket.

"How do you do it?" he asked.

She glanced over at him. "Do what?"

"I've watched you the past couple of days, and I'm amazed at all you do. The store's running far better than when I was here, the garden's stunning, your sisters are happy...When do you have time for yourself? For fun, or even sleep, for that matter?"

"I've always done what I have to do."

Catherine cringed, wishing she could melt the icy currents around her heart. The conversation sounded more like an exchange with one of her customers than a heart-to-heart talk with her father.

"What about the raspberries?" he asked. "Seems like a bit of a venture for a busy storekeeper."

"Emily's husband gives me all the fruit jars I need from his factory in exchange for my making raspberry preserves every summer. I love raspberries."

"I remember more than once having to get onto you and your sisters for coming home with empty baskets, which meant I missed out on eating many a good pie because of the lack of filling."

Catherine couldn't help but smile at the memory of the scoldings and how she'd been unable to eat her mother's supper because she was so full of raspberries.

"That Grady O'Conner spoils your sister, doesn't he?" he asked.

"He's very good to her."

"I'd say so. Like, for example, ostriches. Who ever heard of raising those crazy birds here in Ohio? I'd half decided to tell him it couldn't be done; that they'd all freeze to death come winter, but have you seen what he has planned..."

His voice faded into the background. Catherine felt another surge of anger rise to the surface as she thought about Emily. Where had Isaiah Morgan been when Grady came to the house to ask permission to marry Emily? Or the day Emily walked down the aisle on her wedding day? She'd been the one to hold her sister's hand when she'd cried over the loss of a mother who was never coming back and a father who didn't want to come back.

"Catherine?"

She dropped another berry into the basket and blinked away the painful memories. "I'm sorry. It's been a rough few days with the break-in, preparations for Audrey's wedding, and now…"

And now your being here.

"I know that my return hasn't been easy for you. Or for any of your sisters, for that matter." His gaze dropped to his black boots that peeked from under a pair of worn trousers. "Coming home wasn't easy for me, either. I spent the entire trip here fearing you wouldn't even let me in the back door."

Catherine popped another berry into her mouth. Her father had returned like the prodigal son, but instead of embracing his return, she'd continued to let resentment fester and grow like the weeds she'd pulled this morning. "I suppose I didn't give you the welcome home you were hoping for."

He set the basket between them and turned to her. "I know it's not enough, Catherine, but I am sorry. I don't know what else to say. Only that I hope you will one day forgive me."

Catherine squeezed her hands into fists at her sides, wishing the words she knew she should say were easier to speak. Jesus would have welcomed her father with a feast and spoken of forgiving a

man seventy times seven. Hadn't her father come to her with words
of repentance? Except Isaiah Morgan's words had never been worth
anything. He knew how to say what one wanted to hear.

*Is that the kind of forgiveness you meant, Jesus? Forgiving even
when the other person has no intention of changing?*

"Catherine?"

She glanced up at him, her emotions a tangled web of confusion.
She couldn't do this. Maybe if he'd been as determined when it came
to keeping his family together, she'd have been able to find the words.
But in her mind, he'd given up the title of Father years ago. "I don't
know if I can."

"Then I'll wait until you can."

She moved down another foot and started picking berries again,
thankful that they were far enough from the store that no one would
overhear them. "Why should I believe that you've changed? You've
always known what to say, but that's not enough anymore."

"All I want is your forgiveness."

"So that's why you came home, is it? To ease your own conscience."

"Yes…no." He dropped down onto the grass beside her and rested
his arms against his legs. "I'm back because I spent my life as a coward.
Staying in Alaska was the easy thing, because I knew if I came back I'd
have to explain. And now…I just need you to understand that."

She spread out her dress and sat beside him, feeling drawn to his
words, but still unable to let her heart completely believe him. "Why
now? Why come back at all?"

His deep laugh fell flat. "You always were the one full of questions."

Catherine pressed her hands into the soft grass. "I'm the one who
spent my life raising my sisters. I'm the one who promised Momma

I'd take care of them and make sure they married decent, Christian men." Harrison flashed before her, but she shook away the image. "And I'm the one who gave up marriage and children to make sure that promise was kept."

"So that's why you lost Corbin? Because he wasn't ready to take on a ready-made family?"

Catherine fiddled with the edge of the basket. "What happened wasn't Corbin's fault."

"Then what happened? Because it seems to me that I'm not the only one who's spent most of his life running from someone I love."

"How dare you compare what I've given up with your selfishness?" Catherine stood before grabbing the handle of her basket. It tipped over on its edge, sending berries scattering across the grass. She reached down to pick them up, irritated that his presence could affect her so much. That wasn't supposed to happen. She'd learned long ago how to wrap up her emotions so tightly no one saw them. "This is completely different."

"Then tell me what happened."

"Why?"

"Because something tells me I'm not the only one who needs forgiving. Sometimes we end up being hardest on ourselves."

"No." Catherine shook her head. She dropped the last berry back into the basket then started for the house. He didn't deserve to know. Just like he didn't deserve to walk back into their lives and think he could suddenly be a father to them. It was too late for that.

Just like it was too late for her and Corbin.

He followed right behind her. "I know it's not going to be easy for you to believe me, but I never meant to hurt your mother, or any of you girls."

No matter how many lines he tried to feed her, or how many excuses he gave, she'd never believe his leaving was for anything other than selfish reasons. "You left us here alone. She was sick…"

"We knew the risks."

Catherine spun around. "We? You're telling me that this was a decision you made together?"

"She knew I was too restless to be tied down to a store—"

"And a family?"

"It was never because of you, but she supported my decision. We thought it might be the way to something better."

"So you're telling me that she let you go? Just like that?"

"It wasn't easy on either of us."

Catherine turned to face him. "This is what I don't understand. You act as if she just let you go. Like she had no reservations about you leaving her alone with four children and a store—"

"She wanted me to follow my heart."

"With no regard to those around you or your responsibilities? No regard to the consequences left behind by your leaving?"

"She understood me and who I was."

She shook her head. "My mother was everything you're not. Kind, gentle, faithful…"

"And because of that, she was willing to let me follow my heart." His gaze pleaded for her to understand. "Then, when she died, I didn't know how to return to a house without her. Surely you know what it's like to lose someone."

Catherine swung her basket around and started again for the house, wishing she could ignore the twinges of understanding. But even that didn't change anything. He'd abandoned her and her sisters, and forgiveness wasn't something she could simply switch on and off like the telephone.

"What about your heart?" he asked.

"What do you mean?"

"Maybe it's time you followed yours. Marry Corbin without feeling any regrets of neglecting your sisters."

"Marry Corbin…" Catherine shook off the ridiculous notion. "Mr. Hunter and I…whatever was between us all those years ago is gone. It's been gone for years."

He let out a deep chuckle. "I might be a fool in every sense of the word, but I know love when I see it."

"Love? You just don't understand love. While you were off chasing some hollow dream, I was here keeping the family together. I had a promise to keep, and I…" Catherine dumped the basket of berries beside the back door and pushed away the tears. "I let Corbin go."

"Tell me what happened, Catherine."

She jerked her head up. "Why?"

"Because just like me, you've got to find a way out of the past. You've got to forgive yourself."

Catherine shook her head and swallowed the sob trying to work its way up her throat. The past didn't matter any longer. Hadn't she reminded herself of that very fact a hundred times this week?

"I told you, whatever there was between Corbin and I was over years ago."

"I don't believe you."

"Why does it matter to you? Don't think you can waltz back in here and make everything right."

"What happened?"

Catherine slumped her shoulders, defeated. The turmoil of emotion pressed against her from every side. "We'd planned our wedding to be a simple celebration in the spring. But with you gone and Momma sick, we decided to put off the wedding. At first it was postponed temporarily, but then one day I knew that she wasn't going to live."

Catherine watched the cloud of emotions pass through her father's eyes and for a moment wondered if he really did regret what he'd done.

"I'm sorry."

"I remember the night she died. I sat the girls down in the parlor and told them that Momma wasn't coming back. And that the four of us were going to have to work hard to keep things running."

Feelings of loneliness and fear swept over her. Feelings she never wanted to admit to him, because he was the one who had left her.

"I would have thought Corbin would have wanted to help," he said. "I remember how good he was at bookkeeping."

"His father was good at bookkeeping, but I don't think that was ever what Corbin wanted."

"What did you want?"

A house, a family...a husband.

Catherine avoided his question. "Corbin came to the house later that night. Mrs. Morrilton was in the kitchen playing chaperone. Corbin promised me that nothing had changed between us. He told me we could still get married, but I knew it would never work. I had Audrey, Emily, and Lily to care for and a store to keep up. I had no idea how to add marriage to my plate."

"So you're the one who broke things off?"

Catherine squeezed her eyes shut for a moment, wishing she could erase the one regret she'd had to live with her entire life. The whole town of Revenge believed that Corbin had walked out on her so that he wouldn't be saddled with a ready-made family, but the truth was far from what she'd allowed them to believe. He hadn't fought to keep her, but she'd been the one who'd sent Corbin away.

Catherine wiped her cheek with the back of her hand, unable to stop the flow of tears. "I…told him that I didn't love him anymore."

"Why?"

"Because I'd promised Momma I'd take care of my sisters. There wasn't time for love. Corbin had a job offer in Lancaster, and I knew he'd be happier there than working here at the store and feeling obligated to provide for all of us."

Her father pulled off his hat and clenched the brim between his fingers. "Something I should have been doing."

Catherine heard the defeat in her father's voice, along with guilt and regret. But that didn't change anything. Because he was right. He should have been the one to ensure that his family was cared for.

"I think part of me believed he would stay despite my protests," she continued. "To stand up and fight for me. Instead, he walked away."

"Does Corbin know the truth?"

"I never told him. A few days later, he left Revenge. I heard later that he was working on a ranch down in Texas." Catherine leaned against the side of the house, feeling the emotional fatigue of the confession. "Then, I barely had time to miss him. I was so busy making sure we had everything we needed, I didn't have time— or take the time—to think about what I'd lost. Momma had taught me all she could, but it was a struggle not to lose customers. Few thought I could make the store survive that first year."

"Seems to me that you proved yourself."

She shot him a wry grin. "We're still in business."

He tugged on his beard. "Was it worth it?"

"Losing Corbin?"

He nodded. "You don't have to do it on your own."

Irritation loomed its head again. Couldn't he see that losing Corbin had broken her heart? "What would you have had me do?"

"Tell Corbin the truth. That you loved him. That you still love him. You know I was right when I said that we both have a lot of forgiving to do."

"While I did what I felt I had to do at the time, how I felt all those years ago has no bearing on my life today. It would only dredge up a bucketful of emotions better left buried." She shook her head. "It's too late for the truth."

"Like it's too late for us?"

She looked up at him. "Isn't it?"

"I regret so many things. I missed watching you and your sisters grow up. Emily and Audrey's courting, and for all that you've lost, Catherine. I'm sorry. I never imagined my actions affected so many people."

"How could you not? We were a family. Not perfect, but a family."

"And that's what I want for all of us again."

Catherine fought reason. "Like I said. It's too late."

"Why?"

"Because…because I don't know if I can forgive you."

"Then I'll give you time. All I want from you is a second chance. Your sister's wedding will be here before you know it, and I want to see my first grandchild. I want to make up for everything I've missed."

Catherine met his steady gaze for a moment then turned toward the house.

"There is one other thing."

She turned back to him.

"I have something I want to give you." He pulled a necklace from his pocket and handed it to her. On the end of the thin gold chain was a small key.

Catherine held the gift in her palm. "I don't understand. It's a key?"

"Yes."

"To what?"

He closed her fingers over the key. "You'll know when the time comes."

"I don't—"

"Trust me." He brushed back a loose strand of hair from her face like he used to when she was little. "I'll leave if you want me to, Catherine."

She squeezed her eyes shut. She'd seen the joy on her sisters' faces. Emily wanted him to be a part of her child's life; Audrey wanted him to walk her down the aisle. She was the only one ready to forget that Isaiah Morgan had ever been a part of their lives.

God, I just don't know how.

She opened her eyes. "You can stay, but please don't expect me to act as if the past didn't happen, because I don't know if I'll ever be able to forgive you."

Catherine fled into the house, fearing she was making yet another mistake by not forgiving him.

* * *

Lunchtime on Saturday, Catherine took another bite of fresh corn and watched Penny Martin flirt with Corbin. The younger woman rested her hand briefly on his arm and laughed. Scandalous, if one were to ask her. Not that anyone would. But this was supposed to be her father's welcome-home party, not a matchmaking social. Penny was only one of a line of unattached women who had set their eyes on the new sheriff. And, as if their overt ploys to snare him weren't obvious enough, Corbin appeared to be enjoying the fresh banter. Catherine's frown deepened as Penny stood on her tiptoes and whispered something into Corbin's ear. This time he laughed.

"You look positively jealous, Catherine Morgan." Lily flopped down on the quilt beside her in a most unladylike manner.

"Jealous? Of whom?" Catherine turned back to her piece of corn. "Can't a girl finish eating her lunch in peace?"

"I can see how you've been keeping your eye on Corbin. Just like every other single girl in the county."

"I'm nothing like every other single girl in the county, because I'm sitting here enjoying my lunch and the beautiful late-summer weather instead of making a complete fool of myself like Penny and all the others."

Lily flicked an ant off the corner of the blanket. "So you're telling me that you have no claims on him?"

Catherine shook her head resolutely. "Absolutely not."

Even her father's bold statements regarding her former engagement hadn't been enough to convince her that things could ever be different between her and Corbin. She might not have told Corbin the entire truth the day she told him she didn't love him anymore, but neither had he stayed around to try and prove her sentiments wrong. Instead, he'd walked out of her life when she'd needed him the most.

Lily leaned back on her elbows. "Then what do you expect Penny and the others to do? He's not only single, but very handsome. And face it, there are few men in this town who are handsome, intelligent, and single."

Catherine poked at her baked beans with her fork. Why was it that conversations involving Corbin always tended to squelch her appetite? "There's John."

"Who's already taken."

"True." Catherine dropped her fork onto her plate, ready to change the subject. "Have you spoken to Father yet this afternoon?"

"Yes, and he's ecstatic about the whole party."

Despite the uneasiness that had settled between them since his return, Catherine had worked hard to make sure her father's welcome-home party was a success—even though she had decided to avoid any more personal conversations with him.

Lily reached out and squeezed her hand. "I know all this has been hard on you, but I want you to know how much we appreciate your going along with this party. You really helped a lot."

"I wanted to help. I know how important it is to you." Catherine stared at her plate. There was no use taking out her frustration on Lily, but neither could she find it in her to tell her father she forgave him. "I keep waiting to feel at peace over his arrival, but I haven't. Nor do I know if I'll be able to."

"I understand that forgiving him is hard, but we all have a second chance to be a family." Lily snatched a cupcake from Catherine's plate and licked the frosting from the top.

"Lily!"

"You know I can't resist one of Mrs. Master's desserts."

Catherine eyed the stolen cake, wondering if there were any left. Lily wasn't the only one who found them irresistible. At least she'd managed to change the subject. "Fine. Tell me about you and John. You know I'm waiting for the announcement of wedding bells in your future, because he certainly has my approval. Just yesterday he helped me hang three new shelves in the back of the store. He's quite a handyman."

"He does have a knack for fixing things. I think that's why he's enjoying working for his uncle so much at the blacksmith shop." Lily leaned back on her elbows and smiled. "And he makes me happy. He's such a gentleman, and so handsome with his dark blue eyes and curly blond hair. Even the thin scar that runs across his jaw line manages to make him all the more rugged and appealing, don't you think?"

"That's certainly not for me to say." Catherine caught her sister's dreamy expression. "You're going to say yes if he asks you to marry him, aren't you?"

Lily took another bite of cupcake. "Everything's happened so fast, but it's strange how I feel as if I've known him forever."

"Then follow your heart. You'll know when the time comes if it's right."

Lily wiped her mouth with a napkin then frowned. "What if I don't know?"

"Then maybe the time's not right." While she thought John to be the perfect fit for Lily, it certainly wasn't her place to make that decision.

Lily leaned back on her elbows and stared out across the rolling landscape that offered a mixture of dense trees and wide, open spaces.

"I suppose part of it is that there's still so much I want to see in life. I want to travel and see some of the world beyond Revenge, but if I get married, there'll be babies and housework and no time for anything else."

Which was exactly what she'd once dreamed of. "And that's so bad?"

"It's what's expected, isn't it?"

"I suppose."

Catherine looked up across the green lawn at Corbin, who now stood in the middle of an animated conversation with the town doctor. Marriage and family might be what every young girl dreamed of, but Catherine hadn't followed her heart or done what society expected. Still, no matter how hard she tried to ignore them, seeing Corbin brought back the same emotions she once held. Was there ever a chance—even a small one—for a second chance with love? And was that a chance she even wanted?

"He's coming to talk to you."

Catherine's chin dipped, and she felt her face flush. "I'm sure he's just being polite."

"I've seen the way he looks at you, and it's certainly not a man attempting to be polite."

Catherine forced a wide smile and prayed that he hadn't overheard Lily's last words as he stopped beside their quilt.

"Sheriff Hunter," Lily jumped in. "How nice to see you."

"Good afternoon, ladies." he began. "I'm sorry to interrupt."

"Would you care to join us?" Lily asked.

"Thank you, but I was wondering if I could speak to your sister alone for a moment?"

Lily nudged Catherine with her elbow. "Of course you may. She's all yours, Sheriff."

Catherine stood awkwardly then straightened her skirts. How could she look at him like he was just another man when everyone assumed that the sparks between them had never died? She pressed her hands against her sides as the answer surfaced. The truth was that anything that had been between them had long since died away, and any well-meaning encouragement from her father or her sisters, or even the townspeople of Revenge, couldn't change that.

Corbin shoved his hands into his front pockets as he led her toward the edge of the picnic clearing. "I'm sorry to take some of your time, but I promised I'd tell you if there were any further developments in the case."

Dread replaced any remaining thoughts of romance. "What happened?"

"One of the gang members was shot during the latest holdup," Corbin told her. "I just found out that Sheriff Robinson from Lancaster managed to pick up a lead this morning. I'm heading out there in a few minutes to check out the situation. Apparently Frank Sutherland is holed up at a farm outside of town. If we're lucky, we'll catch him, and he'll identify the rest of the gang."

"And you think he'll do that?"

"We can hope. I've learned to be rather…convincing."

"What about Harrison? You still think he's involved in all of this?"

"That's one of the things I plan to find out."

Catherine's stomach roiled at the thought of something going wrong. She may have told him once that she didn't love him anymore, but these men killed anyone who stood in their way. "There is one more thing."

"Yes?"

"The last time we spoke…the day my father arrived…" She lowered her gaze, still ashamed by the unladylike behavior he'd been forced to witness.

Corbin shook his head. "Forget about it."

"I can't." She forced herself to look him in the eye. "I never should have lost control of my emotions the way I did."

He shot her a half smile. "Only goes to show that you're human like the rest of us."

Catherine studied his expression, trying to determine if he was mocking her…though, of course, he wasn't. Corbin never would have treated her the way she'd treated him. "Then just promise me you'll be careful."

"I will." Corbin smiled, tipped his hat, and was gone.

Chapter Thirteen

Corbin rested his finger on the trigger of his Colt .45. He kept his gaze steady on the open window of the VanLeer homestead, which sat thirty yards directly in front of him. A yellow curtain blew in the breeze, but beyond that, there was no movement in the house that he could see. Sheriff Robinson had been right about the location of Frank Sutherland. What he hadn't expected was their pursuit to turn into a hostage situation.

Corbin rested his arm against the thick log that he'd stayed burrowed behind the past thirty minutes alongside the Lancaster sheriff and two other deputized men. So far, the situation was at a standoff, as Sutherland had already made it clear his plan was to hunker down and wait things out. But surely the felon knew he'd never win.

Unless Sutherland had decided to take down as many hostages with him as he could. The Masked Gang had never stopped to worry about the number of dead bodies they'd left behind. Which meant no false moves. It was up to them to ensure this situation ended well.

Corbin flicked a bug off the tip of his nose then reached for his father's brass binoculars. The only thing on their side was that Sutherland was purportedly injured. Shot in the shoulder two days ago by one of Sheriff Robinson's men, the felon had to have lost a lot of blood. A close-up glimpse inside the house could give him a clue about how to proceed. Sutherland was weak and vulnerable, but despite his clear disadvantage, he still refused to back down. If they could find a way to separate him from the hostages, they could end this with little or no bloodshed.

"What do you see?" Sheriff Robinson asked from farther down the fallen log.

"Still nothing yet." Corbin wiped away the beads of sweat from his forehead. "Are you sure we're only looking at two hostages?"

"Mason VanLeer lives here with his spinster daughter, so I wouldn't expect more than the two of them. They both tend to stay to themselves."

"What else do you know about them?"

Sheriff Robinson repositioned himself behind the fallen log. Fifteen minutes had passed since their last communication with Sutherland, but none of them could dismiss the possibility of a bullet headed their way.

Robinson cleared his throat. "Mary used to be the town school teacher until her father got sick and demanded she stay home and take care of him. That was ten years ago. They're both quiet and not very social. The only time anyone sees them is at church once a week. Needless to say, they're not likely to put up a fight of any kind."

Good. Corbin set down his binoculars so he could recheck how much ammunition he had. At least they shouldn't have to deal with a cocky hostage who wanted to play hero. The last thing he needed was for this to turn into a bloodbath. And the way the odds were stacking up, Sutherland probably figured he had little to lose.

Sheriff Robinson rose slowly from his hiding place.

Corbin motioned for him to get down. "What are you doing?"

"We've waited long enough." The sheriff pulled out a second revolver.

"No, we haven't." Corbin's jaw tensed. "We need to wait this one out to ensure no one gets killed. There've been enough lives lost in this battle to take down the Masked Gang. If you rush out there half-cocked, you're only going to get yourself or someone else killed."

"I said we've waited long enough." Sheriff Robinson glared back at him. "I'm headed for that oak tree and a better shot of the house. Cover me if you have to." He darted ten yards, then crouched behind the oak tree. "Frank Sutherland, we know you're still in there, and we're through playing games. I want you to come out of that house with your hands up."

The sheriff's demand was met with silence.

Corbin watched as Robinson fired a shot, and the front window shattered into a hundred pieces.

Corbin yelled at the sheriff to hold his fire. "I want this man alive."

"This is my territory, which means we'll do it my way."

A breeze hit the back of Corbin's neck. He pressed his lips together and bit back the reply he knew he'd regret. All he wanted to focus on right now was saving the hostages and getting the information he needed out of Sutherland. If he got lucky, he'd be able to clear Catherine's future brother-in-law at the same time.

Catherine. He'd watched her at the picnic today while Penny Martin and half a dozen young, single women tried to catch his attention. He couldn't help but smile at her when she'd stumbled over her apology. She'd always been a fiery mixture of pluckiness and stubbornness, but those had been some of the very things that had drawn her to him—and had eventually made him fall in love with her.

Corbin tightened his grip on the butt of his gun. But that had been years ago, and today, he had to shake her image and concentrate. One mistake and they all could end up dead.

A shot rang out from the direction of the house and yanked Corbin from his thoughts.

Sheriff Robinson signaled toward the house. "I'm moving in."

"Don't be a fool."

Corbin's response fell on deaf ears. Robinson ran toward the side of the house.

Before the sheriff could find cover, Sutherland walked out the front door with a gun and Mary VanLeer in his grip.

"What do you want, Sutherland?" Robinson called out. "You know this is the end of the road for you."

Sutherland yanked Miss VanLeer closer to his chest. "I don't think so."

Corbin grabbed his binoculars and peered out over the neglected front yard of the property. He stopped at the framed image of the terrified women then moved to Sutherland. The man's hollow expression stared back at him. He wasn't going to make it much longer.

"I want a horse and two hundred dollars."

Corbin kept his gun aimed at the man's temple. He wanted the man taken alive, but not at the cost of other lives. "That isn't happening, Sutherland."

"Then I'll kill the woman." He pushed her out in front of him, held out his hands, and pressed the muzzle of his gun against her head.

"Don't do it, Sutherland," Robinson said. "You'll force me to shoot you myself."

One of the other deputies maneuvered beside Corbin. "If you keep him talking, I'll crawl around the eastern side of the house where I can get a clean shot."

Corbin weighed the situation. Robinson had wanted to come in like an army with a wave of bullets, but Corbin hadn't agreed. He'd insisted they evaluate the situation and make a plan before jumping into a gun battle.

He peered through the binoculars again and shook his head. "Don't do anything yet. You'll end up hitting Miss VanLeer."

"I'm the best marksman in the county. Give me thirty seconds to set up the shot then distract him."

Corbin shook his head. "Sutherland's been shot and doesn't look like he's going to make it much longer. If we give him a bit more time, he's going to collapse."

And with the way things stood at the moment—with a loaded gun aimed at Mary VanLeer, that was the only sure way they were going to get out of here with no one else getting hurt.

"If you think I'm foolin' around, you're wrong." Sutherland's voice cracked. "I'll give you a minute to make your choice. After that, the woman's as good as gone." Sheriff Robinson had a reputation for being hot-tempered and trigger happy, and he was living up to the locals' claims of always having to play the part of the hero.

Miss VanLeer pleaded with them. "Please, do what he says. He'll kill me."

Corbin caught the woman's terrified expression. He needed to keep Sutherland talking. "I've got the horse, but not the cash. That'll take time."

"I don't have time."

None of them did. If Sutherland was as weak as he looked, he'd end up dying before Corbin could get any information out of him.

He needed him in custody, because without Sutherland, he'd be back at square one, a place he couldn't afford to be.

The sound of gunfire ripped through the mid-morning air. Corbin searched for the source. Robinson. Sutherland fired his weapon. Two more shots followed, then silence. Sutherland loosened his grip on his hostage and dropped to the ground.

Robinson clutched his right leg. "I'm all right. Go see what you can get out of that no-good scoundrel before he dies."

"You shot him!" Corbin jumped up from his position and ran across the dirt yard toward the house. If the man was dead…

"He'd have killed her and you know it," Robinson shouted.

"No. This didn't have to happen. He was so weak, he was about to pass out." Corbin knelt down beside Sutherland, ignoring the Sheriff's excuses. Already a trail of crimson soaked through the outlaw's white shirt and stained Corbin's hands. The man let out a raspy breath of air. Corbin grasped Sutherland by the collar and raised him a couple of inches from the ground. This would be his only chance to get the truth. "Who's behind the Masked Gang robberies?"

"Why should I tell you?" The man's throat gurgled as he choked on his own blood.

"Why? Because I need the last act you do in this world to be decent." Corbin shook him by the shoulders. Time was running out along with every lead he'd followed the past few months. "Tell me now."

"I need…doctor…"

"It's too late for a doctor, and I, for one, wouldn't want to die with a string of cold-blooded murders on my conscience."

"It's too…late…"

"No!" Corbin tightened his grip. "Tell me, who is it?"

Sutherland choked then slumped back onto the hard ground, mumbling something unintelligible.

Corbin lowered his face toward the dying man's. "What did you say?"

"Har...Harrison Tucker. He's...he's who you want...but..."

Corbin let the dying man drop back against the hard earth. A sick feeling washed over him as he watched Sutherland take his last breath. A vacant stare looked up at him. Whatever else he had to say had just been forever silenced, but Corbin now held the one piece of evidence he'd sought. He'd been right. Harrison was the leader of the Masked Gang. A bank robber, womanizer, and con man, all wrapped up in one package.

Audrey's world—as well as Catherine's—was about to crumble.

He wiped his blood-stained hands against the dusty earth. What was Catherine going to say when she heard the truth about Harrison?

"Sheriff, please." The choked words came from behind him. "My daughter."

Corbin jumped to his feet. Mr. VanLeer hovered over his daughter. Corbin searched her still body for signs she'd been shot, but saw nothing. "She's fainted—"

"No. She was hit in the crossfire." He rolled her over onto her side to show Corbin what everyone had missed in the confusion. His heart pitched. Blood was seeping through the waistline of her dress. "Please, you've got to help her."

"Get your wagon hooked up. We've got to get her into town to see the doctor." He signaled at the sheriff, who was nursing his injury across the yard. "We'll get you patched up at the same time."

Corbin lifted the woman into his arms and headed for Mr. VanLeer's wagon. How had this happened? Everything he'd prayed wouldn't happen had just played out in front of him. He glanced down at Mary VanLeer's lifeless form. If it wasn't too late, they might be able to avoid another death, but he wasn't sure that was possible. The body count was rising…and so was his thirst for revenge.

"Is she going to make it?" The sheriff shuffled beside Corbin as they hurried toward the wagon.

"I don't know."

What he did know, though, was not only could this have been avoided, but that Catherine's life was in danger. She'd wandered far too close into the circle of a murderer, and someone else was going to get hurt. It was time he put a stop to the senseless killings.

* * *

Horace Baldwin slid a small bottle across the counter toward Catherine later that afternoon and grinned. "Miss Morgan. I think we've finally done it." His beaming smile reached his eyes as he glanced at his brother, who stood beside him with a small bandage on his forehead. "Behold, Horace and Harold's Effervescent Cold Remedy."

Harold cleared his throat. "Harold and Horace's Effervescent Cold Remedy."

Horace nudged his brother with his elbow. "We haven't done the label yet, but we thought you'd like to be the first one to see it."

"I'm honored." *I think.* Catherine picked up the jar and opened it cautiously before taking a whiff. "It smells like…licorice."

"That would be one of our ingredients," Horace said. "And what do you think about the bottle? Mr. O'Conner sold it to us.

He promised us as many as we need."

"For a small price, of course," Harold added.

Catherine held up the jar, wishing Corbin would walk in the door and let her know he was all right. At least the Baldwin twins and their latest experiment was a distraction. "What exactly is inside the jar?"

"Vaseline, a bit of camphor, eucalyptus, licorice extract—"

"And our secret ingredient."

"Which is?"

Horace leaned forward. "We can't tell you, of course."

"It's a secret," Harold added. "How many do you want to purchase? You know, as our favorite customer, you will get a reduced price."

Catherine coughed. "How…thoughtful of you."

"You can resell them for a profit, of course."

"I see." Catherine pressed her lips together. "May I ask you a question, Mr. Baldwin?"

"Anything, Miss Morgan," Harold said.

"I was simply wondering why your forehead is bandaged. " Harold glanced at his brother. "Oh, that."

"Yes. Does it have anything to do with your cold remedy?"

"No—"

Harold dropped his gaze. "Horace, I told you we couldn't lie to Miss Morgan."

"What happened?" Catherine asked again.

"It was the last batch of cold remedy," Harold began. "Not this one, of course."

"And it's not serious," Horace continued. "Just a few blisters."

"Nothing serious at all," Harold repeated.

Nothing serious? Right. This wasn't the first time the twin's cold remedy had come with questionable results. One formula had exploded, while another had burned off the top layer of skin.

"I'll make a deal with you," Catherine said.

The two brothers leaned forward. "You continue working on your Magical...Effervescent...Cold Remedy."

"Horace and Harold's Effervescent Cold Remedy," Horace said.

"And once you have a formula that doesn't burn, or explode, or... dye the skin blue, I'll promise to consider it again. Why don't you go help yourself to a handful of penny candy? On the house."

"Catherine?" Lily signaled Catherine from the switchboard.

Catherine bid Horace and Harold good day, then slipped into the back room. She pressed her hand against her chest and whispered to her sister. "Your timing couldn't be more perfect. Horace and Harold are trying to sell me their latest invention."

"At least it didn't explode this time."

Catherine laughed. "You have a point."

"There's a phone call for you. It's Mr. Peterson."

Catherine frowned. "Is something wrong?"

"He won't tell me anything. Insists on speaking only to you."

Catherine hurried to the phone. "Mr. Peterson, how are you?"

"Fine, thank you. I promised I would look into that matter we spoke of earlier."

Catherine lowered her voice. "Please, go ahead."

"I found out something interesting you might want to know."

Catherine frowned as she scribbled a few notes on the back of the ledger before hanging up. There was only one thing left to do. It was time she had a talk with Harrison herself.

Chapter Fourteen

....

Catherine approached Harrison's saltbox farmhouse on the outskirts of town, knowing she was blatantly ignoring Corbin's warnings of not getting involved in his investigation If he would have made an ounce of progress in the past couple weeks, she might think differently, but he'd yet to find any real proof of Harrison's guilt—or innocence. And time was running out. More than likely, his trek to find one of the bank robbers—like every other lead he'd followed—would prove to be nothing other than a dead end.

With her sister's life at stake, taking things into her own hands seemed to be the only logical thing to do. If Harrison proved to be guilty, as Mr. Peterson's phone call implied, she wouldn't stand in the way of his arrest, but neither would she break her sister's heart needlessly. She had to know the truth for herself. And to get to the truth, she had to get Harrison to talk—whether he was the face on the Wells Fargo wanted poster or not.

She fingered the Colt hidden in the folds of her skirt. Her father might have failed as a father in a number of ways, but he had taught her to hit a target as well as most men she knew. Letting out a slow breath, she sent up an extra prayer for courage. Something that was irrefutably missing at the moment.

Swallowing any doubts of her mission, she turned her attention to the house that had been built three generations ago by Randall Tucker. Fresh paint and a few repairs had gone a long way. It was hard not to be impressed with the amount of work Harrison had put into the place. But a well-kept place did nothing to prove one's innocence.

Harrison crouched on the shaded eastern side of the barn, repairing a loose board. Clad in a white band-collared shirt, tan cotton trousers, and a pair of suspenders, he looked the part of a farmer. Of course, if Corbin was right about him, that was all Harrison was doing. Playing a role.

"Good morning, Harrison."

"Catherine?" Harrison stood before lifting his hat. "I didn't hear you coming. This is an unexpected surprise."

Catherine shielded her face to block the afternoon sun. "I'm sorry to disturb you."

"You almost missed me. I was getting ready to head out to one of the fields. Need to repair some fencing on the west side before it gets dark." Harrison dropped his hammer into a bucket, then slapped off a layer of dust from his trousers before approaching the buggy. "Is Audrey all right?"

"Of course. She's fine."

"Good. I just…" He shrugged a shoulder. "I just assumed if you came by, whatever you needed to speak to me about would have something to do with her, or the wedding."

"The wedding?"

His Adam's apple bobbed. "Audrey wouldn't be the first woman to have second thoughts about the man she's going to marry, and I know that I can be a bit—"

"You don't have anything to worry about. Audrey loves you."

From outside appearances, it was clear why Audrey wanted to marry the man. He was handsome, thoughtful, always a gentleman.

All characteristics of a womanizing con man. Catherine reeled in her thoughts—for Audrey's sake.

"You've really taken to farming."

"I guess it's in my blood. Both my grandfather and great-grandfather farmed this land. Though I have to say that I never imagined I'd follow in their footsteps."

Catherine eyed a squawking hen with her brood in tow as they ran from the shelter of the barn. "From all your stories, you do seem more the adventurous type than say a…a farmer." She studied his expression. Was that a sign of guilt on his face?

Harrison rested his hands on his hips. "Is there something I can help you with?"

"I promise not to take up much of your time, but I do need to speak with you."

Harrison pulled his hat back on. "I suppose I could take a few minutes, though I do need to head out soon. I've got quite a bit of work left to finish, and it won't be long before the sun sets."

Catherine tried not to read anything into his hesitation. She wanted him to be innocent, but even more so, she wanted to find out the truth—because the evidence Corbin had that connected Harrison to the Masked Gang was hard to ignore. She glanced out across the endless rows of wheat to the east. Quiet. Solitude. The Tucker farm was fifteen minutes from town…and off the main road. Catherine drew in a quick breath as her gaze traveled back to the corner of the barn wall where a Winchester lay propped up. She rested her finger on the trigger, prepared to make the first move if necessary. If Harrison really was William Marker, she'd likely just walked into a peck of trouble.

"The place looks fantastic." She worked to keep her voice steady. "Audrey told me you've been putting a lot of time into it."

"This year's crops are doing well, and the house is livable."

"Your grandfather would be proud of you."

"I'm guessing that my farm isn't the reason you came by."

Catherine studied a crease in her skirt, as second thoughts resurfaced. "No."

"So what is it you wanted to talk to me about?"

Catherine hesitated. "I'm not sure exactly how to begin."

She lifted up a short prayer that God would forgive her for going ahead with her unconventional plan. A confession from Harrison that he'd never set foot in Alaska was the final proof she needed, but confronting the man straight out seemed far too risky. Which meant if the Good Lord had a better way to handle the situation, He was going to have to speak up now.

Harrison drummed his fingers against his legs and shifted his gaze to the ground. "I suppose the beginning tends to be the best place."

"All right then." She took a deep breath and plunged ahead. "I'm considering going to Alaska."

"Alaska?" Harrison's eyes widened. "You're not serious, are you?"

Catherine plunged ahead with her plan—one that suddenly sounded anything but rational. "I know I'm not the first woman to consider heading west to seek out a bit of adventure."

Harrison sat quiet for a moment. "You're serious?"

"It's simply a business proposition I've been thinking about. I have experience with numbers and selling, and I'm considering a change of scenery." Which at the moment was at least partly true. While Alaska might not be at the top of her list, there were certainly

days when she considered going away for a while. Lily wasn't
the only one in the family who'd ever considered seeing life outside
of Revenge.

"But your family is here. I guess I never saw you as the
adventurous type."

Catherine chose to ignore the comment. "With Audrey getting
married and Lily not far behind her, I've fulfilled my promise to my
mother to raise my sisters. I've always wanted to see more of the
world, and since you are obviously familiar with the terrain, I thought
you'd be the perfect person to talk to."

It wasn't a lie. Not really. The thought had crossed her mind
at least twice. Once while reading one of Emily's dime novels about
the West, and another time when she'd heard Harrison tell a story
about Mabel Mason, who had opened a general store for a bunch
of prospectors and returned home with a fortune a year later.

"Why Alaska?"

"You seem surprised."

"I hate to disappoint you, Miss Morgan, but I don't believe that
the Wild West is the place for a lady of your...your position."

Catherine tried to read his expression. Caution? Intrigue? Or
perhaps he simply wanted to discourage her. Of course, reading the
expressions of a storyteller like Harrison was, more than likely, going
to prove to be quite challenging.

She pressed her hands together. "What do you mean, a lady
of my position?"

Harrison tugged on the open collar of his shirt. "While this can't
be said for all the women who live on the frontier, many of them
have...sordid reputations."

"I've heard there are women who have invested in the gold mines." Catherine plunged ahead in their defense. "And that doesn't include those who run perfectly respectable businesses that help society. If I'm not mistaken, there's always a need for good food when there are hungry men around."

"Of course, but you must understand that those women are few and far between. And without a husband, I'm afraid…"

So they were back, once again, to the state of her unmarried bliss.

"And there's always the very real possibility that you'd never find gold," Harrison continued.

"That is a risk I'd have to take."

"Do your sisters know about this?"

"I felt it important to gather more information before I made a decision."

Harrison's gaze flickered toward the horizon. Perhaps he was praying for a rescue. But Catherine hadn't gotten what she'd come for yet.

"Why are you asking me all these questions?"

Catherine frowned. Wasn't it obvious? "Because you've been there and you know what it's like."

"There are challenges," he continued. "Both physical and emotional. You can't imagine how much time and preparation it takes for a trip like this."

"All things I'm quite prepared for. I simply thought you could recommend a town for me to set up a store as well as the best place to stake a gold claim."

Harrison's Adam's apple bobbed. "You want to set up a store and invest in a claim?"

"I have managed to save up a bit of a nest egg. Not a huge one, of course, but enough, I believe, to get me started, and from what I understand, there's plenty of need for supplies."

He shook his head. "I'm not sure if I'm qualified to advise you in such matters, to be quite honest. If anything were to happen to you on account of what I told you…surely you understand my position. Perhaps you should ask your father as he's just returned from Alaska."

"My father and I are not presently on speaking terms. Besides, I'm not asking for you to ensure my safety if I decide to go. Simply to share with me some of your connections."

His glance dropped, his nose quivered, and his ears turned pink. Interesting. Harrison was no longer the suave storyteller who had wormed his way into the lives of the Morgan women.

Catherine forged ahead. "I don't know why you wouldn't see yourself as qualified. You know more about Alaska than anyone else in this town."

"I suppose that's true, but…"

"I've read a few dime novels, and while I realize they are only fiction, there must be some truth to them. But not enough, I'm afraid, to tell me all I need to know if I decide to go."

"You've been reading dime novels about Alaska?"

A rooster crowed. They had to be as bad as Emily's ostriches.

"They're almost as entertaining as your infamous stories. You must have traveled extensively in order to tell the kind of stories you tell. Met dozens of colorful prospectors. Panned for gold by the hour and listened to their stories."

Harrison leaned forward. "What exactly is it you're trying to say, Miss Morgan?"

Catherine nodded. She would tell him the truth. That the only thing he knew about Alaska came from the pages of those novels. The rooster's squawking increased, but she ignored it.

"I know for a fact that you've never gone to Alaska."

"Hold on." Harrison spun around and grabbed the gun from the side of the barn.

Corbin's words hit her like a slug from a rifle. *He won't let you walk away once he knows you know his secret.*

Catherine pulled out her gun and aimed, hoping Harrison Tucker was prepared to meet his Maker.

* * *

Corbin finished washing the dried blood from the back of his hands then slid on the shirt the doctor's wife had graciously given him. His was going to have to be burned.

Sheriff Robinson sat across the small room in the back of the doctor's house, his injured leg now cleaned and bandaged. "Is Miss VanLeer going to make it?"

Corbin avoided the man's gaze. "Probably not."

"We did what we had to do."

Corbin said nothing.

"And I saved myself the trouble of a hanging," the sheriff continued.

Corbin slid his gun into his holster. "And we just lost the best lead we had, along with a woman who didn't deserve to die."

"We'll find them."

"When?" Corbin crossed the wood-planked floor, stopping far enough away so he couldn't give in to the temptation of giving the man the beating he deserved. "When their leader is as infamous as Jesse James, or when he's murdered another dozen people? You had no right to start a shootout. Now we don't have anything."

"And you would have had us sitting there all day, waiting?"

"The man was badly injured and we put him in a corner. He wasn't going to last."

Corbin turned away. There was no use explaining his actions. Nor did he plan on sharing Sutherland's dying words. He'd keep them to himself for now. The last thing he wanted to do was have Robinson back on the case. The man had proved himself to be impulsive and irresponsible when there were lives at stake. He couldn't afford for that to happen again.

The sheriff draped a sheet over Sutherland and stood back. "We'll find the rest of them. For now, I've got a man to bury."

Corbin headed for the town telephone at the Lancaster General Store. He'd made a promise to tell Catherine before he arrested Harrison, but more importantly, he wanted to make sure that she and her sisters were out of harm's way when he confronted the man.

Lily answered the call and must have heard the tremor in his voice. "Is there a problem, Sheriff?"

"Yes…no…" He gripped the counter. "Nothing that I can't take care of. Where is Catherine? I need to speak to her."

"She had an errand to take care of, out at Harrison's farm. Said she wanted to drop off a few jars of peaches."

Corbin froze. "Harrison's farm?"

"Yes. It's funny, isn't it? He and Audrey will be married next week, but I think Catherine is the one who worries most about him not getting enough to eat."

Corbin sucked in a breath. Catherine had no idea who she was dealing with. If Harrison found out that she knew who he was, he'd show her no mercy. Regrets of how he'd handled things gripped him. He'd told Catherine to let him take care of things, but she'd never been one to listen. He should have realized that.

"Sheriff, are you still there?"

"Yes, and I need you to do something for me."

"Of course, what is it?"

It wasn't the first time he'd been grateful for the invention of this newfangled communication device. "Is Audrey with you?"

"Yes, she's working in the store right now."

"Good. I want you to close the store for the day and wait in the house for me to return to town."

There was a long pause on the line. "I don't understand, Sheriff. If something's wrong—"

"Just do as I say. Please."

Corbin hung up the telephone then headed for Revenge. Anger still seared through him at how the sheriff's stupidity had managed to cost them their one lead because he'd insisted on playing the role of a hero. The town was already celebrating the capture and death of one of the infamous gang members, but no one seemed to realize that Sutherland had held key information. And with him dead, Corbin knew little more today than he had yesterday.

Unless he could get to Harrison in time.

Otherwise, the Masked Gang would strike again, and perhaps seek revenge for Frank Sutherland's death. Which could put Catherine and her sisters in the middle of a bloodbath.

Corbin smacked his thighs against the horse and raced toward

Revenge. His talk with Harrison the week before had convinced
him that the man was hiding something. Now Sutherland's words
confirmed that Harrison was nothing more than a dirty bank robber
who had no more claimed a stake on the Alaskan soil than Corbin's
great aunt Beulah.

Thirty minutes later, he approached the farm, praying he wasn't
too late. He should have brought a posse with him, but with the
possibility of Catherine's life at stake, there hadn't been time to seek
additional help. Besides, few in town were capable of facing the leader
of the notorious gang. The day-to-day activities of a sheriff in a town
like Revenge normally left little need for deputies. If he wasn't on the
trail of this gang, his time would be filled with mundane tasks like
investigating petty theft crimes and the occasional street brawl. Not
chasing down killers and bank robbers.

Catherine's buggy sat near the barn, confirming what Lily had
told him. He slowed down to weigh his options. There was the slight
chance that Sutherland had set him up, meaning this was nothing
more than a social call, but his gut told him not to take any chances.
The last thing he needed was another hostage situation, especially
with Catherine involved.

A shot rang out on the far side of the barn.

Corbin jumped down from his horse. His boots crunched
through a strip of gravel as he made his move toward the barn.
Any doubts of who Harrison Tucker really was vanished. Harrison
stood beside Catherine with a rifle in his hands.

Chapter Fifteen

Corbin held out his gun. "Harrison Tucker, I've got a gun aimed at you. I want you to throw your rifle down in front of you then drop to the ground."

Harrison turned toward him without dropping his weapon. "Sheriff, what's going on?"

"That's exactly what I was about to ask you." Catherine stepped between them. "Corbin Hunter, put that gun down."

"Get out of the way. Now." Corbin took a step forward. His jaw twitched. Why did she always have to be so stubborn? "Mr. Tucker, I want you to drop to your knees and put your hands where I can see them."

Neither moved.

"Catherine, I'm only going to ask you one more time. Move out of the way now, or so help me, I'll arrest you both."

Catherine stood her ground. "You wouldn't dare."

"Try me. Tucker, slide the gun across the ground toward me." Corbin fired a shot over Tucker's head, all formalities lost in the moment. "Now."

Harrison complied then dropped to his knees.

Catherine moved aside. "You're making a big mistake."

"No, you're blinded to the truth. What am I going to have to say to convince you that this man isn't the man he claims to be? He's robbed half a dozen banks and is responsible for the murder of at least five innocent victims."

Harrison's face paled. "You've got to be kidding. Miss Morgan, please. You know me. Audrey can vouch for me."

"Which is simply a part of your plan, isn't it?"

"I think it's time to clear the air once and for all." Catherine pushed her shoulders back and nodded at Harrison. "Mr. Tucker is not involved with the Masked Gang, Sheriff. And if you could find a way to get past this vendetta of yours, you'd see that he's nothing more than a farmer who happens to love my sister."

Corbin frowned, not buying a word of it as he picked up Harrison's rifle off the ground and threw it toward the barn before pulling out a pair of metal handcuffs. "Of course he's going to try and convince you that he's innocent."

"I just spent the past thirty minutes asking my own questions. He told me the truth."

"You want the truth? The truth is that I just watched Frank Sutherland breathe his last breath."

"Who's Frank Sutherland?" Harrison asked.

"Cut the act. He confessed you were the ringleader of the Masked Gang."

Harrison's face paled. "Does this have something to do with the conversation we had?"

"I've managed to tie together a few more pieces since then."

Corbin grabbed Harrison's wrist. "Give me your other hand."

Harrison's shoulders slumped as Corbin snapped the metal cuffs into place.

"Corbin—"

Corbin grabbed Catherine's arm and pulled her out of Harrison's earshot. "I told you not to get involved, Catherine."

"But I am involved." Her expression darkened. "Why are you doing this?"

"Because, like I said, I finally have the proof I need to arrest him." Corbin kept his gun on Harrison to ensure he didn't move. "I want you to go get back in your buggy and ride back into town. Wait for me at your house."

"I really don't think—"

"Catherine!"

She didn't budge. "First tell me what you found."

"When we arrived at the VanLeer homestead, Mr. VanLeer and his daughter were being held hostage by Frank Sutherland, one of the gang members."

"So you took him into custody?"

"I wish. Sutherland was killed in the standoff, along with the woman he took hostage."

Catherine pressed her fingers against her mouth and let out a soft groan. "She's dead?"

"Murdered."

Catherine choked down a sob. "Which is all the more reason to find the truth. Harrison's not the man you're looking for."

"Catherine—"

She set her fists against her hips and raised her chin. "What if I can prove his innocence?"

"He's a con artist, Catherine. He can make you believe anything he wants. And besides that, I show up and find him with you and firing a rifle. What do you expect me to believe?"

"That there was a weasel in the chicken coop."

"A weasel?"

"What do you think he was doing?" Catherine demanded.

"Game's over, Miss Morgan." He lowered his voice, praying he could control his temper. "I've got the evidence I was looking for, and I'm going to arrest Harrison."

* * *

Catherine felt a wave of nausea shoot through her at Corbin's announcement. "He didn't do this." She moved back toward Harrison. "You've got to tell him the truth."

Harrison gritted his teeth. "You promised."

"And I promised my mother that I'd protect my sisters. You can stop this."

"I don't think I can. You've got to find Audrey. I can't have her finding out about this from one of the townspeople. Tell her everything will be fine. That all of this is nothing more than a big mistake."

Corbin let out a loud whoosh of air. "Except everything's not going to be all right. At least not for you. The law in this town doesn't take too kindly to bank robberies and murders, which means justice will be fair but swift."

"I'm not a murderer."

Catherine gripped Corbin's forearm. "You've got to believe him. You're chasing after the wrong man."

"So you've said." Corbin shook his head. "But I've got the confession of a dying man who admitted to me who his ringleader was."

"Who? One of the gang members shot during the last robbery?" Catherine continued her defense, determined to convince him of the truth. "I'm sure his word is worth a lot."

Corbin gripped Harrison's arm and led him toward his horse. "I don't have time for this."

Maybe not, but she wasn't done with him yet. "Did you ever stop and think that Harrison is being set up? All your evidence against him is based on anonymous tips and the dying word of a known bank robber and murderer."

Corbin stopped in front of his horse. "Listen to me—"

"No, you listen to me. Harrison's no more a criminal than you or I are. If you go through with this, all you're going to do is destroy his life along with my sister's. And in the meantime, the real leader of the Masked Gang is out there free somewhere, planning to strike again."

Corbin helped Harrison onto his stallion before turning back to her. "William Marker's gang killed my father."

Catherine felt her knees buckle beneath her as the reason behind his determination fell into place. So his quest *had* been personal. "When?"

"Eight months ago the gang was terrorizing Kentucky. My father was living in Frankfort." Corbin avoided her gaze. "He tried to help one of the hostages and they shot him."

"Oh, Corbin. I'm sorry. So very sorry." She brushed her hand against his arm then pulled away. It all made sense now. His ragged determination to hunt down the leader of the Masked Gang at all cost.

But there was still one serious problem. Revenge for the sake of revenge was as big an evil in her eyes as murder. Harrison sat on the horse, jaw clenched, mouth shut, and looking straight ahead. He was as stubborn as Corbin. And she wasn't going to let this happen. She raised her chin in determination. "Please understand how very sorry I am about your father, truly I am, but please don't go through with this arrest."

Corbin grasped the reins of the horse tighter. "If I don't do this, I'll be endangering all of you. You, your sisters…the entire town."

"Think about it. Harrison just willingly surrendered. Do you think the leader of some rogue gang would have done that without a fight?"

"He's a con man, Catherine. And the evidence points to—"

"The word of some anonymous tipster and a dead convict. That's not real evidence."

Corbin's jaw tensed. "I have all the evidence I need, and I don't have time to stand here and argue with you. Can you get back to town all right on your own?"

Her frown deepened. "Of course. Especially now that you've captured a mass murderer. I shouldn't have anything to worry about."

Harrison looked down at her and caught her gaze. "Talk to Audrey for me. Please. I can't have her finding out about this from someone in town."

She nodded. "I'll find her. Then I'll come to the jail to see if I can talk some sense into our sheriff…and into you."

Corbin swung up onto the horse, ignoring her comment.

"You've got to make sure Audrey knows that I didn't do this," Harrison repeated.

"Don't worry. She loves you. You've got a wedding to attend in another week."

"Catherine," Corbin said. "You're only making this harder on everyone."

Catherine stood at the edge of the yard and watched them ride away until they disappeared behind the hundreds of rows of corn framing Harrison's field. Another piece of her world had just crumbled away. Which promise was she bound to keep? The one she made at her mother's deathbed, or the one she'd just made to Harrison?

* * *

Corbin yanked William Marker's wanted poster off the wall behind his desk and waited for the surge of relief he should feel after catching his father's murderer. He'd followed the gang across hundreds of miles of lonely prairie and through a dozen towns, and now William Marker, Harrison Tucker, or whatever alias the man chose to go by, was locked behind bars. And he'd avenged the death of his father.

So if he had the right man, why did he feel so empty inside?

Revenge had turned out to be a persistent companion that had haunted his dreams at night and kept him focused during the day. How could it have forgotten to bring with it the deep reward of satisfaction he'd expected? Corbin crumpled the poster between his fingers and thrust it into the trash bin beside his desk. Of course, until the rest of the gang was brought in, there was still a chance that the Masked Gang would strike again, even without their leader.

Tomorrow he'd put together a posse with several of the lawmen from the surrounding towns. With the ringleader behind bars, the odds of the group sticking together were small. They would track the criminals down before another night passed.

Corbin glanced at the closed door that led to the jail. Catherine was right about one thing. Harrison Tucker wasn't the ringleader he'd expected to bring in. He'd prepared himself for a man who thought nothing about shooting anyone who got in his way.

Not that he was having second thoughts about bringing Harrison in. He couldn't forget that the man who killed his father was a smooth-talking con man. A charlatan wolf dressed in sheep's clothing. No doubt he found it to his advantage to continue playing the role of innocent farmer, believing it would somehow help him get off. No. He wouldn't let Harrison's smooth exterior and cunning ways cause a moment of weakness on his part. That very identity was one Harrison had taken on in order to charm everyone around him. He was simply playing another role.

Give it up, Corbin. The man you've been looking for is behind bars. Period.

Catherine's image surfaced again in his mind's eye, uninvited. No matter how hard he tried, he couldn't get her out of his head. Her stubbornness made him madder than a hornet; her insistence that Harrison was innocent made him question his own professionalism; and her presence...her presence made him wonder why he hadn't ignored her protests and married her all those years ago.

Because she'd made it clear she didn't love him, and that there could never be anything between them.

He let out a deep sigh. And nothing had changed since that day. He had let Grady O'Conner's comments the night of the party and the town's whispers since then mingle in the recesses of his mind until he'd convinced himself he'd seen something in her eyes. But he'd been wrong. And as soon as the last member of the Masked Gang was hanged, he was going to leave Revenge forever.

The front door of his office slammed open, jerking him away from his turbulent thoughts.

Audrey stormed into the room, slammed her handbag onto his desk, and planted both fists on her hips.

Corbin caught her insolent stare. "Miss Morgan. Can I help you?"

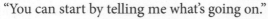
"You can start by telling me what's going on."

Corbin moved behind his desk, suddenly feeling the urge to run. Two women after him in the course of an hour was two too many. "You talked to Catherine?"

"Catherine? No. I ran into Mrs. McBride in front of the hotel. She saw you ride into town with Harrison in handcuffs."

His Adam's apple bobbed. "She's right."

Audrey's face colored. "You arrested him?"

"I had no choice. I've been hired to uphold the law—"

Audrey smacked her hands against the desk. "Harrison had nothing to do with those robberies, and if I have to find a way to knock some sense into you personally, Sheriff, I'll do it."

Corbin pressed his lips together. Apparently Catherine wasn't the only Morgan in this town who harbored a temper. He motioned to the chair, offering her a seat. With his track record, he'd prefer tangling with a copperhead over fighting one of the Morgan sisters.

"I'll stand, thank you." Audrey rubbed the base of her neck with her fingertips. "Harrison had nothing to do with those robberies."

"So you've just said." Corbin proceeded cautiously. "But I'm afraid I have evidence that says otherwise."

"What kind of evidence?"

"An eyewitness, for starters."

"They're mistaken."

"I also happen to know that there is no record of him staking a claim in the Alaskan territory."

For the first time, Audrey seemed at a loss for words. "Harrison— Harrison likes to tell stories. We all know they're often embellished, but that doesn't make him a murderer."

"It's not his stories that put him here."

Audrey looked up at him, her lashes laced with tears. "So you believe he's guilty?"

"I have no doubt that he's guilty, but that's not up to me to decide. My job is to follow the evidence and, with that knowledge, to make an arrest. Which is exactly what I've done. Harrison will have to defend himself, but Miss Morgan…you're going to have to prepare yourself that there's a good chance he will be found guilty."

Her shoulders slumped in defeat. "I…I don't think I can do that."

Corbin combed his fingers through his hair. He didn't want to hurt her, but her love for her fiancé didn't change the circumstances. "Miss Morgan, please. I understand how upsetting this is, but you must realize that when I find evidence regarding a crime, I must follow through with it. Harrison's real name is William Marker. He's a con man who knows all too well how to weave his way into the lives of young women."

Her face paled. "What are you implying, Sheriff? That this isn't the first time he's done this?"

Corbin proceeded cautiously. "I'm sorry, Miss Morgan. I truly am. But it's far better to know the truth now than wait until you're married."

Corbin pressed his lips together. He knew the promise Catherine had made to her mother, and knew that what happened to her sister would be just as painful as if she'd had her own heart betrayed. Even the sweet satisfaction of revenge did little to salve his guilt. Audrey Morgan wasn't the only one ready to hang him on the nearest tree for doing his job. Catherine had made it quite clear that he'd arrested the wrong man. The problem was, neither of them realized just how convincing a man like Harrison could be. He knew what to say and

REVENGE
1884
OHIO

when to say it. Everything necessary to make the very women they were conning come forward and defend them with their lives.

Tears began to roll down her face. "I just don't understand. We had plans to expand the farm…to add wheat next year…have children. I know Harrison. He's not that kind of man."

"I am truly sorry."

The sobs increased.

"Miss Morgan, please don't cry." He reached into his front pocket and handed her his handkerchief.

"I want to see him."

"He…he requested no visitors."

"What?" Audrey dropped into the chair. "But I'm his fiancée."

"I realize that, but Harrison made it quite clear that he doesn't want any visitors," he repeated. "Including you."

"You must be mistaken."

"Please, Miss Morgan, don't make the situation more difficult than it already is."

She dabbed at her face with his handkerchief then grabbed her purse off the desk. "You're wrong about Harrison, Sheriff Hunter, and I'll find a way to prove it."

A moment later the door slammed behind her as she slipped outside into the humid afternoon air. Corbin knew that Audrey Morgan wasn't the only person determined to prove Harrison's innocence. But while Catherine was resolute in her stance, he also knew that there was something she wasn't telling him. And it was up to him to find out what it was.

Chapter Sixteen

....

Corbin glanced up from his desk at the unannounced visit from the second Morgan sister in a space of less than thirty minutes. He pushed his chair backward, not relishing the anticipated confrontation. Besides, he was the sheriff, and it was his responsibility to ensure the safety of this town. Something Catherine was going to have to accept.

Dismissing her obvious irritation, he beat her to the punch. "Your stubbornness this afternoon could have endangered both of us."

Her eyes widened. "My stubbornness?"

"You refused to obey a direct order from an officer of the law."

The look of exasperation on her face grew. "Have you questioned Harrison yet?"

"Yes."

"And…"

Corbin folded his arms across his chest. "He continues to claim that he had nothing to do with the string of robberies."

"But you don't believe him."

"How can I? I have a witness who identified him as the leader of the Masked Gang. Frank Sutherland ran with them for the past eight months. If anyone knows, he does."

"He could have been lying."

"Why? The man was dying."

"He lied for the same reason someone gave you the anonymous tip that pointed to Harrison. To take the heat off himself and keep you running in the wrong direction."

"And you have evidence for this. Clear, solid evidence that will hold up in a court of law."

She folded her arms across her chest and frowned. Obviously not.

"Can I talk to him?" she asked.

"No."

"Please, just let me talk to him. I'm the only person who knows the truth about Harrison."

"Then tell me. What do you know that you haven't told me?" He moved around the desk, feeling torn by her presence. "You have an obligation to divulge any information you have regarding this crime. If not for my sake, do it for your sister's sake."

Catherine's gaze flickered. She was wavering. "And I have an obligation to my family."

"As I have an obligation to uphold the law."

"Let me speak to him."

"No."

"Just give me five minutes."

"Miss Morgan…" He combed his fingers through his hair. He needed any information she had.

"Please, Sheriff. You want the truth as much as I do. Just let me talk to him."

* * *

Catherine stepped to the edge of the jail cell and pressed her hands against the black iron bars. Harrison sat on the one wooden bench, shoulders slumped, hands in his lap.

"Better not get too close. You're talking to a hardened criminal," Harrison told her. "Besides, I told the sheriff I didn't want any visitors."

Catherine ignored his protests. "Why didn't you tell the sheriff the truth?"

"The sheriff doesn't care about the truth. Or so it seems."

"Sheriff Hunter's a good man. A bit stubborn at times, but—"

"His stubbornness is going to get me hanged on charges of murder." Harrison combed his fingers through his hair then stood. "Murder. I didn't even want to shoot that weasel this afternoon."

"If you ask me, it's your own stubbornness that's about to get you hanged for murder."

Harrison paced the small space. "You know what's going to happen when Audrey finds out the truth. I'll lose her."

"So you'd rather be hanged by a lynch mob than tell her the truth?"

"Yes…no…I don't know."

"Harrison, look at me. You've made some mistakes, but you're lucky. Audrey loves you. If you're willing to tell her—and the sheriff—the truth, you have a chance to put all this behind you."

"I can't tell her."

"You have to. Don't you realize the odds you're facing? They're not good. The Masked Gang killed Sheriff Hunter's father. Do you think he's going to simply let you go because he feels sorry for you?"

"Just give me some time to think."

Catherine shook her head. "You don't have time."

She left the small hallway and slammed the door between the two rooms. Corbin sat at his desk, holding a cup of coffee.

"Did he talk to you?" he asked.

"He's as stubborn as you are."

"Meaning?"

Her hands clenched at her sides. "Give him twenty-four hours to come to his senses. Maybe then the reality of his situation will finally sink in."

"He may not have twenty-four hours. Do you realize what will happen once word gets out that I have the leader of the Masked Gang in custody?"

"He'll tell you," Catherine insisted.

"And if he doesn't?"

"I said, he'll tell you."

"I could arrest you, too, you know. After your stunt at the farm and now this. You need to tell me what's going on."

"And I need you to trust me."

Corbin pressed his lips together.

"Just give me twenty-four hours. And if he hasn't told you the truth by then, I will."

* * *

Catherine connected the call at the telephone switchboard the next afternoon then glanced up at the clock that hung on the wall beside her. Three o'clock. How much more could change in the scope of twenty-four hours? While Audrey stayed with Emily, Harrison sat in the town's jail cell refusing to speak. She had no idea what motivated him. If he was worried that he'd lose Audrey with his confession, not telling the truth was a guarantee that was going to happen. Yet the man refused to swallow his pride and confess what he'd done.

Not that he was the only man in this town who couldn't get beyond his pride. Corbin was so intent on arresting his father's killer that even if she did tell him the truth, and he discovered he had the wrong man, she wasn't certain he'd listen. According to him, he had all the evidence he needed to hang Harrison. Including several triangular-based bullets found at the Tucker farm.

Which had to have been planted, because as far as she was concerned he was innocent.

The front door of the store jingled. She looked up from her post. Where was Lily? She'd invited their father for dinner in hopes of distracting Audrey. Something she'd been unable to do so far. With Harrison sitting in a jail cell and the wedding temporarily postponed, nothing had helped soothe her sister's despondent mood.

Pressing down the folds of her skirt, Catherine got up and glanced into the store. Ike Larrick stood by the counter. Catherine cringed. All it would take was a word of encouragement on her part and she wouldn't have to be the town's twice-jilted spinster any longer. Except that Ike Larrick was twice her age, had three boys, and lived with his mother on a pig farm. Life as a spinster suddenly didn't seem so bad.

"Miss Morgan. You're looking lovely today." Mr. Larrick pulled off his Derby hat, revealing too much grease.

"Can I help you with something this afternoon?"

His smile widened, revealing two missing front teeth. "It's been awhile since I've seen you, Miss Morgan."

"So it has."

"I've been in Lancaster the past three weeks on a bit of business."

Catherine forced a smile. "How nice."

"I was wondering if you'd like to accompany me on a buggy ride this afternoon? The weather is perfect and—"

"While I do appreciate the offer of the ride, I'm afraid I have quite a lot to do today." Catherine cut him off before he could finish his sentence. She searched for a better excuse but came up empty-handed. No matter. Her excuse was perfectly valid.

"What about tomorrow?"

"And tomorrow...I have to work tomorrow." While she didn't want to hurt the man's feelings, neither did she want to encourage him. She quickly changed the subject. "Was there something specific you were looking for? Something for the farm, or your mother perhaps? We just received some lovely fabric she might like."

"No, thank you. Though I might have her come by later this week."

"That would be fine, Mr. Larrick." Catherine glanced at the door. Where was Lily? She'd never been good at dealing with pushy men.

"You can call me Ike if you'd wish."

Catherine suppressed a groan. Kindness obviously wasn't working. "Mr. Larrick is fine."

"Nails. I need half a pound of nails and a pound of coffee." Mr. Larrick leaned against the counter and chewed a wad of tobacco, not seeming to realize she was putting him off. "Have you heard the news?"

Catherine reached for the coffee. "What news?"

"There's a stranger in town."

"Who?"

"Care to guess?"

Great. He was going to make her drag it out of him. "Not really."

Mr. Larrick's smile faded, but only momentarily.

"A Pinkerton agent just showed up in town. I understand he hails from Chicago."

A Pinkerton agent? Catherine's mind reeled as she closed the lid on the coffee. She'd gambled on keeping Harrison's secret for twenty-four hours, believing it would give Harrison time to come to his senses. She'd never dreamed the law would move that fast. She turned back around to Mr. Larrick. "And what would a Pinkerton agent be doing in Revenge?"

"Must have something to do with the arrest of Harrison Tucker, though the sheriff's managed to keep things pretty quiet. I heard from my ma that you're friends with the sheriff."

Mr. Larrick leaned forward. So that's what he wanted. Not to give out information, but to get it. Something he wasn't going to get from her. She was the one who needed information at this moment. She had to talk to the sheriff.

She set the package of coffee on the counter then turned to the bucket of nails and eyed the front door. Where was Lily? "I'm sure the sheriff has a reason for keeping things quiet."

"The sheriff better realize that none of us want a murderer sitting in our jail."

"I'm sure that the sheriff is doing everything he can to ensure that justice takes place."

The bell jingled again, and Catherine sighed with relief as Lily burst through the door.

"I'm sorry I took so long, Catherine." She turned to Mr. Larrick without taking a breath. "Mr. Larrick. How are you today?"

"I'm fine, thank you."

Catherine coughed. "I'm sorry to have to leave so quickly, but I have something I need to take care of now that Lily's here."

Lily took her place behind the counter.

"The phone's been quiet this afternoon, and I promise I won't be long," Catherine told her.

Mr. Larrick turned his wide smile to Lily. Apparently anyone who hadn't walked down the aisle was fair game in Mr. Larrick's mind. Catherine hurried from the store, praying it wasn't too late to save Harrison.

* * *

Corbin poured a second cup of coffee then slid it across the table to the man sitting across from him. Tailored suit, derby hat, and New York smile—the man didn't belong in a town like Revenge.

"I didn't expect you to get here so fast. It's not even been twenty-four hours since I contacted you."

"I wouldn't have, except I've been working nearby. Your timing was perfect." Brad Sanders took a sip of the coffee. "And I want to add how pleased I am, along with the rest of the company, of your involvement in catching this murderer."

Corbin strummed his fingers against the desk. "There is something I need to talk to you about regarding our prisoner."

The front door flung open, and Catherine flew into the office. Her hat sat askew atop her head and her cheeks were bright red. Whatever had her in a tizzy had her running like her skirts were on fire.

"Sheriff Hunter, I need to speak with you immediately."

Corbin sat back in his chair and took a calm sip of his coffee. Surprisingly enough, his coping skills with women seemed to be improving. He set the cup on the table and smiled. Mrs. McBride's gossip pipeline was running slow today. He'd expected Catherine thirty minutes ago. "Catherine Morgan, this is Brad Sanders. He's a Pinkerton agent working on the Masked Gang case who has just arrived from the capital."

Mr. Sanders dipped his head. "It's nice to meet you, Miss Morgan."

Catherine's gaze traveled from Mr. Sanders then back to Corbin. "This visit has something to do with Harrison, doesn't it? Ike Larrick said he saw—"

"You know you're interrupting official business of an officer of the law."

"And I apologize, but...

"But what, Miss Morgan?"

"I made a mistake."

Corbin leaned back against his chair, taken aback by her apology. He'd expected her to arrive ranting and raving over Harrison's innocence, not admitting to a wrongdoing. "You made a mistake?"

"I thought I was making the right decision by staying quiet, but I have proof that Harrison had nothing to do with these bank robberies—"

"Miss Morgan—"

"Wait... you have to understand that if Harrison is convicted for this crime, then the real William Marker will still be free, which means that more robberies will take place, which means that more people will get killed, all because I didn't—"

"Miss Morgan—"

She continued without taking a breath. "Everything you have against him is completely circumstantial, but I can prove he's innocent."

Corbin leaned back in his chair and suppressed a grin. Mr. Sanders sat, jaw dropped at the display. "And what evidence do you have to the contrary, Miss Morgan?"

"For starters, you were right about him never being in Alaska. Harrison Tucker worked for a newspaper, writing fictional serials. He was on his way to Alaska when his stagecoach was involved in an accident outside Chicago. Three people were killed, and he ended up in the hospital with a dozen broken bones."

"That would explain his slight limp," Corbin threw out.

"Not wanting to lose his job, he read everything he could get his hands on to make his stories more authentic."

"Then the newspaper found out."

Catherine nodded then paused. "How did you know?"

"I have my sources, too, Miss Morgan." Corbin steepled his hands in front of him.

"But please, continue with your story. I'm sure this is as entertaining for Mr. Sanders as it is for me."

Catherine glanced at Mr. Sanders then back at Corbin before plunging ahead. "The problem was, he couldn't pull it off. The newspaper wanted someone who was actually living in Alaska and fired him. It was about that time he received word his grandfather had died and the farm had been left to him. A farm in Ohio was far less appealing than an adventure in Alaska, but once he'd recovered from his injuries, he made his way to Revenge."

"He never planned to stay," Catherine continued. "He was going to fix up the place and sell it. But then he met Audrey, and they fell in love."

"And they lived happily ever after," Corbin injected. "Or, at least that was the original plan."

Catherine frowned. "He knew enough about what was happening to make us all feel as if we were there, but his tall tales about the frontier were just stories. He's a storyteller at heart. Not a murderer."

"Are you done now?"

She folded her arms across her chest. "I'm done."

"Are you sure?" he asked.

She opened her mouth, but he cut her off. "Never mind. I was just telling Mr. Sanders, before I was so rudely interrupted, that you were right. I believe Harrison was set up."

Catherine blinked twice. "You what?"

"I told him that you were right."

"You believe he's innocent?"

"Like you said, there have been too many things that haven't added up. Anonymous tips, confessions from a known criminal, and in fact, as you stated so eloquently, everything we have on him is circumstantial. Which made it clear to me that someone was trying to set him up. Even so, I talked to Harrison and had to force his hand to get at the truth. I convinced him that if he didn't come up with an alibi, he was going to hang in the morning."

"You what? Why?"

"You know as well as I do, Miss Morgan, that if I didn't hang him, the town would ensure he did. At this point, the truth is the only thing that has a chance of saving him. I also contacted the newspaper people in Boston, and they assured me that Harrison did work for them, and had been fired after they found out he'd been writing his serial from a hospital bed."

Catherine's chin dropped. "He didn't want Audrey to know that the stories he tells were simply stories."

Mr. Sanders took a final swig of his coffee, then rose to leave. "If you're right about Harrison Tucker, then I'd say we both have our work cut out for us."

Corbin shook the agent's hand. "We're going to get the real outlaw."

"I always do. And if you ever change your mind, just let me know. We could always use another good man in the agency."

Catherine plopped onto the empty chair across from Corbin as Mr. Sanders left the office. "If you change your mind about what?"

"He thinks I'd make a good Pinkerton agent."

She shook her head. "Why didn't you tell me you knew the truth?"

"Because you wouldn't stop talking." Corbin suppressed a grin. He liked a woman with a mind of her own, even if it seemed to get her into trouble most of the time. Like Catherine? No. He ignored the unsolicited thought and forced himself to focus on the problem at hand.

She pressed her lips together. "So you are going to release Harrison?"

"I'll let him know he's free to go, but I'll suggest he stays out of sight until the real crook is snagged. I don't want to have to deal with a town lynching."

Catherine's stomach soured at the thought. "Surely you don't think—"

"It's just a possibility, but we have to be careful."

She let out a slow breath. Not too long ago, Harrison had spent his time courting her sister and entertaining a captivated crowd with stories of the frontier. Today he sat in a jail cell to save him from an angry town. "He didn't want Audrey to know he was nothing more than a reporter who never struck gold—or a story for that matter. All he wanted to do was win Audrey's heart."

"There's only one problem with all of this." Corbin tapped his fingers against the desk. "I'm back to the beginning."

"Not completely." Catherine leaned forward. "We know that William Marker is probably someone working close to Revenge. It's the only way he could have set up Harrison."

The door opened and Lily appeared in the threshold. "Catherine, I'm sorry to interrupt, but I just received a phone call from Emily."

Catherine stood up. "What is it? The baby?"

"No, it's Father. He's…he's missing."

Chapter Seventeen

....

Why was it that Isaiah Morgan managed to affect their lives whether halfway around the world or right here in Revenge? Catherine paced the small expanse of the sitting room, her emotions teetering between the worry on Lily's face and an intense anger that her father could have done this to them again. It had been almost a week ago she'd stood in this very same room, wishing Isaiah Morgan had never shown up. But even despite her anger, she'd do anything to see his face again. Even if it were only for the sake of her sisters.

Corbin stood near the doorway, arms folded across his chest, obviously taking seriously his role as sheriff. "Did you stop to consider the idea that he simply left?"

"Of course."

Catherine stopped in front of the patterned settee, wishing her words hadn't been so biting. And wishing he hadn't spoken her fear out loud. But it was something that had to be considered. It wouldn't have been the first time Isaiah Morgan had walked out on them. She squeezed her eyes shut and, for a moment, she was there again. The last time she'd seen her father and mother together. He'd kissed her mother on the cheek with promises that he'd return soon, stepped out onto the front porch of the store with the rising sun behind him, and with one last look, he was gone.

Corbin took a step closer to her. "Catherine."

She opened her eyes and drew in a staggered breath as feelings of loss tore at her heart.

"I'm okay." She dropped onto the settee beside Lily. As much as she didn't trust her father, she still wasn't ready to admit that he'd simply deserted them. Not again. "I think Lily's right. He was so excited for Audrey's wedding and the birth of Emily's baby. I can't see him just leaving and missing all of that. And besides, while he didn't bring much with him, everything he owns is still in Emily's guest room. He didn't take any personal items with him or the small amount of cash he has. Why would he leave without taking it with him? Without saying good-bye?"

"That's what we have to find out."

Catherine pressed her lips together. No matter how many bitter feelings she still harbored against her father, even she didn't want things to end like this. Not with him walking out the door, never to return.

Corbin sat down across from them and waited silently. How was it that he was, once again, the one giving her the support she needed? Just like she'd one day planned. She looked up at him, wondering how they'd come to this point.

She still loved him.

Catherine felt her lung compress. Loved him. Once...not now.

"So tell me again exactly what happened."

Lily nodded. "Emily told me that he left to take a walk down by the creek after breakfast. He never returned."

"And he didn't take anything with him?"

Lily shook her head. "Nothing. He just walked out..."

Corbin rested his elbows against his knees. "We're going to find him, Catherine."

"I don't think my sisters can handle his leaving again."

"Where's Audrey?"

"She's at the O'Conner farm with Emily right now, waiting for Father." Lily looked up at Corbin, her eyes brimming with tears. "Where is he?"

"I don't know, but I promise I'll do everything I can to find him."

"Maybe we're all overreacting," Catherine threw out. "It's only been a few hours. Maybe he just needed to get away for a while and think. He's used to being independent."

"I don't think we know enough to make a fair judgment about the situation," Corbin said. "There could be a hundred explanations. He could have fallen, gotten lost, or maybe he's visiting a friend. We could start with any close friends he had in town."

"I suppose it's possible," Lily said. "Emily said he was on foot when he left, and I can't see him going far without a horse or wagon."

"Someone could have dropped by to see him and taken him out for a while."

Catherine turned and caught his gaze. "Or your first instinct was right. He decided to simply walk out on us again."

"Catherine." Lily shook her head. "He couldn't do that. I know it."

But no matter how much Lily tried to justify his disappearance, it was the only one that made sense to Catherine. And it was one they all might have to come to terms with. "We both know it's a question we can't ignore. And one I should have seen coming. Don't you see? Despite his noble words, he hasn't changed at all."

"You don't know that," Corbin said.

"Then give me a better explanation."

Corbin combed his hands through his hair and shook his head. "I'm sure your father will show up. He probably just got lost."

Catherine walked to the window and peered out on the quiet street. "My father lived half his life here. He isn't lost." She pressed her fingers against her temple. Three weeks ago she'd been sitting on Emily's porch with no worries other than a mean ostrich and a worn-out hat. At what point had everything begun to fall apart?

I don't understand, God…

Praying had helped, but there were some things she had to do on her own. She turned to Corbin. "We need to put together a search party, before it gets dark, and go look for him."

He nodded. "With the telephone in place, we should be able to round up some men."

Lily grasped her arm. "I'm coming with you."

"I need you to stay here, in case he simply got sidetracked and shows up for dinner. And you can make the phone calls," Catherine said. "I'll ask Mrs. Morrilton to stop by and keep you company."

"We'll need at least half a dozen men to help with the search," Corbin told Lily. "Have them meet at the O'Conner farm as soon as they can get there. We'll leave from there since that was the last place your father was seen."

"John will want to help as well," Lily said. "I'm sure of it."

Corbin grabbed his hat from the table. "Have him join us when you see him. We can use all the help we can get."

"What about Harrison?" Catherine asked.

"He can come with us. That way, I can keep my eye on him and help ensure he's safe."

Catherine gave Lily a reassuring hug. "Are you going to be all right?"

Lily nodded. "Go. I'll make some phone calls and send as many men as I can."

* * *

Twenty-five minutes later, Corbin pulled the wagon up in front of the O'Conner house. The roar of an ostrich from the corral only seemed to add to the eerie mood of the cloudy afternoon. The lanky bird stood silhouetted in the prairie. He'd heard Grady's explanation about the experiment and his plan to use the warming techniques of glassblowing to incubate the eggs and chicks, but the whole setup seemed a bit farfetched to him. It was a lot of expense and effort for a bunch of feathers.

Catherine sat silent beside him on the wagon.

She gazed at the floorboard. "Thank you."

They were the first words she'd said since they left for the ranch. Why did it seem as though all he'd brought her was heartache—something that seemed to go hand-in-hand with his return to Revenge.

His Adam's apple bobbed. "For what?"

"For letting Harrison go. For coming out here with me. For not telling me that I'm crazy to try to find a man I didn't want to be here in the first place."

"You're not crazy. And besides, it's my job."

She looked away.

He stopped the wagon in front of Emily's house. "What I meant was—"

"It might be your job," she said, "but I still appreciate all you've done for my sisters and me."

Not waiting for him to help her down from the wagon, she lifted the bottom edge of her skirt and hurried toward the wraparound

porch. He jumped down from the wagon. Independent…feisty…
beautiful. It was enough to drive a man crazy. And when was that
woman going to realize that she didn't have to do everything herself?
That it was all right to depend on other people?

Like himself. Which meant maybe he should just come out and
tell her that he wasn't doing this because he had to. Whether he
wanted to admit it or not, this had become far more than just a job to
him. Catherine Morgan was the girl who'd stolen his heart and never
given it back when he walked out all those years ago.

He followed her toward the porch, knowing it was no longer
worth trying to deny the subtle feelings she stirred in him. She had
no idea how much her presence affected him, or how much he
wanted to ignore it. But it was strong enough to make him want to
gather her into his arms and promise her that everything was going
to be okay. And that he wasn't going to walk away again like he'd done
so long ago—the way her father had done.

He paused at the bottom stair. Except that was something he
couldn't promise, because everything might not be okay. He had no
intention of sticking around this town longer than he had to. He took
the porch steps two at a time and joined her at the threshold. If the
search for his father's killer took him to…to Alaska…he'd go there.
Something he wasn't sure she'd ever be able to understand.

"Catherine!" Audrey stood just inside the doorway. "Sheriff.
Thank you so much for coming."

Audrey paused at the sight of Harrison, who exited the wagon
behind them, then went back into the house. Corbin caught
Harrison's crestfallen look. Obviously he wasn't the only one haunted
with mistakes from the past.

Corbin entered the O'Conner home behind Catherine, wishing the occasion were less somber. He could see the worried expressions on the faces of Emily and Audrey as they welcomed him into the house. He wished he were more optimistic about the situation, but either way he looked at it, something wasn't right about Mr. Morgan's disappearance. Corbin wasn't sure why, but he'd had that uneasy feeling in his gut since the first moment Lily had told them about it. And if it turned out that he had simply walked out on these young women, Corbin was going to be the one wringing some sense into the man.

Anything he did was going to tear up the family who'd experience more than their share of heartache lately. Especially Catherine. As the matriarch of the family, she bustled around her sisters, assuring them that everything was going to be all right. According to Mr. O'Conner, if they were lucky, Isaiah Morgan would be back at the dinner table for supper, though any man who walked out on his family like he had didn't deserve a second chance, in his opinion. Actions always did speak louder than words.

"Sheriff." Mr. O'Conner stepped up and shook Corbin's hand, interrupting his thoughts. "Thank you for coming. Lily just telephoned and already has six men on their way here who have volunteered to help with the search."

"That's great," Corbin said.

"Where do we start?" Catherine asked.

Corbin cleared his throat. "I need to know anything you can think of. Any sign that he might have left on his own accord. Any notes he left. Any unusual behavior the past day or so."

"He didn't leave a note," Emily began. "All he told me was that he was going to go for a walk. Said he had some thinking to do."

"Did he seem upset?"

Emily looked to Audrey before speaking. "He'd been quiet, but no different from when he first arrived. I think he was still trying to find his place back in the family. Something we all realize will take some time. The last thing he said to me was that he'd be back in time for us to head into town for supper with Catherine."

Audrey hovered beside her twin sister. "I don't see how he could be lost. He knew this land better than any of us. Even eight years can't change that. If he fell and injured himself…"

"Which is exactly why we need to get started," Catherine said. "It's been almost twelve hours, and it's going to be dark soon."

Corbin took the lead. "As soon as the men get here, we'll divide up in groups of two and leave from here, reporting back every hour."

Catherine took a step forward and addressed Corbin. "I'm coming as well."

"That's not necessary."

"It is for me."

"Catherine—"

"I can ride as well as any of the men joining the search and you know it."

Corbin looked to Mr. O'Conner, who only shrugged. The man was right. There was no use trying to talk any sense into her. If she wanted to come, neither Grady nor he could stop her.

"Fine. You'll ride along with me." At least he'd be able to keep his eye on her.

Corbin caught the look of concern in Catherine's eyes. He knew what it was like to lose a father, and he didn't want her to go through what he'd experienced. Losing him again, no matter what she felt about him, was going to hurt.

Twenty minutes after their arrival, he was heading toward Clear Creek with Catherine beside him. He wasn't worried that she couldn't keep up. He was more worried that the emotional toil of the situation was going to end up being more than she could handle. Catherine had always had an inner strength, but sometimes even that inner strength wasn't enough.

"What are we looking for?" she asked.

"Footprints leading off the main road, signs of a struggle, anything out of the ordinary."

"Do you think something happened to him? This land isn't free from outlaws who will kill a man over the change in his pocket."

"There's no way to know at this point. All I know is that we don't need to give up now. We'll find him."

She was quiet for a few moments before speaking again. "What if he just left again? He could have hitched a ride to Lancaster and taken the train halfway across the county by now. And if he left…"

"I don't think that's what happened." Corbin hoped his words were as convincing as he felt. "He's got too much holding him here. A new grandchild, a wedding… He's not going to miss those things."

"Then where is he?" Catherine's voice caught.

Corbin glanced over at her. Her hat created enough of a shadow that he couldn't read her expression, but he knew that was what she really feared. Isaiah Morgan knew this land as well as anyone and the chances that he'd gotten lost were slim. She had the same fear he'd seen written on the face of each of her sisters. Isaiah had walked out on them once. What if he had done it again?

* * *

Three hours later, darkness had begun to settle across the Ohio landscape. Catherine arched her back in the saddle, trying to work out the tight muscles that had formed. They'd traveled across miles of terrain without a sign of her father.

"It's time to head back to the ranch again and check in with the others. It's going to be too late to go out another time."

Catherine glanced up as dark clouds drifted over the half moon. "Grady will have lanterns. Father's got to be out here somewhere."

"We'll never find him in the dark."

She didn't answer. She knew he was right. But that did little to lessen the dread she felt at going back to the house and seeing the disappointment on the faces of her sisters when they realized that their father wasn't with them.

"There's still the chance that one of the other groups found him," Corbin offered.

Catherine nodded. He was right again. She was giving up too soon. Her father could be sitting at Emily's table right now eating supper.

The porch lights were lit, and inside, Milena had set out fried chicken and biscuits for those who had been out searching. Catherine's gaze swept the room. All but two of the searchers had checked in, and there was no sign of her father.

Catherine looked at her sisters and felt the last thread of hope begin to disintegrate.

"It's too dark now." Grady gathered his wife into his arms and held her tightly. "If Samuel White and Clint Faulkner don't find him, we'll have to start looking again at daybreak. There's nothing more to do at this point—"

Mr. White burst through the front door then stopped short in front of the group. He took off his hat and dropped his gaze to the floor.

Catherine stepped forward. "What is it?"

"We've found him." Mr. White looked up at Catherine. "Along Clear Creek, about four miles to the east...I'm sorry to be the one to have to tell you this, ma'am, but your father's dead."

Chapter Eighteen

....

Corbin entered the O'Conner home for a third time this evening, wishing he had different news. What had been a simple missing-person case had turned into something far more serious. His investigation had been clear. Isaiah Morgan had been murdered.

He stood at the threshold of the open doorway, uncertain how he should proceed. The last thing he wanted was to add pain to the already grieving family. They sat huddled together in the large room. The smell of fried chicken lingered in the air, but no one had touched Milena's dinner. Dealing with their father's death was going to be difficult enough, but knowing how he died was like rubbing salt into the open wound.

Catherine glanced up, and he motioned for her to join him on the front porch.

Neither spoke as she closed the door behind her and followed him out to the railing. Crickets chirped their unscripted melody in the background, competing only with the occasional roar of an ostrich. Corbin's gaze wandered across the shadowy horizon. The mammoth bird made an odd silhouette—the Ohio landscape was known more for its corn and wheat crops than exotic wildlife. Emily O'Conner was the only woman he knew who could convince her husband to defy the laws of nature and raise a bunch of brainless birds for the sake of fashion.

He turned to Catherine, who stood quietly beside him, seemingly lost in her own thoughts.

A pale beam of moonlight illuminated the side of her face, making her look both vulnerable and determined at the same time. Maybe he understood Grady O'Conner better than he thought.

"What did you find out?" she finally asked, breaking the silence between them.

Corbin stared at the tips of his boots. Even with only the light from the moon and a handful of lanterns, the cause of Isaiah's death had been clear. The answers as to why, however, were not. "Your father was murdered."

"Murdered?" Catherine gasped then pressed her fingers against her mouth. Tears welled in her eyes. "There has to be some sort of mistake. Why would anyone want to kill him?"

He watched as her expression changed from the sadness of knowing her father was dead, to the horror of realizing someone had purposely taken his life. "I'm sorry, Catherine. So very sorry."

Her hands gripped the whitewashed porch railing. "How did he die?"

"He was shot in the heart."

She looked up at him with the look of undeniable grief in her eyes. "It could have been an accident. He liked to hunt. Maybe he took his gun, or one of Grady's guns, and fell, or —"

Corbin shook his head. "The bullet doesn't match his pistol and none of Grady's guns are missing. Besides that, there was another set of footprints. Someone was there on a horse. This wasn't an accident."

Catherine's chest heaved. "I can't tell my sisters our father was murdered. What about Emily and the baby... She's already lost so much. We all have."

"The problem is that they will find out, Catherine. If not from you, from someone else. You've got to tell them." He drew in a ragged breath. "I'm sorry. I have no right to—"

"No." She reached up and brushed the sleeve of his jacket before pulling away. "You're right. I just...I just can't believe someone would want to harm him."

"There's something else." Corbin rubbed his chin, wondering how much he should tell her. She was strong, of that he had no doubt, but even Catherine Morgan—while she'd most likely go to her grave denying it—had her limits. "No one else knows about this, but I found a possible connection..."

"What are you talking about?"

He shoved his hands into his front pockets. He had to tell her the truth. "I found the bullet that killed your father. It had a triangular base."

"I don't understand."

"It was a .69 French Dragoon bullet. Just like the bullets used in the robberies."

"You're telling me that there's a connection between my father and the Masked Gang?"

"There are too many things that don't add up, Catherine. Why did your father return now, after all these years? I can't say for sure, but yes, there could be a connection."

"At least Harrison has an alibi for the murder." She rubbed the back of her neck. "And if the same bullets were used, doesn't that clear his connection to the robberies as well?"

"Maybe, though I'm not ready to dismiss anything entirely. There's always the chance that someone else in the gang used his gun."

She looked up at him. "So what do I do?"

"Nothing—"

"I won't stand by and do nothing."

"I will find out who did this. I promise."

Catherine shook her head. "The Masked Gang is still on the loose and my father's dead. Don't make me any more promises you can't keep."

Corbin reigned in his temper. "I will find them, Catherine. They killed my father, too, and nothing is going to stop me until I find out the truth."

* * *

Catherine sat down on the edge of Emily's settee and clenched her hands together. Emily and Audrey sat across from her, their eyes laced with tears. She might not have welcomed her father back to Revenge, but neither did she want him dead. "I've just spoken to Corbin, and he's given me some disturbing news. I believe that you all need to hear the truth from me—before you hear it from someone else."

Harrison stood across the room, a longing in his eyes as he looked at Audrey, but they would have to find time to talk later. Their father's death was going to have to be dealt with first.

Please, God…give me the words to speak to them.

Catherine pressed back a strand of hair from her damp forehead. "I know that this news about Father came as a shock to all of us. But Corbin found out something more." She watched their reactions carefully, wishing there was something she could do to take away the sting of what she was about to say. "Father was shot in the heart. He was murdered."

The room fell silent.

"We just got him back, and now you're telling me that not only is he dead, but that he was murdered?" Emily rose from her seat. "No. I can't accept that someone shot him in cold blood, for…for what? We need to get a posse together and find out who did this."

Grady tugged her back down onto the couch. "Emily. You've got to calm down."

"I want to assure you, Mrs. O'Conner, that I will do everything in my power to find out who did this." Corbin spoke from the doorway. "But for now, it's too dark, and we won't be able to track whoever did this until morning."

"So you're giving up?"

"Of course not, but at the moment I have little to go by other than a few sets of footprints. But I assure you, we will do everything we can to find out who committed this atrocity."

Catherine stood, agonizing over the thought of leaving her sisters. "I've got to get home to Lily. She needs to know what's happened. I can't have her finding out from someone else."

Emily nodded. "Audrey can stay here tonight, and if we need anything…I'll call."

Catherine's arm shook as she picked up her hat.

"You're in no condition to go anywhere, Catherine," Audrey said.

Corbin spoke from across the room. "I'll take her home."

* * *

Corbin gripped the reigns of the horse and headed toward town. "I meant what I said earlier. We're going to find who did this."

"What if we don't?" She shook her head. "I just don't understand why. He hasn't been here for years. He doesn't have any enemies, and certainly doesn't have anything to do with these robberies. It doesn't make sense. What has this world turned into if we have to constantly worry about our family members being murdered in cold blood?"

Corbin's jaw tensed. He stared straight ahead through the darkness ahead of him, lit only by a handful of stars and the half moon. On any other night he might relish the fact that Catherine sat beside him. If only circumstances were different. He let out a soft sigh. He'd learned a long time again that all the wishing in the world couldn't change things.

He felt her gloved hand on his forearm and felt a burning soar through his veins. Catherine's love for him had dried up years ago, and no matter what a few lingering emotions might tell him, he wasn't going to try to change things between them.

"All of this must bring back memories of your own father," she said. "I remember how close you were to him."

"He was a good man who only wanted what was best for his family."

"How did you get through it? At the moment, I'm so numb I don't know what to feel. Guilt, for not making things right. Loss, for the years without him that are forever gone. Relief, that he'll never hurt me or my sisters again…"

"Forgiveness is a choice. Sometimes you have to forgive others. Sometimes you have to forgive yourself."

Unfortunately, he hadn't taken his own advice. He still harbored regrets over not being there to stop his father's murder. Or his inability to take down the murderer. It was easier to say the words to someone else then to follow them himself.

"Tell me what happened."

Corbin sat quiet for a moment, lost in resurrected emotions from the past. "We'd just planned a hunting trip the week before. I was excited because it had been years since I'd gone with him. The next thing I knew, the sheriff was knocking at my door with news that he'd been murdered. I'll never forget the crash of emotions that overcame me. The denial, the anger, the grief, knowing that I wouldn't stop until the man who had killed him was hanged."

"And you're still trying to avenge his death."

"He never should have died." Familiar seeds of anger rose. Why was it so easy to tell someone else the importance of forgiveness, when he'd yet to find a way in his own life? "He died because of another man's greed. It's something I don't think I'll ever be able to forgive."

"You just told me that forgiveness is a choice."

"My father told me that once. It's good advice."

"But hard to do." Catherine gripped the edge of the seat and shook her head. "Why would God bring Father back to us only to take him away before things were made right between us?"

"God wasn't the one who took your father's life." Corbin reached out and grasped her hand as they approached the edge of town. "I promise I'll find out who did this, Catherine."

"You can't make that kind of promise. Sometimes evil simply triumphs."

"Not this time."

He set the wagon's brake in front of the store then turned toward her. The moonlight caught her wide eyes full of pain. The myriad emotions he had been trying unsuccessfully to ignore since his arrival in Revenge returned full force. The day he told her he wanted to court her... The day he asked her to marry him... The day she told him she didn't love him...

Looking into her eyes, he could almost forget the damage she'd done to his heart and the resentment she'd left behind that day.

Her face hovered in front of his—full lips, blushed cheeks, unspoken expectations. Without thinking further, he slid his hand around her neck and pulled her toward him. His heart exploded with emotions left dormant for too long. This was what he'd dreamed of. This was what he'd been missing.

For a moment, he felt her respond.

"Please...not now." Catherine pushed away from him and shook her head. "It can't work between us. It's too late."

"You never stopped loving me, did you, Catherine?"

Her eyes welled with fresh tears. "I can't love you."

He gripped her wrists. He needed to know. "Tell me the truth, Catherine."

Catherine pulled away from his embrace and stumbled from the buggy toward the store.

Corbin watched her flee toward the house. He'd made his first mistake in courting Miss Catherine Morgan all those years ago, and now he'd just made his second. But he'd been right all along, and this was something he wouldn't do again. Her actions showed all too clearly how she felt. And he, for one, wasn't going to make the mistake of falling for her again.

* * *

The feel of Corbin's touch still burned on Catherine's lips while she worked to erase the memory of his kiss. But no matter how hard she tried, she couldn't. With it had come a torrent of emotions tied together in an odd-shaped package that she didn't know how to deal with. Anger, hurt, loneliness, pride…

She'd told him the truth. That she didn't love him. That she couldn't love him. Or was it merely a deception she'd tried to make herself believe? She closed the door behind her and entered the house.

"Miss Morgan?"

Catherine peered into the lamplight. John Guild stood in the doorway of the kitchen. "Mr. Guild, I'm sorry. You startled me."

"I apologize. I wanted to stay until I knew you were home safely."

"Thank you. Where's Lily?"

"Mrs. Morrilton took her upstairs. She was so tired, but I didn't want to leave her until I found out what had happened."

"Yes. Thanks for staying with her. I appreciate it."

"Mrs. Morrilton wasn't too pleased that I was here so late— or that I'm still here. And while I suppose I should have joined the posse, I felt that Lily needed me here."

"Mrs. Morrilton makes an intimidating chaperone, I'm sure."

"We were allowed to sit across the room from each other and talk."

Catherine laughed despite the somber events of the evening. "Thank you. For staying with her and putting up with the antics of the doctor's wife. She does care."

"Did you find your father?"

Catherine glanced at the bottom of the staircase, dreading what she was going to have to tell her sister.

"He's dead."

"Dead?"

"Murdered." Fresh tears began to flow.

"I'm so sorry. And Lily…" John pressed his lips together. "I don't know how she's going to take this."

"I know you care about my sister."

"I'm in love with her."

"I know."

"There's something I need to speak to you about." John waited while she poured them both a glass of water. "I know the timing for this isn't right. I'd planned to speak to Mr. Morgan, but now…"

Catherine handed him a glass of water. "You want to marry her, don't you?"

He took a sip of his drink. "I'd take care of her. Provide a good home."

"You have my permission. All I ask is that you wait until after the funeral to ask her. Give our father the respect he deserves."

"Of course." John set the glass on the counter. "Does the sheriff have any leads? Anything that might point in the direction of whoever did this?"

She shook her head. "Not enough to catch the person. There was a set of other footprints, but it was too dark to follow them. I suppose if they got lucky, they might be able to pick up the trail tomorrow, but by then I'm afraid it will be too late."

Catherine thought about sharing the possible connection between her father's death and the leader of the Masked Gang, but decided to respect Corbin's wishes.

"I'll go now. Please tell Lily that I'll come by and check on her in the morning. Perhaps we can go for a ride to help clear her mind."

"Thank you, John. For everything."

Catherine locked the door behind him before mounting

the stairs. A peek in Lily's room showed that she was fast asleep.
At least she was able to rest. The news could wait until morning.

"Mrs. Morrilton. Thank you so much for staying. "

The older woman got up from the rocking chair. "It was no
problem. And your father. Did they find him?"

Catherine stepped from the room with Mrs. Morrilton,
wondering how many times she was going to have to repeat what
had happened. "They found his body near the creek. I'll tell Lily
in the morning."

"Oh, my dear, I'm so sorry. Many of us have fond memories
of him from years ago. I can't imagine how difficult this must be.
If there is anything you need…"

"Thank you. I'm fine for now."

"Then I'll let myself out."

Catherine stood in the doorway of her room for a moment then
knelt in front of her mother's hope chest.

*Why, God? I might never have told him I forgave him, but this isn't
what I wanted.*

Catherine lifted the lid of the wooden chest that was full of the
few treasures she had of her mother's. Handmade baby clothes,
embroidered tea towels, her mother's wedding dress… There were a few
things she'd already passed on to Emily the day she'd married Grady.
Others she planned to give Audrey and Lily on their wedding days, but
for now, she simply needed to find a connection with all that she'd lost.

In the bottom corner of the chest was a stack of letters from
her father. The week after her mother had died, she'd considered
burning them, but in the end had decided to keep them, even
though she'd never been able to bring herself to read them. But

things had changed. And while she knew they might never find out who had killed her father, it was a place to begin. If there was any record of him finding gold, this was the one place she knew where to start looking.

She slid off the pink ribbon that held the letters together, opened the yellowed paper of the first envelope, and began reading.

September 12, 1877
My dearest Sarah,

It's only been four months since I left Revenge, but it seems more like decades. I am well, but I miss you and the girls so much, I often wonder if I made the right choice in leaving. If it weren't for the chance of giving us a better life, I think I'd be headed back to Ohio.

I'm sending this letter with a man who came through camp selling newspapers today. I have no idea how long this letter will take to get to you, or even if it will. But if you do eventually receive it, don't worry about me. I have a place to sleep at night and enough food...

Catherine continued reading through references of freezing cold temperatures, long days of hard labor, and little food, but nothing about what he'd found. Or that he'd ever come to understand that family would always be more important than a better life financially. But all she needed now was something that might give her a clue to someone who might have wanted revenge against him. Or perhaps something that might distract her from Corbin's kiss.

There have been enough secrets in this family.

She squeezed her eyes shut remembering Corbin's words. Why hadn't she been able to tell Corbin her own secret? Today might have been filled with a tangle of emotion that had ended with him kissing her, but Corbin hadn't returned to Revenge for her. Nothing had changed between them. When all this was over, he'd realize his mistake and leave Revenge forever.

She pulled open another letter dated the following spring from the last she'd read, not long before her mother died.

My dearest Sarah,

How time passes quickly. To think that last spring I was helping you plant the garden, and this spring, I've yet to thaw out. I staked a second claim on the outskirts of Juneau, and in less than three months, it's already yielded two thousand dollars. More than many people find in a couple years. I know it's been long, but I just need a little more time. I hooked up with a partner. We're certain that given a bit more time, we'll strike it big. I'm planning to be home before winter comes, so watch for me, but this could be the big one, Sarah. I can feel it. Remember I love you. Just wait a little bit longer.

Catherine read through the remaining letters. She needed a name, or a clue…anything that might give her an insight as to who might have killed him. Her father had never mentioned a partner to her, and it was more than likely that their relationship had dissolved years ago. Or could it have something to do with his murder?

What her father hadn't expected was that their mother would be buried by the time those first letters arrived. And he'd never kept his promise to return by winter. Catherine shoved the letters back into the chest, wishing she'd had the chance to ask him about his partner. And if they had struck it rich, where was the money?

Chapter Nineteen

....

Catherine wrapped her arms around her waist and stood alone at the newly dug grave beside her mother's, still holding the handful of wildflowers Lily had picked for her. She missed her parents. Both of them. Sometime during the past couple of weeks she'd seen a side of her father she'd never known. He'd gone from the selfish drunk she remembered to a doting father and soon-to-be grandfather. Yet she'd never acknowledged his changes, because she hadn't been able to get beyond her own anger and hurt over what he'd done to them.

I didn't know how to, God...

She knelt down beside the sandstone marker, picked up a handful of the loose dirt with her free hand, and let the dark soil fall between her fingers. The entire morning had progressed in slow motion as Pastor Landon led them through the ceremony meant to put Isaiah Morgan to rest. But none of his words could subdue the discontent stirring in her heart. Instead, while the morning sun had cast its warm rays on them, and her sisters had wept over the father they'd lost, she'd stood beside them like the matriarchal figure of the family, wrestling with her inability to forgive her father's betrayal, and at the same time, vowing to find the man who killed him.

When the last of the procession had left, she'd promised her sisters she'd join them later at the house, but for now, there were simply too many things left unsaid. So many emotions left to sort out. She'd gone over what had happened to her father a thousand times and asked herself at least that many questions, because the connection between her father's killer and the leader of the Masked Gang continued to haunt her. Whoever had murdered him had to have known both Harrison's habits and those of her father. Which narrowed it down to someone who lived in Revenge. Someone who knew how to con a town into thinking he was a loyal member of the community when, in reality, his only goal was to plunder the surrounding towns—with no regard to anyone who got in his way.

A horse whinnied behind her. Catherine looked up. Corbin sat atop his gray stallion, making the perfect silhouette in the Ohio landscape. Her heart quivered. Why did her heart always come back to that one regretful moment between them when she'd told him good-bye? And now his kiss had brought those turbulent emotions to the surface all over again.

"Miss Morgan."

"Sheriff. I was just…saying good-bye."

She stood and brushed the dirt from her skirt. Why was it whenever she was feeling the most vulnerable, Corbin showed up? And why hadn't she been able to bury her memories of him like she'd buried her father?

"Are you all right?"

She wanted to laugh at the question. "Am I all right? In the past two weeks, my prodigal father returned, my future brother-in-law was arrested, then my father murdered." She shook her head and tried to stop the flow of tears she'd managed to hold at bay so far. "No. I don't suppose I am all right."

* * *

Corbin dismounted his horse, wishing for the dozenth time
that he could undo the past and set things right for her. But he, too,
had lost his father by the hand of a murderer, and there was nothing
he could do to change any of it.

She stood in front of him, her face pale above her dark funeral
garb. He tried to erase the image of the last time he'd dared to hold
her in his arms, but instead of sealing away the past as her rejection
should have, the memory only managed to stir up feelings from the
past that were better left forgotten.

He jammed his hands into the front pockets of his jeans and
caught her tearful gaze. "I was headed out to the Baldwin farm for
supper and saw you here. I thought everyone had left."

She brushed away a tear. "Everyone else did. I just had…a few
more things to say before leaving."

"I can't tell you how sorry I am. If there is anything I can do…"

"As a sheriff or as a friend?"

"Both."

She laid the handful of wildflowers on the fresh grave and started
walking up the slight hill on the other side of the graveyard. Corbin
followed her toward the grassy embankment that met the lazy creek
below and waited for her to speak.

"A couple nights ago, I read through my mother's letters from my
father. I don't know if they're important, but they mention the fact
that my father had gone into business with a partner, and that they
had started finding a decent amount of color from their claim."

"Who was his partner?"

"I don't know. There was no mention of any names. And the money
could have kept coming in for years, or simply a matter of weeks."

"What if his partner came and killed him for his share of the money?"

"After all these years?" She shrugged. "I don't know. It could make sense except for the fact that as far as I know, my father returned to Revenge with little more than the clothes on his back. According to him, there was no fortune, and I don't know why he would lie about it."

"But whether he actually had the money or not might not be the real issue, if someone thinks that he had it."

"Which means, for all we know, that person could be the same one who ransacked my house looking for the money."

Corbin watched a small-bodied veery as it skimmed the top of the water and sang its loud, whistling call. There were simply too many odd pieces to the puzzle that didn't fit with the rest of the picture. "If your father was hiding a fortune, and someone wanted his share, wouldn't Revenge be the first place he would check?"

"Perhaps. And there is also the question about the bullet that killed my father and his implied connection to the Masked Gang."

They started walking back toward the small cemetery. "I spoke with the sheriff in Lancaster. It's definitely the same type of bullet, down to the letter marking on the base, which makes it unique. And while I can't guarantee that the same gun was used, the odds of it being two different people are slim."

"But all that does is bring up the question again as to how was my father connected with a gang of bank robbers." She pressed her fingers against her temple. "None of it makes sense. I may not have liked the man my father was, but that doesn't mean I believe he was connected to a gang of criminals."

"The only conclusion that makes any sense to me is that someone assumed he returned from Alaska because he'd found a fortune."

Corbin studied her profile. "You look tired, and staying out here won't answer any of your questions."

"Questions like does the pain ever lessen?"

"After losing someone you love?"

She gestured toward her parents' graves as they passed. "That empty feeling of loss, along with wanting whoever did this to hang. I may not have agreed with all the choices my father made, but he was my father. And my sisters loved him. They were so excited for him to be back home."

"There will always be a hole left in your heart for what you've lost, but one day, the pain will lessen."

"I don't know if mine will." Fresh tears welled up. "I never forgave him. He asked me to, but I wouldn't."

A rush of grief swept through him. Words left unsaid. Others he could never take back. He knew the feelings all too well. "Don't do this to yourself, Catherine."

"You don't understand." She shook her head and stopped beneath the shade of a towering oak. "He came to me one afternoon. I was picking raspberries to make preserves for Emily. All I could think about was how he'd left us alone, and how if he'd never returned, we wouldn't have to deal with all the hurt he'd brought us in the past. But he just wanted me to forgive him. I couldn't even do that."

He grasped her shoulders and turned her toward him, so she had to look at him. "He's gone, and nothing's going to change that. What you can change is how you react from now on. Forgive him then let him go. For your sisters' sake, and for your own, you can't let this destroy you."

Because that was exactly what he'd done—vowed not to stop until he found his father's murderer at whatever cost.

"How can I forget what happened?" Catherine's blue eyes peered up at him. "It was as if he were here one moment and now…he's not coming back this time."

Corbin dropped his arms to his sides. "I know how hard it is to lose someone you love. I lost my father."

I lost you…

Her smile tugged at the corners of his heart.

"Thank you," she said.

"For what?"

"For telling me what I needed to hear." She took a step back and pressed her fingertips against her lips as if she, too, were thinking about the last time they'd been together. Then she turned to leave. "I need to get back to my sisters."

He swallowed hard. There was still one more thing he had to tell her. "Catherine, wait."

She turned back to him.

"I was wrong the other night when I brought you home and kissed you. With all the emotions of the evening…" He hesitated. There was no excuse for what he'd done. He no longer had any claims over her. "I'm sorry."

A blush crept up her cheeks. "Please, you don't have to apologize. With all that has happened, I'm sure it's natural for emotions from the past to come to the surface."

He nodded. She was right. And once he found answers, and was no longer personally involved, he'd see things differently.

"Just promise me one thing," she continued.

"Anything."

"I want you to find the man who murdered my father."

Corbin nodded. She was right. There was only one thing that was important right now. He had a killer to catch.

* * *

Catherine sat at the end of the long table in the dining room, not missing the significance of the moment. The last time the four Morgan women had eaten together at this table had been the night she erroneously announced that their father had been killed in a mining accident. How was it that two weeks later, they were burying his body?

The clicks of silverware on plates and the occasional shuffling of a chair filled in the silence of the moment. There was little to say. Their father was dead. Murdered. How did one respond to such horror? She glanced across the table at her sisters and, for a brief moment, wished she'd invited Corbin to join them. Emily sat beside Grady, and Lily next to John. Only Harrison's seat sat vacant, with the wedding postponed indefinitely.

"I spoke to Father about what we were going to name the baby." Emily broke the heavy silence surrounding them, reminding Catherine that life continued even in the face of death.

Grady nodded at her, and she cleared her throat. "I told him that Grady and I had decided if our child was a boy we would name him Mark Isaiah. Now that he's gone..." Grady reached for her hand. "We...we've decided to name him Isaiah Morgan O'Conner."

Catherine set her fork on her half-empty plate. "Father would be proud to know he had a grandson carrying on the family name."

Audrey wiped the corner of her eyes with her napkin and nodded. "We have many things to celebrate. I think that's what Father would have wanted."

"Speaking of things to be thankful for…" John pushed back his chair and stood. "I have something I'd like to say."

The room fell silent.

"I've sat with you the past few days and listened to you share memories of your family and life with your father. And I've realized how much I want to be a part of this. Not just of memories from the past…" He looked down at Lily. "But of future memories. Our future."

Catherine tried to gauge Lily's reaction. Her sister gasped and pressed her napkin against her lips as he took her hand.

"Lily, you've known how I feel about you for quite some time, and while I know that my timing might not be the best, I'm tired of waiting. I want to be the one who loves and protects you. What I'm trying to say is that I want you to be my wife, Lily Mae Morgan."

Lily began to sob.

"Lily?" Catherine began.

"I'm sorry." Lily shoved back her chair and ran from the room.

John stood up. "I'm sorry. I thought…I thought she loved me."

"She does love you." Catherine rose from the table. "But let me go to her. She just needs time."

Catherine found Lily upstairs on her bed, face down, crying in her pillow. "Lily?"

"Oh, Catherine." Lily sat up and wrapped her arms around Catherine. "I couldn't help it. How can I think about getting married when Father's just been buried?"

"Don't worry. He's just an impatient man in love."

"I don't want to lose him, but—"

"You have nothing to feel bad about. He should have given you more time to deal with Father's death. He'll understand."

Lily hugged her pillow to her chest. "I hope so."

"Do you want me to read to you like I used to? Maybe that would help you get your mind off things for a while."

Lily shook her head. "Go back downstairs. Audrey and Emily need you right now. I'll be okay. I just need some time to think."

Catherine kissed her sister on the forehead. "Are you sure?"

Lily nodded. "Tell John I'm sorry. It's not him."

"I will. Try and get some sleep."

Lily lay back down on the pillow as Catherine slipped from the room and went downstairs. John stood at the threshold waiting for her.

"Is she all right? I never should have proposed like that. I just thought…" He shook his head. "I suppose I didn't think."

"Everything will be fine. Just give her some time. I'm sure she'll feel like talking to you tomorrow."

"Catherine?" Audrey stood in the doorway.

Catherine's heart pounded. "What's wrong?"

"There was another robbery. This time it was in Amanda."

A sick feeling washed over Catherine. The robberies were becoming more and more frequent. There had to be an end to all of this. "And the sheriff? Did he go to Amanda?"

Audrey nodded. "I thought you would want to know."

Catherine pressed her hand against her mouth and fought the fear, wondering why her heart felt as if it were about to break in two.

Chapter Twenty

....

Catherine listened to the familiar hum of the store while distributing the mail in the partitioned shelf on the back wall. Harold and Horace drank their morning coffee and played a game of chess at the table near the front door while Stanley Phillips hovered above them, watching the long-standing competition. Mrs. Long searched through several new bolts of fabric that had just arrived from Cleveland, and Gregory Allen stood at the front counter, begging his mother for licorice. Catherine glanced at the chubby-faced seven-year-old, already knowing who would win the battle. She couldn't remember a day when the boy had left her store without a handful of penny candy in his pocket.

It might be a day like any other day, but even the normalcy of the scene couldn't keep Catherine's mind off Corbin.

"Any word from the sheriff yet?"

Catherine's stomach clenched at Audrey's question. She shouldn't let her heart feel so much, but she couldn't help it. She dropped another letter into its slot then turned to Audrey, who'd spent the morning dusting the shelves and arranging a crate of dry goods. "Far as I know, he didn't return to town last night."

"Maybe they're trailing the robbers."

"Maybe." As much as she wanted the Masked Gang arrested, she didn't want Corbin caught in the middle of a shootout. She knew the danger involved in sending a posse to capture a gang as notorious as this one. And knew that there was always the chance they wouldn't all return alive.

She went back to sorting the rest of the mail. Whoever was behind the robberies had become arrogant after months of avoiding capture. Holdups had become more frequent as the death toll rose. Which was why she understood Corbin's determination. But until they were captured, his life was at stake, along with the innocent bystanders who happened to be in the wrong place at the wrong time. And this part of Ohio had already seen enough trouble lately.

Audrey pulled Catherine toward the far corner of the store and lowered her voice. "You know what everyone is saying."

"About the sheriff?"

"They're saying he let Harrison out of jail and then another bank was struck. In other words, Harrison is guilty."

"That's nonsense, and you know it."

Audrey shook her head. "What if it's not? What if they're right and it's not a coincidence? We both know he could be simply covering up his tracks by another one of his tall stories. Even his working for the newspaper could be a lie."

"If all that were true, don't you think he'd be long gone by now?"

Audrey dropped her gaze. Her refusal to see Harrison since his release from jail had spawned numerous attempts on his behalf to win her back. Which, in Catherine's mind, meant Harrison Tucker was simply lovesick, not a robber and murderer.

"Neither of us know where he was yesterday afternoon when that bank was being robbed," Audrey continued. "He left the funeral early, giving him plenty of time to make it to Amanda."

"Think about it. If Harrison was the real leader of the Masked Gang, do you think he'd stay in Revenge and risk getting arrested again? Because I can guarantee if that happened, he'll be swinging from the end of a noose, and he knows that. And if that were the case he'd be halfway to Texas by now, or...Alaska for that matter."

Mrs. Long appeared behind them. "Any mail for me today, Miss Morgan?"

Catherine glanced up at the woman's empty mail slot. "I'm sorry, but not today."

"It's my son." Mrs. Long pressed her hands against the front of her cotton skirt. "He's gone to Cleveland, you know, to find work. It's been almost a full month now, and I haven't heard anything."

"Maybe next week," Catherine said. "You know how slow the mail can be."

"I suppose you're right." Mrs. Long turned to Audrey. "I was so sorry to hear that your wedding was called off, though I can understand. You certainly can't marry a man who's been accused of murder."

Fresh tears welled in Audrey's eyes.

Catherine stepped forward, intent on stopping the wave of gossip in its tracks. "In case you hadn't heard, Mrs. Long, the sheriff released Mr. Tucker because he has proof that he had nothing to do with the exploits of the Masked Gang."

"That might be true, but it still seems—"

"My belief has always been that, until convicted of a crime, a man deserves a bit of grace," Catherine retorted.

"I suppose, but—"

"I almost forgot to mention it, Mrs. Long." Catherine forced a smile. "There are several other new bolts of fabric I don't think you noticed toward the front of the store."

"Oh?"

"I have them on display in the front corner. I think you'll like the blue patterned one in particular." Catherine ushered Mrs. Long toward the front of the store where she'd laid out some of the fabric the day before.

Once Mrs. Long was settled, Catherine returned to Audrey.

Audrey shot her a half smile. "Thank you."

"Harrison loves you."

"I used to believe that. But now, I don't know how I can ever trust him again."

"Just give it time. He might have made some bad choices, but he really does love you."

The door jingled in the front of the store and Harrison walked in.

"It's Harrison." Audrey ducked down. "Tell him...tell him I'm not here."

Audrey dashed into the house, leaving Catherine to deal with the guilt-ridden suitor—again.

Harrison took off his hat and shot Catherine a sheepish smile. "Will she see me yet?"

"I'm sorry. You have to understand her point of view. You lied to her."

"And I've made a complete mess of things, haven't I? All in hopes of winning her heart." Harrison fiddled with the rim of his hat. "Have you seen the sheriff?"

Mrs. Long signaled from the counter with a bolt of fabric. Apparently, she'd been correct about the blue fabric.

"I'll be right there, Mrs. Long." Catherine turned back to Harrison. "Why do you need to see the sheriff?"

"Because if he's going to catch those scoundrels, he's going to need extra men to back him up. I'm planning on volunteering for the job."

While she might agree with Harrison's assessment, she was quite certain Corbin wouldn't accept help from Harrison. "All you'd manage to do is get yourself killed. Do you think that's what Audrey needs right now?"

"It's the fastest way for me to prove to her—and to this town—that I had nothing to do with the robberies."

Catherine caught Harrison's gaze. "And the fastest way to die trying to prove it."

* * *

Corbin stood inside the small bank lobby, wondering what he'd missed. He fingered the triangular-based bullet he'd found. He wasn't surprised they'd left behind the clue, because the Masked Gang never went anywhere without a rally of gunfire. But this time the good guys had been lucky. Three shots had been fired during the robbery, but the only damage left behind was the small holes left in the ceiling by the bullets. And, of course, the missing two thousand dollars in cash.

There had to be a common thread connecting the robberies. Some clue that they'd all missed. Nobody was this lucky. At some point, they'd make a mistake that would be their final downfall, but until then, he was getting tired of chasing ghosts. It was time he found a way to gain control of the situation.

The banker, Miles Sherman, sat on a chair in the far corner of the room, his bald head cradled between his knees, about to be ill.

Sick or not, Mr. Sherman was the only witness he had at the moment. "Tell me exactly what happened."

The pale-faced banker glanced up. "I've already told you."

"I want you to tell me again. If we're ever going to catch this gang, I need to know everything you saw, heard, and said in the past hour."

"They came in with those masks over their heads, aiming their guns straight at my heart." Mr. Sherman held up his shaking hands. "All they said was 'hand it over,' and I wasn't going to argue. The money had just been dropped into the safe, so I opened it up and gave it to them. All of it."

Corbin frowned at the familiar story. "There has to be something we're missing. Some sort of identifying mark on one of them."

"I already told you. Black masks, nondescript manners." The banker pushed up his spectacles. "I was lucky they didn't blow a hole through me with all the guns they had pointed my direction. There's nothing more to say. They walked in, took the money, and then they were gone."

Corbin paced the eight-by-eight entrance of the bank. There had to be something here. The sun cast a ray of yellow light across the floor. Corbin bent down to check beneath the three-inch-deep lip of the bank counter. Something glistened. He reached down and picked up a man's pocket watch. The fob was broken and the cover cracked.

He held up the watch. "Is it yours?"

The banker pulled his from his pocket. "Could have been dropped by anyone."

"Maybe."

"I sweep in here every morning before I open the bank. I would have noticed it."

Which meant the owner of the watch had been here today. Corbin opened the cover and studied the engraving.

Mr. Sherman sat up in his chair. "Is there an inscription?"

Corbin's heart pounded. "H.T."

"Someone's initials."

Harrison Tucker.

Corbin snapped the watch shut then shoved it into his pocket. "This has gone on long enough."

"What do you mean?"

"It's time someone put an end to all of this." Whether he liked it or not, Harrison Tucker was the common denominator in all of this, and it was time he found out just who was playing them both.

* * *

Catherine unplugged the phone line before readjusting her clunky metal headset. Lily's first impressions of the new telephone system had been correct. Already this afternoon, she'd had two requests for a recipe, another for tomorrow's weather, and Mrs. McBride had called to see if Mrs. Watson had been by the store today. And Catherine hadn't given in to the temptation to listen to the longwinded conversation between the two women an hour later. If she had, she'd have no doubt caught up on half the gossip in town, but that's not what she wanted to hear. Not the way things were going.

Another call came through. Catherine plugged in the connection then paused before hanging up at the unfamiliar voice.

"I'm waiting for my shipment of goods from Revenge."

"When do you expect them to arrive?"

"Noon tomorrow."

The call ended.

Strange. It was almost like some sort of…code.

Code?

Hadn't Lily mentioned someone speaking in code? Catherine shook her head. Dealing with secret codes and spy talk belonged to organizations like the Pinkertons, not an ordinary telephone operator from Revenge. She'd already spent far too much time worrying about who was behind the Masked Gang. She didn't need to let a strange call complicate her life.

Lily entered the room with a book in one hand and an apple in the other. "I'm back, and Mrs. McBride just walked into the store."

Catherine frowned. "I'm happy to handle things here if you want—"

"That's quite all right." She slid into the empty seat Catherine had vacated. "Any strange calls?"

"Strange calls? Let me see." Catherine handed Lily the headset. "If you count calls regarding the weather and requests for recipes as strange, then yes."

"That's not strange, it's normal."

Catherine laughed. "Outside weather and recipe requests, there was one that struck me as odd."

"What did they say?" Lily grabbed a piece of paper from the edge of the desk and held it up.

"Nothing important."

"I need to know exactly what they said."

Catherine stood in the threshold. Mrs. McBride was studying the barrel of pickles. "Why?"

"Because I'm keeping track of certain calls. I need you to think. Tell me everything they said."

Mrs. McBride moved onto the row of iron pots Catherine had recently discounted. "I wasn't paying that much attention—"

"Were any names used?"

"No." Catherine shook her head and tried to remember. "I suppose one of the things I found odd was that there was no typical greeting or names used."

Lily scribbled something on her paper. "What else?"

"They only talked for a few seconds. It was about a shipment of goods. Something about it being delivered."

"Where were the goods from?"

Catherine snatched the slip of paper from Lily's hand. On it, she'd scribbled a list of dates, locations, and hours. "What is all of this?"

"I told you I've been taking notes."

"Of phone calls? Why?"

Lily rubbed her forehead. "I thought it was just a crazy suspicion at first, but not anymore."

"What do you mean?"

"What was the location?"

"Right here."

"Revenge?" Lily's face paled as she grabbed the paper back.

"What's going on, Lily? It was nothing more than a quick call by a cheap customer who didn't want to spend money."

"I don't think so." Lily tapped the pencil on the paper. "Was there a time mentioned?"

"Noon."

Lily dropped the headset onto the desk and stood up. "I need to see the sheriff."

"Not until you tell me what's going on."

Lily held up her notes. "Can't you see? It's a pattern that has something to do with all the robberies."

"The robberies?"

"And I've got to see the sheriff. Now."

* * *

Corbin grabbed one of the extra rifles then threw open the door of the sheriff's office, barely missing a collision with Catherine and Lily.

"When did you get back from Amanda?"

As always, Catherine was full of questions. "Just now. I'm on my way out."

Lily stood in the door, blocking his way. "I have some information for you regarding the robberies."

"It's going to have to wait until I get back." He shoved his hat on and made sure he had enough bullets.

Catherine grasped his arm. "What's going on?"

He hesitated. "Nothing for you to worry about. I'm headed out on official business."

"Lily might have found a way to capture the Masked Gang."

"Catherine, I really—"

Lily shoved a piece of paper toward him. "I never made the connections until I started writing things down. The phone calls were always the same. They mention a town and a time. It has to be how they are coordinating the robberies. Amanda was the last one mentioned, and the last robbery."

No matter how pressing his business, he needed to hear them out. Corbin quickly ushered the women into the sheriff's office and shut the door behind him. "I think you better slow down and start from the beginning, Lily. What exactly are you talking about?"

She perched on the edge of the chair he offered, still clasping the paper between her fingers. "I noticed it for the first time a few days after the telephone was installed, but at first, I didn't think anything about it. I connected a call between two men, both from public phones. The conversation was brief, only a couple of exchanges before they hung up. They never identified themselves. That was the first thing that struck me as odd. Most people exchange names and a handful of pleasantries before revealing the true reason for their call. Mrs. McBride for example—"

"Lily." Catherine shook her head.

"Sorry." She handed Corbin the paper. "In each phone call, they mentioned a place and a time. About ten days ago, I noticed that what I'd written down in my notes corresponded with the time and place of a robbery. I figured it had to be a coincidence. But then the same thing happened again."

"It could be a coincidence. Lots of things are delivered across the country every day."

"True." Catherine reached out to tap on the end of the paper. "But I overheard the last conversation. Tomorrow they're delivering to Revenge. I'm not sure I'd be willing to just assume it's nothing more than a coincidence. If Lily's right, we could finally be one step ahead of the gang."

Corbin scratched his forehead. "Then what do you propose I do?"

The way Catherine smiled at him, Corbin knew he was in for trouble. "I've got a plan."

Chapter Twenty-one

Corbin's jaw tensed as he walked the breadth of the boardwalk across the street from the bank. He held his finger on the trigger of his cocked gun and watched a dust devil swirl down the main street of town before dissipating into the warm, midday air. Senses alert. Heart pounding. He could feel it in his gut. Today was going to be the day he brought the Masked Gang to justice.

And the day he avenged his father's death.

He glanced down the street, looking for anything out of the ordinary. He'd debated over clearing the streets, but knew that if the gang arrived and felt they were walking into a trap, they'd disappear. And if he lost this chance, they'd strike again and even more people would be in jeopardy. Which wasn't a risk he was willing to take.

Corbin glanced at his watch. Eleven fifty. He'd brought in three men to even the odds. Four doors down, Samuel White sat outside the barber's office reading a newspaper. Clint Faulkner, with his arms as thick as railroad ties, stood posed inside his blacksmith shop due east of the bank. Fred North swept the boardwalk outside his shop, his Colt .45 poised at his side.

Subtle and inconspicuous, which was exactly what he was looking for. He expected the Masked Gang to ride into town and assume that today was just another day in Revenge. Except they'd be wrong, because Corbin had what he'd been missing for months—the element of surprise. And he planned to use it fully to his advantage.

He swung open the door of the bank and eyed Norman Morris. The banker's left eye twitched. In his checkered vest and tan trousers, Mr. Morris looked more nervous than the banker he'd dealt with in Lancaster. Perhaps because he knew he was about to be robbed. Something that would understandably fray anyone's nerves.

Mr. Morris wiped his brow with a white handkerchief then stuffed it back into his vest pocket. "I'm not sure about this, Sheriff."

"It's going to be fine."

"Don't go making promises you can't keep. Every time I open these doors for business, I realize that this could be the day someone shows up with a rifle in his hands and demands the contents of my safe, but knowing ahead of time that you're about to be robbed… well, that's a different feeling altogether."

"And you're a brave man for agreeing to help." Corbin popped a lemon drop into his mouth, praying Catherine managed to stay out of the way. Her stubbornness and determination had already proven to be a lethal mixture more than once, which had been the one deterrent to his plan. He glanced across the street at her store and prayed that God would keep her safe—just as fervently as he'd prayed all morning that they'd be able to capture the gang without an exchange of gunfire.

Corbin turned back to Mr. Morris. "Do as I say and everything should be fine."

"Should be fine." The pudgy banker shook his head. "Therein lies the problem, Sheriff."

Corbin took his place by the front window and watched for the signal. The noisy second hand of the clock behind the counter frayed his already frazzled nerves. He wiped the beads of moisture at the back of his neck then glanced up at the clock again. It was ten minutes past noon. His heart pounded. Of course, Lily could be wrong. Her list of presumed robberies could be nothing more than actual deliveries by a perfectly legitimate businessman. Which meant he was once again back to square one. Either way, they'd know soon enough.

Samuel White dropped his newspaper, his predetermined signal, and then reached to pick it up. Fifteen seconds later Corbin saw them ride into town. Four men, unmarked mounts…and black masks.

He swallowed hard then nodded at Mr. Morris. "It's time."

The banker's face paled. Corbin hurried into his position behind the counter.

The scenario had been relatively the same in every town. Three stayed outside the bank while two marched into the bank with their weapons raised, spouting their demands for money. With Frank Sutherland dead, Corbin was gambling on the belief that William Marker would enter the bank alone. After all, no one expected Revenge's small bank to be built like Fort Knox.

Corbin held his position, unseen, from behind the counter. His temporary deputies would take down the masked men who were guarding the door, then join him inside. If everything went according to plan, they'd take William Marker alive. The bank door opened then slammed against the brick wall. Mr. Morris held out a shaky hand and held up one finger. Corbin smiled. He'd been right.

A shot rang out on the street, followed by two more in quick succession. Corbin jumped up, but not before a fourth weapon fired and Mr. Morris slid to the ground beside him, his checkered vest now stained red.

O Lord, this can't be happening...

Where were his backups?

Corbin flew across the counter and slammed into the masked assailant, knocking him off his feet in one fluid motion. The element of surprise might be in his favor, but obviously the four robbers weren't going down without a fight. Corbin swung his fist to the right and made contact with Marker's jaw then pulled his gun. Marker swung at him, and both weapons went flying across the room. Marker went down with a heavy groan. Corbin lunged toward his gun, but Marker was up again, swinging at Corbin. Corbin felt his nose crack at the impact. His head hit the wall full force, and he fell to his knees.

Marker jumped him from behind. Corbin pinned him against the wall, hesitating only when someone else entered the bank. The man standing in the doorway wore a black mask. Corbin's heart hammered. Where were his men? He swung Marker's body around in front of him as a shield from the armed man and eyed his own gun that lay between him and his second attacker. The odds had just shifted, and he wasn't getting any help from Mr. Morris. All he could do at the moment was pray that the banker—and his backups—were still alive. Because if his men had been injured in the exchange of gunfire...

Corbin took another punch to the ribs and groaned as the air whooshed from his lungs. His body slammed against the counter. His father's lifeless face flashed in front of him and adrenalin surged. He wasn't going down without a fight.

His fist made contact with the second attacker's jaw as Marker lunged toward him. The second man staggered for an instant, dropped to the ground, and didn't move.

One down, one to go.

Corbin spun around to face Marker for another round. The man was tough and resilient, which might explain his success. Up until today, that is. Corbin dodged a punch to the chest then dived again for his gun. Marker slammed into him from behind and knocked him to the ground—with his gun still out of reach. Corbin swiped at Marker's mask, revealing a jagged scar running across the man's chin. Recognition flickered as the man jerked away and grasped the gun. Corbin sprung toward the counter, but he was too slow. The gun went off. Corbin felt a bullet sear through his shoulder. He grabbed for his opponent, then everything went dark.

* * *

Catherine stood over Corbin in the doctor's front office and dabbed a wet cloth across his forehead. She wished she'd never overheard that wretched conversation. For all she cared, the Masked Gang could have their money without anyone trying to stop them. At least then the robbers would have been long gone before anyone knew what had happened. And maybe no one would have gotten hurt. But somehow, the plan had backfired, leaving two of their men dead and the gang's leader missing. Even the banker, Mr. Morris, had taken a bullet.

"You going to be all right, Miss Morgan?" The doctor stepped into the room, the front of his shirt stained with blood. A visual reminder of how much had gone wrong.

Catherine nodded.

"I appreciate your help. I've got to stitch up Mr. Morris."

Catherine winced. "Is he going to make it?"

"We'll know soon enough."

What had happened out there?

"How long before the sheriff comes to?"

"Can't say for sure, but he's strong. Even a bullet to the shoulder shouldn't be enough to keep him down for long, though I can't say the same for the other two bodies laying in my back room."

Catherine tried not to relive the scene she'd witnessed from the store window. The gang had picked off Corbin's deputies before they'd had a chance to respond. They had to have been tipped off to the ambush. But by whom?

Corbin stirred as the doctor left the room.

Catherine took his hand and sent up a prayer of thankfulness that he was alive, something that caused a deep stirring of guilt. God was giving them a second chance, but Clara North had just lost her husband. "How do you feel?"

He groaned and blinked his eyes. "Like I've been run over by a herd of cattle."

"Do you remember what happened?"

"The Masked Gang. They attacked me in the bank."

"The doctor said a couple punches to the jaw and ribs then a bullet to the shoulder."

"What went wrong? North and White never came to back me up."

Catherine's gaze flew to the open window where a pair of white curtains fluttered in the breeze.

"They're dead."

Corbin groaned. "What about the gang?"

"Two are dead, and the other two are missing."

"And the leader? William Marker?"

Catherine pressed her lips together. "He escaped."

"This isn't what was supposed to happen." Corbin tried to sit up. "They were tipped off."

"I don't know about that." Catherine eased him back down on the bed. "But what I do know is that you're not going anywhere. You've been shot, and I think you've seen enough action today."

Corbin squeezed his eyes shut for a moment. "It was him…"

"Shhh. You've lost too much blood and you need to rest."

Catherine wiped Corbin's forehead with the wet cloth. The fact that the Masked Gang had once again outsmarted the law was maddening. This killing spree had to end.

"The good news is that we may not have taken them all out, but the gang's finished." Catherine searched for something—anything—good that might have come from the massacre to boost his spirits. "Which means that more than likely, he's halfway to the Ohio border by now. There's no way he'd stick around."

"I know who it is."

"It doesn't matter anymore."

"I saw his scar, Catherine. The thin, jagged white line that runs across his jaw line. John Guild is the leader."

"John…I don't understand." Her voice caught. "You're not thinking clearly. John is no more a murderer than Harrison. He's been fixing my porch steps and he…he fixed the fence. He loves Lily, I know he does. He's going to marry her."

Corbin gripped her hand and she stopped babbling. "You're wrong. We had it wrong all along. He's the traitor. I pulled his mask back, and saw his scar. I know it was him."

"You've got to be mistaken. I…" Nausea gripped her stomach in waves. It simply couldn't be John.

"He couldn't have gone far." Corbin started to sit up. "Now that I know who he is I can find him."

"Corbin Hunter, you get back in that bed right this minute."

"I've got to…" He tried to stand then fell back against the bed.

Catherine scoured her mind for a plan on the off chance he was right. "I'll telephone the sheriff in Lancaster and see if he can put together a posse."

Audrey bustled into the room. "Catherine, I've been looking everywhere for you. I heard what happened to Fred North and Samuel White. Are the two of you all right?"

"I'm fine."

"And I'm thankful to be alive," Corbin added.

"It's Emily," Audrey continued. "She's gone into labor."

Catherine pressed her hand against her forehead, wondering what else could happen in the scope of twenty-four hours. "The doctor's in surgery, but you can go back to the store and call Mrs. Peal. She's birthed a dozen babies in this town."

Audrey nodded.

"I'll ride out to the ranch as soon as I know Corbin's out of danger," Catherine said.

"She's not out at the ranch, she's here in town at the house. Grady drove her in for a couple of hours."

Catherine couldn't breathe. She'd told her sisters to stay inside today. The last thing she'd counted on was Emily coming into town. "Where's Lily?"

"She's at the house with Emily. John's there as well—"

Catherine felt her legs buckle beneath her. "No."

"What's wrong, Catherine?"

All the scrambled pieces merged together. If Corbin was right, the robberies, the break-in at her house, her father's death...they were all connected.

And her sisters' lives were in danger.

"John is the leader of the Masked Gang, and there's a good chance that he's got Lily and Emily," Catherine rushed on. "I want you to ride quickly and find Mrs. Peal. Bring her back into town with you."

"I don't understand," Audrey began. "John—"

"There is no time to explain, just do as I say, please. And stay away from the store until I raise the shade on the front door. That will be the signal it's safe." She knew all too well that there was no telling what she was walking into. "You can wait here if you'd like, or at the sheriff's office."

Corbin caught her elbow as she turned to leave. "Catherine, what are you doing?"

"I'm going to do what should have been done a long time ago."

Catherine felt for the gun she carried in her bag then rushed from the room. The fact that John Guild had spent the past few months courting Lily would no longer be of consequence to him. He obviously wanted something that had nothing to do with the string of bank robberies. Which tied John to her father's death. And the gold he'd presumably found.

The yellow tint of sunlight greeted her on the empty street. After the rounds of gunfire and two deaths, the streets had cleared quicker than a spring shower. Catherine entered the house through the kitchen, holding the gun behind her as she entered the sitting room. John sat beside Lily on the settee, while Emily leaned back in a chair on the other side of the room. Her face was flushed with pain from a contraction, but Catherine had been around enough women to know that it could be hours until the baby came. At the moment, getting them out of this room alive was her first priority. She glanced at John's hands. They were red and swollen, and he held a bag of ice against his jaw.

Corbin had been right. For whatever reason, he was still playing the role of charmed suitor. What a fool they'd all been.

She glanced back at Emily, her heart pounding. "Are you all right?"

"The baby's coming." Emily rested her hands in front of her. "Though that almost pales in comparison to what just happened. John just told us that several men were shot and the leader of the gang escaped in another robbery."

"News travels fast." Catherine kept her voice even. "Looks like you were in the middle of it, John."

"He tried to help," Lily said. "One of the Masked Gang made their escape from the bank, and John tried to take him down on the other side of the store, but he got away."

"Turned out to be a bit tougher than I expected." John held up the ice. "Guess I'm not the agile fighter as I used to be."

Liar.

"Everything's going to be fine." Catherine reigned in her temper. "Audrey's getting Mrs. Peal, and we'll call Grady."

She weighed the situation. She'd seen enough today to know that John wasn't going to simply walk away from all of this without getting what he wanted. And he wasn't afraid of killing. He'd take hostages and shoot his way out if he needed to. The one thing in their favor was that he didn't appear to realize she now knew the truth. Which meant she would have to take the element of surprise and use it to her benefit. Of course, Corbin had assumed he had that same element of surprise and now two of his people lay dead.

The first thing she had to do was to get Lily away from John. Emily sat closest to the kitchen. If she could get between her sisters and John, they might have a chance. "John, if you'll excuse Lily, I need to talk to her in the kitchen." Catherine matched his steady gaze. She wasn't ready to play her hand until Lily was safe. "I promise it will just take a minute."

Lily started to rise, but John gripped her arm. "Can't it wait?"

"John…" Lily began.

Catherine forced a carefree smile. "Come on, John. Just for a second."

He kept his hand on her forearm. "Where's the sheriff? I understand he was one of the men shot."

Catherine's grip on the Colt tightened. Her father had taught her how to shoot, but taking out John when he had his arm on her sister wasn't worth the risk.

Show me what do to, Lord.

"The sheriff?" Catherine forced herself to breathe. "He was shot in the shoulder, but thankfully, it's not too serious."

"That's wonderful news," Lily said.

"Yes, he'll be on his way over here in a few minutes, in fact."

"Really." John frowned. "I'm surprised he's able to get up so quickly."

"He's a strong man."

John pulled Lily toward him. "Your sister and I were just speculating on why your father came back suddenly after so many years."

Catherine gripped the gun between her fingers. She'd been right. All he wanted was the money. Like the stash from a dozen bank robberies weren't enough to fill his coffers. "A strange topic at a time like this, don't you think?"

"My theory is that he stumbled across a bit of a fortune," he continued, "and finally found what he was looking for."

"The realization that his family was more important than any strike?" Catherine countered.

John's smile sent a passel of shivers down Catherine's spine. "No. Gold."

Lily tried to pull away. "John, you're hurting me."

"You know I never intended to hurt you." John kissed her cheek.

"Really?" Catherine asked. "Then what was your intention?"

"Catherine, what are you talking about? What's going on?"

"She knows who I am," John said.

Lily looked to Catherine. "I don't understand."

Catherine steadied her hands and aimed the gun at John's heart. "John Guild's real name is William Marker, isn't it, Mr. Marker?"

"Now where would you have come up with a piece of information like that?" His laugh rang shallow. "I suppose it was your sheriff friend. The only problem with him is that he's so caught up in avenging his father's death that he can't see clearly. And as for you, I really am sorry, Lily." He wrapped his arm around her waist and pulled her toward him. "The sad thing about all of this is that I really liked you."

Lily's eyes widened as she fought to swallow the truth. "John, tell me she's mistaken. You asked me to marry you. I...I was going to say yes."

Catherine held the gun steady. "Let her go, John."

"And I thought we were friends, Catherine. Surely a gun's not necessary."

"I said, let my sister go." Emily let out a gasp from behind Catherine. "Hang in there, sweetie."

"And why would I let any of you go? Because, Miss Morgan, you're not the only one here who has a gun." John pulled out a gun and pressed it against Lily's head. "Unless you want your sister to be the next unfortunate causalty in this town, I suggest you stop playing hero and put yours down."

"John!" Lily screamed.

Catherine fought a wave of panic. "Don't do this, John. All you have to do is take what you want and go."

"Then tell me where my money is."

"What money, John?" Lily's voice rose. "You knew when we met I didn't have anything other than my part of the store."

"Surely you don't think your father came back simply because he wanted to see you."

Catherine felt all her insecurities sweep over her. So it had been true all along. Isaiah Morgan hadn't returned to see his four daughters.

"He never told us about any money," Catherine said.

"And I don't believe you. So you can answer me before the sheriff and his incompetent posse arrives and everything will be fine, or we can do it the hard way. All you have to do is hand it over and I'll be gone."

"I don't think so." Catherine held her gun steady at his heart. She could do this. Kill the man who murdered her father, massacred countless other innocent men, and who was right now in the process of breaking her sister's heart. "My father didn't have any money. But that's not the real issue right now."

"Really?" John shot her a wry grin. "Then it looks to me as if we have a problem."

All the frustration and anger that had been growing within her surfaced at once. "You're the one who has a problem, because you killed our father." Catherine signaled at her sister. "Lily, I want you to come stand by me."

"I don't think so." Unrelenting, John pressed the gun against Lily's temple. "Because, like it or not, I'm the one in control here, and like I said, I want the money."

"Catherine?" Emily's breathing grew more rapid behind her. "It's the baby. It's coming…now."

Chapter Twenty-two
....

Catherine searched for an escape. Before she could prepare a defense, John had confiscated her gun and forced her and her sisters to sit in a row on the settee. So much for her grand plans of confronting the leader of the Masked Gang and ensuring he ended up behind bars in the local jail. Instead, he'd trumped any ace she'd held in her hand and held them in a precarious situation.

Corbin had been right. She should never have tried to handle things herself.

The fact that John now held them all at gunpoint wasn't the only problem she faced. What if Audrey didn't wait for her signal and ended up walking into the trap as well? And then there was Emily's baby, who apparently had no intention of waiting for a more opportune time to arrive. Catherine glanced at Emily's swollen stomach and sent up an extra prayer of petition because, quite frankly, aiding her sister in the childbirth process was not something she was prepared to handle. She understood numbers and mathematics, not the complexities of bringing a child into the world.

Though helping her sister seemed the least of her worries at the moment.

John, William, or whatever his real name, had some insane belief that her father had struck it rich and had brought a fortune with him back to Revenge. But the truth seemed to matter little to

John. And if he had his way, she expected him to kill them all before this was over. A thought that brought with it another large dose of panic.

Out of all her options, the voice of sympathy seemed her best ally, but she wasn't sure it would be enough ammunition. "Emily needs the doctor."

Catherine eased from her seat then stopped as John aimed the gun her direction.

"John, please." Lily sobbed beside her. "You can't do this—"

"No one is going anywhere until I get some answers." John's hard gaze was anything but benevolent. "And besides, from the way I look at things, a baby on the way gives all three of you a bit more motivation to talk, don't you think?"

Catherine grasped her sisters' hands, her fear quickly turning to anger. "I don't know what you want from us, because we've told you that there isn't any money."

John leaned back in his chair, seemingly confident that there was no immediate danger of anyone coming to capture him. Something Catherine feared was correct. With Corbin incapacitated and his best men dead, it seemed unlikely that an imminent rescue party would arrive and put the felon where he belonged. "I happen to know your father actually made quite a fortune."

Catherine didn't buy his declaration. Especially since the con man Corbin had described had been full of tall tales and lies. "How would you know about an alleged fortune when he never mentioned it to any of us?"

"I happened to be in Alaska last fall where I was presented with a unique opportunity."

Catherine leaned forward. "What kind of opportunity?"

"I overheard a conversation one night between your father and his business partner about how their luck had finally turned and realized that I'd just struck gold." The arrogant smile on John's face widened, as if he were enjoying the confession. "I had planned to dispose of both men and take the gold, but after his partner died in an unfortunate accident, your father vanished with the money."

"You killed his partner?"

John shrugged. "I knew Isaiah Morgan was from Revenge, so I decided to come here, figuring he'd show up at some point."

"And in the meantime, made sure you had access to our family." Catherine's stomach roiled.

John paced the room in front of them. "I know he arrived here with the money, and I intend to find it."

Catherine felt trapped. Emily's labored breathing continued beside her, while Lily sobbed on the other side. How had she ever let this bank robber and con man weasel his way into the Morgan home?

"So the money is why you came to Revenge?"

"It was simple, really. Ohio not only provided new territory for the Masked Gang, it was also a chance for some easy money."

Catherine had to stall for time. The longer they took, the greater the chance of someone showing up with help. Corbin might be injured, but he knew that John was a murderer and that she'd gone on her own to confront him.

She squeezed Emily's hand. "Can you hang in there a bit longer?"

Emily nodded and Catherine turned back to John. "What about Harrison then? How did he play into this drama of yours?"

"Harrison turned out to be the perfect scapegoat, with his wild stories about the Alaskan frontier. All it took were a few well-placed red herrings to point the sheriff in the wrong direction."

"And you killed my father?"

"Your father was foolish enough to deny there was any gold, something I knew to be untrue, so the confrontation ended with Isaiah Morgan's death." John brushed aside the curtain and glanced outside before turning back to them. "It was an unfortunate consequence. One of us had to die, and it certainly wasn't going to be me. I figure he had to have told one of you about the money."

"I trusted you. I told you..." Truth dawned on Lily's face. "I told you everything."

Catherine's stomach tightened. Unbeknownst to Lily, she'd become the perfect turncoat.

John's chilling smile was back. "You were very helpful."

Lily rose from her seat. "I think I might know where the money is."

"Lily, don't..." Catherine began.

"Where is it?" John stood in front of Lily. All his charm and charisma had disappeared, and in its place surfaced the man who'd just confessed to killing Isaiah Morgan.

God, please help us.

"My father," Lily began. "He...he never told me he'd struck it rich, but he did say several things that made me wonder if there was more to his return than simply a change of heart."

Emily's face reddened as she squeezed Catherine's hand through another contraction.

"What are you talking about?" Catherine asked.

"He said he had plans to expand the store and the house," Lily continued. "To travel back East to see his mother's family."

John smiled. "All things that take money."

Catherine tried to absorb her sister's words. The thought that their father had returned to Revenge for reasons other than the fact that he simply wanted to make things right stung. Surely Lily was wrong.

Forgiveness is a choice.

Catherine's jaw tensed. Forgiveness might be a choice, but it certainly wasn't an easy one. Especially when her father had done little to deserve her forgiveness. And if he'd come back with a cache full of gold, he was the one responsible for this situation.

Not that she wanted his money. All any of them had ever wanted was his love. Maybe nothing truly mattered anymore, because now that he was dead she might never know the truth.

Except for the truth that, whatever he had, someone was willing to kill for it.

John clapped his hands together, drawing her back to the present. "Where's the money, Lily?"

Lily closed her eyes and breathed slowly before opening them again. "I don't know for sure—"

"I think you do." He leaned into her until his face was merely inches from hers then ran his thumb down her cheek. "All you have to do is tell me where the money is, and I'll let you go. I promise."

Catherine caught the flicker of conflict in his eyes. John Guild— or William Marker—was a con man who knew how to woo a woman without involving his heart and who could shoot a man without thinking of the consequences of his actions. But was there a chance that he'd really cared for Lily? If he had, it was a card that could play in their favor.

"If there is any money," Lily began, "it's buried out behind Emily's barn, near where they keep the ostriches. I saw him digging out there one day. He wouldn't tell me what he was doing, but there's a chance it's there."

"There's still something I don't understand. If he did strike gold, why would he hide it from us?" Emily spoke up for the first time. "Why the secrets?"

"Maybe he wasn't hiding it from us." Catherine turned back to John. "Maybe he was hiding it from those who wanted to get their hands on it. Let Emily and Lily go. I'll come with you to find the money."

John shook his head then grabbed Lily's arm. "I don't think so. I'm taking Lily with me as a guarantee that none of you follow."

"I'll go with him." Lily pushed back her shoulders and raised her chin. "As long as you promise you'll take whatever money is there and never come back."

"Like his promises are worth anything." Catherine clenched her hands beside her, wishing she'd shot him when she had the chance. A man like John Guild didn't deserve to live.

"The sheriff knows who you are now," Catherine began. "They'll come after you. The smartest thing for you to do is get out of town...alone."

"The sheriff's injured, and it will take him hours to form a posse to come after me. And don't try anything on your own. By then, I'll have both the bank roll and your father's gold and be halfway to the next county."

There was no choice. Catherine watched her sister leave without another word. Once the door had shut, she rushed to the window, where John had a horse waiting out back. "We've got to stop this."

Emily lay against the back of the settee. "What are we going to do? I'm about to have a baby, the sheriff's been shot, and his best men are dead."

Catherine stood at the window until the horse disappeared from the horizon. "We've got to come up with something."

"What about Lily?" Emily asked.

"I saw the way he looked at her. I don't think he'll hurt her."

"But we can't just sit here and wait."

"Of course not—"

Emily's breathing quickened. "Catherine…"

Catherine closed her eyes and shot up another prayer for wisdom. "I'll go signal Audrey and Mrs. Peal, and then I'm going after him."

Emily cried out. "No, I can't…you can't leave me."

"I'll be right back. I promise." Catherine's heart pounded as she hurried into the storeroom to pull the shade. *Lord, please don't leave me to deliver this baby alone. I need Mrs. Peal now.*

"Catherine? The baby's not going to wait."

Catherine hurried back into the house and squeezed her sister's hand. "Audrey and Mrs. Peal should be here any minute. What do I do?"

This wasn't good. All she knew about birthing babies was the little she remembered from the births of her sisters. Which was hardly anything. All she remembered was glimpses of her father pacing from the bottom of the stairwell.

"Boil some hot water and find some fresh towels," Emily began.

That she could do. "Will you be all right for a minute?"

"Do I have a choice?"

Catherine rushed to the kitchen to start heating a large kettle of water and search for some clean linens. Her stomach tensed as she began pumping the water into the big iron pot. She'd spent her entire life fighting the odds and had no plans to quit now. She'd made that promise to her mother and now, more than ever, her sisters needed her. But she needed help, and a miracle.

A knock on the door had her hurrying across the room. Harrison stood on the threshold, dressed in his Sunday best and refusing to look her in the eye. "Is Audrey here?"

Catherine's disappointment mounted. The last thing she felt like dealing with today was a love-sick suitor. Unless...

Catherine shook her head. "Audrey's not here, but I need your help."

"What's wrong?"

"John Guild is the leader of the Masked Gang."

"What?"

"There was a shootout in town an hour ago, Emily's in labor, and John took Lily to the O'Conner farm as a hostage."

Harrison's face paled as he took in her words.

"Audrey's gone to find the midwife because the doctor is in surgery."

Harrison blinked. "What do you need me to do?"

Catherine nodded. That was more like it. "As soon as Audrey arrives with Mrs. Peal, I need you to go with me out to the ranch. I've got to make sure Lily is okay."

Audrey and Mrs. Peal appeared behind Harrison. Catherine let out a sigh of relief.

"Thank God you're here. There's no time to explain, but I've got to go, and I need you to take care of Emily. The baby's coming."

"Catherine?" Audrey stepped into the house. "What are you talking about?"

Catherine grabbed her rifle from the top of the kitchen cabinet. "Harrison's going with me to the farm. John's taken Lily there."

"Wait a minute." Audrey grabbed Catherine's arm. "What about the sheriff? You can't do this on your own."

"He's in no shape to fight, and so help me I won't let John do anything to Lily."

Catherine rushed out the door ready to take on an army. And this time she wouldn't hesitate to shoot.

* * *

Corbin forced himself to sit up then waited for the wave of dizziness to pass. He could do this. He had no choice. Catherine and her sisters' lives were at stake, and he wasn't going to let one lousy bullet stop him.

His shirt hung over a chair three feet away. The floor rolled beneath him, but he pushed himself off the bed anyway. Pain took over. He shoved it away. He had to find Catherine. She had no idea just how dangerous a man she was dealing with. William Marker had no conscience. And while Corbin might have lost his father to this madman, he had no intention of losing Catherine.

Catherine, with her rosy cheeks, hair the color of honey, and that sprinkle of freckles that always made him want to reach up and brush them away...

Her image gave him the extra burst of motivation he needed. He grabbed the shirt and managed to stuff his good arm into the sleeve, wincing at the stab of pain that shot across his shoulder. He clenched his teeth and worked to get his other arm into the sleeve.

Dr. Morrilton stepped into the room. He'd shed his bloodstained shirt and now wore a clean one. "Where in the world do you think you're going?"

Corbin fumbled with a button, his injured arm still refusing to cooperate. "I've got a job to finish."

"You've got two men dead and another one hanging on for his life. You're not going anywhere, especially in your condition."

Corbin pulled on his boot and ignored the searing pain in his shoulder. Thoughts of revenge pushed him on. Revenge for what had been done to his father. For what Marker had done to two of this town's finest citizens, and for having ever involved Catherine… "I'll be fine, because that's exactly why I'm going. He's not going to get away with this."

"Then you're a complete fool if you think you can go after the leader of that gang without getting yourself killed."

Corbin managed the last button. Fool or not, he was going. "Miss Morgan went after the man who killed those men in the other room, and I've got to find her before he does the same thing to her."

"So you love her?"

"Gonna ask her to marry me once this is over."

The doctor cocked his head. "Something I can't see you doing if you're six feet under."

Corbin steadied his feet then grabbed his hat off the dresser. "I'm going."

"Fine. Suit yourself, but don't blame me when your stubbornness gets you killed."

"I'll try to remember not to do that."

Corbin walked out the door, feeling like an old man ready to meet his Maker.

* * *

Corbin pounded on Catherine's door, praying he wasn't too late. From what he'd seen, William Marker had never hesitated to put a bullet into anyone, and just because Catherine was a woman wasn't going to make a difference. Audrey opened the door.

"Where's Catherine?" Corbin barked as he stepped into the house.

Audrey dipped her chin. "You're not going to like this."

"Tell me what happened."

Her face paled. "She rode out to the O'Conner farm to find John."

"And you didn't stop her?"

Audrey's upper lip trembled. "What should I have done? I couldn't leave Emily, but John took Lily. He thinks our father buried a stash of gold he found in Alaska."

"And he wants it." Corbin's temper flared. That woman's stubbornness was going to get her killed. "Did anyone go with her?"

Audrey nodded. "Harrison. You've got to help them please."

"Where's Grady?"

"Gone to Lancaster for the day. I wasn't able to get a hold of him."

"I want you to make some phone calls for me. Call the sheriff in Lancaster and explain everything that has happened."

"Where are you going?"

"I'm going to rescue your sister."

Chapter Twenty-three
....

For the second time in a day, Catherine set off with the intent to put a stop to John Guild. But this time she wasn't going to let him slip through her hands. Her stomach felt like a pile of knotted rope as she rode beside Harrison, but she refused to give in to the fear swirling around her. She'd heard the rumors of women fighting beside male soldiers in the War Between the States and risking their lives on daring spy missions for Pinkertons. Her breath quickened as they approached the O'Conner ranch under the cover of a grove of trees. If they could do it, she could do it.

She saw him the moment they reached the slight crest overlooking the ranch. John stood facing away from them beneath the shade of the barn that the good townspeople of Revenge had built two summers ago after a fire tore through the original building. With shovel in hand, he was digging a hole on the east side of the barn. Catherine scanned the adjoining area, still hidden in the thicket of trees.

Where was Lily?

With no time to dwell on the possibilities, she nodded at Harrison, who quickly rounded the far side of the barn and slipped from view. Their plan was simple, but far from foolproof. Harrison had balked at her idea at first, but she'd insisted that she needed to be the one to approach John. He'd be more likely to believe she'd followed on her own, and hopefully less likely to shoot her— a woman—in cold blood.

Or so she hoped. The absence of Lily punched a slight hole in her theory. She knew John wasn't known for leaving witnesses alive, and just because they'd all been of the male persuasion so far didn't mean he'd hesitate to pull a trigger just because his target wore skirts.

Catherine shuddered. If he'd done anything to her sister, a shot in the heart was the least he deserved.

She dismounted from her mare five yards from John and got straight to the point. "Where's my sister?"

John kept digging, apparently not surprised by her arrival.

She took a step forward. "I said, where is my sister?"

John reached for his gun, but she already had hers drawn and aimed at his heart. Not seeing the threat as viable, he again reached for his weapon. Catherine lowered her gun, aimed, and fired.

The bullet missed his left foot by an inch.

John jumped backward. "Now slow down. Your firing that gun is only going to get one of us killed."

"Then you can be assured that it won't be *this* part of us. One of the few things my father did for me was to teach me how to shoot. I can hit the bull's eye of a target at a hundred yards, which means I just missed on purpose. Next time, don't expect to be quite so lucky."

John dropped his gun back into his holster.

Catherine took a step closer. "Keep your hands where I can see them."

He raised them up again, clearly irritated. "Okay, so you've made your point, but what now? You know that in the end your little plan won't work. I'll still ride away with the money I find, because I always win."

"Oh, really? I'm afraid your lucky streak has just ended. Now, I tried to ask nicely before, and you didn't answer. I'm going to ask one more time. Where is my sister?"

John held his hands high. "Lily was right. You really are stubborn. What do you think is going to come of this little…skirmish?"

"You're going to tell me where my sister is, and then I'm going to escort you to the sheriff."

"Just like that?"

Catherine willed her hand to hold steady. "Since I'm the one with the gun aimed at your heart, yes. Just like that."

"And how many people do you think have already tried to do that? Local sheriffs, Pinkerton agents, even a couple of Texas Rangers down south."

"Then it is high time you were brought in, isn't it?"

John leaned against the shovel and laughed. "You know, you're not near as smart as you think you are."

"Think again. I want you to slide your gun to me, followed by the shovel."

"You can't be serious."

"Oh, I'd say she's completely serious." Harrison stepped from behind the barn, with his gun aimed straight at John. "If I were you, I'd do exactly what the lady says. Unless, of course, you'd rather find yourself in the nearest cemetery instead of jail."

John scowled.

Catherine willed her fingers steady. There was only one thing she was concerned about. He could have the money from today's robbery, as well as whatever gold her father had stashed away. She didn't care about that. Lily was the only thing she could think about at the moment.

"Now, I'm going to ask my question one more time, and if I don't get the right answer, I'm going to start shooting again. And this time I don't intend to miss. Where is Lily?"

"I figured you'd do something stupid and come here, though I didn't intend on your partner in crime showing up."

Catherine pressed her lips together. She'd have shot him dead by now, if it weren't for the fact he knew where Lily was, and she wasn't going to take any chances with her sister's life.

"Like I said, I figured you might show up and I might need some insurance."

"What does that mean?"

"I'll give you some credit. You've got a gun trained on me, and I'm weaponless. But I know how much you love your sister. The problem is, I'm the only one who knows where she is right now, and without my leading you to her, I'm afraid...how shall I say it? I'm afraid there could be serious consequences for her if anything happens to me, so put the gun down—"

"I don't believe you." Catherine fired again, hitting his right foot this time.

John yelped and grabbed his foot. "Now you listen to me—"

"No, you listen to me." Catherine fought the urge to simply shoot John Guild. She'd seen the posters and knew that he was wanted dead or alive, so what did it matter if she was the one to kill him? No court of law would prosecute her. In fact, it would likely be a headline story about how a woman took down the leader of the Masked Gang.

"So what happens next?" he asked.

Catherine forced her brain to look logically at the situation. This was a game to John, which meant it was no different than a row of accounting numbers with a solvable equation. John couldn't have arrived much before she did, which meant that Lily couldn't be far. Keeping her gun trained on John, she scanned the surrounding farm and calculated the possibilities. Lily had to be here on the property. In the house, or the barn…

Catherine felt her heart stop as another option surfaced. What if John Guild were only bluffing—because he'd done the unthinkable?

* * *

Corbin approached the outskirts of the O'Conner property with caution. How many times had he told Catherine to let him handle things, and she'd insisted on taking things into her own hands? This time she'd gone too far. No matter what John Guild had done to her father, it wasn't worth risking her life. But if she wasn't careful, she was going to get herself killed.

The pain in his shoulder throbbed with every jolt on the back of his horse, but he gritted his teeth and picked up the pace, despite the pain. The bottom line was—all this was his fault. If he'd figured out who John Guild was sooner, it never would have gotten to the point where Catherine was forced to chase down a murderer to save her sister.

A gunshot rang out in the distance. Corbin pulled on the reins and dismounted near the house, trying to determine where the shot had come from. The afternoon air was still. Too still. An ostrich cried out in the distance. Strange. Where were Milena and the farmhands? And most importantly, where was Catherine? Tying the horse to the porch rail, Corbin eased his gun from its holster and made a quick search of the area surrounding the house.

Nothing.

Something crashed from inside. Catherine? Lily? He took the porch stairs two at a time, ignoring the sharp pain radiating through his body, and rushed through the front door, uncertain of what he would find. William Marker wasn't the kind of man to leave anyone alive who stood in his way.

Lily and Milena sat on the living room floor, hands tied behind them, with handkerchiefs stuffed in their mouths and a broken lamp at Lily's feet.

He ripped out their gags then quickly checked them for injuries. "What happened?"

"I managed to knock off the lamp, hoping someone would hear." Lily shook her head and started crying. "It was all a lie. He told me he loved me—"

Corbin grasped her by the shoulders. "Lily, I need you to focus. Where's Catherine? She came to get you."

Lily's chest heaved. "I heard a gunshot."

"So did I."

She pointed out the window. "I think it came from the other side of the barn. I told him that my father had buried his treasure there."

Corbin set his hands on his hips. Catherine hadn't said anything about a treasure. "A treasure?"

"I made it up." She started sobbing again. "I knew that the only way to keep my sisters safe was to get John out of the house."

"She's here now, trying to find you," he started.

"The gunshot..."

They'd both reached the same conclusion. "Milena, lock the doors and stay here with Lily. I'll be back as soon as I can."

Hopefully, the locked doors would buy them time if John came here next.

Corbin hurried outside. The blues and greens of the surrounding farmland began to spin. He squinted and tried to shake off the nausea

raking his body. Catherine knew how to shoot, but the odds
of her surviving a confrontation with John were slim. And if
Catherine was dead he'd never forgive himself. Or John Guild.
He'd hang the man himself.

He ran toward the barn, arm throbbing, and pondered the
same question he'd been asking himself for weeks. How were his
actions any different than his father's killer? Hatred, revenge, and
unforgiveness had blinded him, and in the process he'd put at risk
the life of the woman he loved.

Which made him wonder what else he was capable of doing.

He'd been so caught up with his agenda to avenge his father's
death, he hadn't bothered to stop and think who else might be hurt
in the process. Or whose lives might be put at risk.

What kind of man had he become?

He rounded the corner of the barn, fearful of what he was going
to find. Catherine held a rifle pointed at John's head.

She flinched at the sight of him. "Corbin?"

Corbin froze. "I thought...I heard the shot and was afraid you
were dead."

"No, I'm fine." Catherine's lip twitched, but she held her gun
steady. "I was just about to shoot him again."

"Again?"

"Trust me, he'll live. For now. The problem is that he won't tell
me where Lily is."

Corbin didn't try to hide the relief that washed through him.
"Lily's fine, and if I were you, Mr. Guild, I wouldn't mess around with
this woman. She learned to shoot when she was barely as tall as the
rifle she's aiming at you. Her father taught her well."

John flung his hat to the ground, showing where the bullet had gone clean through his boot. "I'd say she's plumb crazy."

Corbin pulled out his handcuffs. "Say what you like, but you're under arrest for the murders of Charles Hunter, eight innocent bystanders, and Isaiah Morgan." He turned to Catherine. "You can put the gun down now, Catherine. It's over."

* * *

Corbin signed the form then pushed it back across his desk. "I appreciate your coming so quickly."

"I'm just as happy to take William Marker off your hands." Brad Sanders grinned. "We've put too many man-hours into this case to let him slip through our fingers again. As soon as I can get some information from him, he'll be looking at a swift hanging."

Corbin leaned back in his chair and let out a long, slow sigh. "We found some of the bank money beneath the floorboards where he'd been living."

"Well done."

Corbin brushed aside the compliment. "What about the other matter we talked about?"

"I've got one of my best men standing outside and ready to stand in until Sheriff Lansing is ready to resume his duties. That is if you're sure that's what you want."

"I'm sure." Corbin pulled off the badge from his vest and handed it over, knowing what he had to do. He'd put far too many people's lives in jeopardy and in the process become someone he didn't know anymore. "I don't have time to hang around. There is still

one of the gang members out there, and I plan to bring him
to justice."

"So does this mean you're leaving town for good?" Sanders asked.

"Rumor has it they're headed for Texas." He shoved Catherine's
image aside as he grabbed his hat off the desk. She'd forget all about
him again, once he was gone. Just like the last time. "I've done all
I can do here."

"Suit yourself, though I think I'd like one of these quiet towns
where there's not much more to do than watch the corn grow in the
summer and the snow fall in the winter."

"After all that's happened in the past couple of weeks, that would
be appealing."

But not here. He still had a job to finish.

Corbin nodded his thanks and then headed outside. He gave the
main street of town one final look then rode off, leaving Revenge
behind forever.

Chapter Twenty-four
....

"Corbin Hunter's coming back, you know. As soon as he catches the rest of the gang."

Catherine looked up at Emily from her needlework and shook her head. Isaiah Morgan O'Conner, with his tuft of red hair, lay in his mother's arms sleeping peacefully. The sweet baby was the one good thing that had come of the past few weeks.

"I wasn't enough to hold him here before, and nothing has changed this time. It's something I have to accept."

Life had swept through like a whirlwind and dumped a handful of heartache on the Morgan sisters, and none of them had emerged unscathed. The sudden death of their father was still a constant reminder of all they had missed. For Catherine, the pain emerged late at night or in odd hours of the day when something reminded her of a moment she'd spent with him, reassuring her that there had been good times bundled up with the bad times. Corbin had become simply one more tragic memory she needed to put behind her.

Catherine glanced at Audrey and Lily's neat stitches and compared them to her own uneven row. Emily had insisted that the handwork would get their minds off everything, but all it had managed to do was remind her why she hated the monotonous work—and that no amount of stitches could erase what had happened.

In spite of her good intentions, the despondency she'd felt since Corbin left two weeks ago resurfaced. She'd learned that, in some ways, Corbin was no different than her father. Corbin could never be tied down by a wife and family. His leaving Revenge without saying good-bye had proven as much.

"Would you like Milena to get you a cup of hot tea, Catherine?" Emily asked. "You're positively restless today."

"I'm fine, thank you." Catherine dropped her handwork onto the seat beside her and stood to stretch her legs, wishing she felt as peaceful as baby Isaiah looked. The child had no worries at the moment, certainly not any as enormous as her concerns for Corbin Hunter. She'd been told by the new acting sheriff that Corbin had left for Texas, where the remaining member of the Masked Gang was said to be hiding out. Over the past two weeks, the promise she'd had him make in finding her father's killers seemed far less urgent.

Especially if Corbin were killed in the process.

She shoved aside the bundle of uncertainties she'd collected and stopped at the whatnot in the corner of the room, reminding herself that Corbin Hunter was no longer a part of her life. She'd severed any remaining ties the day she told him she didn't love him anymore.

The shelves were full of glass pieces from Grady's factory and a few knickknacks passed down from their mother. A small, wooden box lay on the middle shelf she hadn't noticed before.

Catherine tapped the edge of the shelf. "I don't remember this box. It's beautiful."

Emily looked up from her work. "It was a gift from Father for the baby."

Catherine picked up the smooth wooden box and ran her fingers across the top.

"He told me he saw it in the window of a shop in Chicago and had to buy it. The strange thing about it is, there isn't a key for it, so I can't open it."

"There's not a key?" Catherine turned over the box and studied the carved top.

"Father simply said that when the time was right, I'd know how to open it. Strange, isn't it?"

Emily's words sent chills down Catherine's spine. "Maybe not."

You'll know when the time comes.

"Why do you say that?" Emily asked.

Catherine sat back down on the settee, still holding the box. "What if Father really did bring back with him a secret from Alaska?"

"What do you mean?" Lily looked up from her handwork.

Catherine slipped the key he'd given her from around her neck. "He gave me a key and told me the same thing. That I would know when the time came."

Lily and Audrey moved in beside her.

"So you think the key is for the box?" Emily asked.

Catherine fingered the key. "There's only one way to find out."

Catherine slid the metal piece into the lock and turned it. A perfect fit. With her fingers trembling, she opened the lid. Inside were five sealed envelopes, the first one addressed to the four of them.

"Open it," Audrey said.

She slid open the envelope and pulled out a letter. Her father's familiar handwriting lay in front of her.

Lily leaned forward. "What is it?"

"A letter from Father." Catherine's eyes misted. There were so many things she wanted to ask him. So many things left unsaid.

Emily nodded. "Read it to us."

Catherine choked back the tears and began reading.

August 7, 1884

My dearest daughters,

If you are reading this letter, then you can be assured that I did everything I could to protect you but have obviously failed. For this I am so sorry. It seems that I have spent my life regretting the choices I've made. All I can ask of you at this point is that you forgive me. My selfishness has cost me far more than I ever imagined.

I never told any of you the complete truth about my time in Alaska, or that I left just over nine months ago. I'd finally made a decent amount of money. Not a fortune, perhaps, as many, but enough that I felt I could return to Revenge with my head held high for all the time I'd wasted away from my family.

When my business partner was killed in a landslide, I had my suspicions that it was more than an accident, but dozens of people die out on the frontier each year, and those in charge have little time to investigate every incident. It didn't take me long to conclude that someone wanted my gold—a common pastime for men who were either too lazy or thought they were too smart to do their own work. Con games run as fast and free as the liquor.

I longed to return home, but believed if someone had overheard a conversation about the gold, they'd also heard

*me speak of the four of you and our home here. I did
everything I could to hide what I carried in my bag. For
the following months, I travelled simply and never spoke
to anyone again about my adventures in Alaska. The only
thing I wanted was to return home to the four of you and
give you what you deserved so many years ago.*

*The problem was, I was still uncertain who was after me,
which meant I was uncertain how to protect you. So, I finally
came up with a plan. I'd bring the money home, but not tell
anyone about it, though I had no illusions that one day, the
man who was after me would confront me.*

*Once here, I did my best to find out who it was. I had
been tipped off before leaving Alaska about a con man who
preyed on innocent woman. This led me to believe that he
was one of the men in your lives—a man who had weaseled
his way into your hearts. Grady was immediately out of
the picture, as I'd rarely seen a man so much in love with
his wife. Corbin seemed an unlikely suspect as well, as I'd
known his parents before he was even born and would
have recognized his face on the Alaskan frontier. That left
Harrison Tucker and John Guild, both men who seemed to
love my daughters. But one, I feared, was an impostor.*

*As I said at the beginning of my letter, I suppose there is
a good chance that if you are reading this letter, then either
I have exposed the impostor and we are all reading together,
or more likely, I fear, the impostor has made real his threats
and killed me. All I can do is pray that I have not endangered
the lives of you and my grandchild.*

There is not much more I can say, other than I'm sorry for everything I have done to you. In this box is an envelope for each one of you containing one thousand dollars. Use it wisely, and never let the love of money take you away from what is truly important. For you are that to me—my four precious diamonds who will always be worth more to me than any cache of gold.

Sincerely,
Isaiah Morgan

Catherine dropped the letter onto her lap, her hands shaking. "So now we know the truth about why Father returned."

"He really did love us," Emily said.

Catherine felt her chest constrict. "I never told him I loved him. I never forgave him."

Audrey reached out and squeezed her hand. "I know he understood."

Catherine held up the other four envelopes, each addressed to one of the girls. "He really did strike gold."

She drew in a staggered breath. Except all the money in the world could never make up for the father she'd never really known. She handed out the envelopes then opened hers. A slip of paper fell from the envelope. Catherine picked it up and recognized her father's handwriting again.

I understand what you went through. Thank you. Just know that I love you.

Catherine excused herself and went outside to the porch and let the tears run freely.

"I forgive you, Father. Not because of the money, but because you loved us."

And for the first time in years, a wave of peace washed over her as she watched the setting sun nestle above the rows of corn in the distance.

* * *

Corbin pulled on the reins and stopped in front of the O'Conner farmhouse. His pulse quickened. How one woman could cause him more apprehension than an outlaw, he'd never know. He slid off his horse then stopped at the bottom of the porch stairs, praying he'd made the right decision.

Five hundred miles of thinking tended to give one plenty of time to contemplate life, and in that time he'd come to one conclusion. Trying to win back Catherine Morgan might result in her sending him packing before the evening was over, but he wasn't going away without one final showdown. If he'd learned anything in the past couple of weeks—besides the folly of revenge—it was that he'd never stopped loving her.

He took the porch stairs two at a time, swallowed any remnants of his pride, and knocked on the front door. A moment later, Catherine answered. He opened his mouth but couldn't speak.

"Sheriff."

"Mrs. Morrilton...she told me you would be here."

"I didn't think you were coming back."

He shoved his hands into his front pockets. "I had some business to take care of."

"Oh." The disappointment in her voice was clear.

"That's not…" Catherine's three sisters appeared behind her like mother hens protecting their young. "That's not what I meant. Could we speak…alone?"

"It's been a long time, Sheriff," Audrey piped up.

Perhaps he'd been wrong in coming. "I'm not the sheriff anymore."

"So we heard." Catherine's frown deepened.

Corbin's heart sank. Had he really expected his coming back to be easy when he'd left without even saying good-bye?

"I know I'd be obliged if you got her out of the house for a few minutes," Audrey rambled on. "She's been running back and forth between here and the store, trying to keep her customers happy while taking care of Emily and her new baby."

Corbin couldn't help but smile. "She is good at that."

"She could use a bit of fresh air," Lily said.

"Definitely," Emily added.

Catherine set her hands on her hips then blew out a quick breath. "Last I looked, I was perfectly able to make a decision myself."

"So?" Corbin's heart faltered as he waited for her answer.

The timid smile she gave him melted away the edges of his apprehension. Maybe his plan would work after all. A moment later, Corbin walked down the quiet lane beside Catherine, breathing in the scent of her lavender as the setting sun exploded in bright rays of yellow and orange along the horizon. In the two weeks since he'd left, he'd found himself missing everything about her. The tilt of her head, the sound of her voice, the blue of her eyes… He'd played the fool once all those years ago when he hadn't been man enough to do anything about it. And now he'd done it again. Except this time, he'd realized that walking out of Catherine Morgan's life wasn't the answer.

"We heard they hanged John Guild." Catherine broke the silence between them.

"Six days ago." The victory from revenge had been swift and subtle, but had left him with little more than a deep sadness over the lives taken in the process. Because as sweet as revenge promised to be, even John's death couldn't bring his father back.

"I'm sorry," she began. "Not that John Guild is dead, but sorry everything had to turn out that way. That broke my sister's heart."

"How is Lily? I've thought about her these last few days."

"It's been hard on her, but she's strong. A friend of my father's, Mr. Peterson, was able to find a job for her in Cleveland, working for the Cleveland Telephone Company. I think the change will help her forget."

"Are you all right with her leaving?"

"I'll miss her terribly, but I think she'll be back as soon as she has time to heal. Although, I'm not sure it's possible to completely get over what John did to her."

"She'll find someone, somewhere, who loves her for who she is without any pretenses. What about Audrey?"

"I think she's about forgiven Harrison. I expect them to be married by next spring."

"I didn't return just to talk about your sisters." Corbin's hand brushed her arm. It was time to get to the point. "I came back to talk about us."

Tears pooled in the corners of Catherine's eyes, and she started walking again.

"Wait a minute. Please." Corbin rubbed the back of his neck. He'd rehearsed his explanation a thousand times, but now that he was here, he couldn't remember anything. "When…when I heard that gunshot and thought John Guild had killed you, I thought I'd lost you again, but that wasn't all. I realized that my thirst for vengeance put you and your sisters at risk."

Catherine stopped at a clump of purple wildflowers on the edge of the road back into town and picked one before breathing in its fragrance. "I made the decision to get involved because my sisters' lives were at stake."

"That's not all. I spent the past two weeks praying and seeking God's will. Something I should have done months ago. In the process, God showed me that men will always have evil schemes, but I have to trust in the One who created me by letting go of the thirst for revenge that had taken over my heart." Corbin searched for the right words. "I thought I could walk away and put you, memories we shared, even the resentment I've felt all these years behind me, but for the past two weeks, all I've been able to think about are all the things left unsaid between us."

Catherine took a step backward. "I don't know—"

"Don't run away from me again. Not this time, because the timing will never be perfect. I thought we decided we were done with secrets." He reached for her hand and grasped her fingertips. "You already broke my heart once, and I know I can handle it again if I have to. All I want to ask is one question."

She fiddled with the flower's stem between her fingers then nodded. "All right."

"Why did you call off our wedding?"

Tears streamed down her face but she didn't pull away from him this time. "What do you want me to say? That I never stopped loving you?"

"I know you loved me, Catherine Ann Morgan." He pulled her closer to him. "I planned to marry you and spend the rest of my life with you."

"My mother couldn't keep my father." Sobs raked her body. "Who was I to force you to stay here and take care of my family?"

"That wasn't your decision to make. I'm not your father. I wouldn't have left you. Nor did I need you to try and protect me. I loved you." His shoulders drooped with the admission. "And no matter how hard I've tried not to, I still love you."

Her chin dipped. He reached out and tilted it up so he could look at her. The last yellow rays of sunlight pierced through the branches of the tree above them, and her eyes sparkled a mixture of blue and gray and gave him hope.

His emotions pulled taut across his chest. "Tell me you never stopped loving me."

Tears rolled down her cheeks. "I never stopped loving you."

There was no going back now. He was going to do what he should have done weeks ago—kiss her properly. Drawing her against him, he leaned down and found her lips, reveling in the softness of her touch. The hollowness in his heart began to fill with every second that passed, satisfying needs long left unmet.

After a long moment, Catherine pulled away, breathless, but she didn't try to escape the confines of his arms. "I'm sorry. Sorry for letting my fears and my pride rob us of what we had together."

"You were wrong about something, you know." His chest heaved with the joy that he hadn't lost her. "It's not too late for us."

A smile lit Catherine's face. "If Mrs. McBride were to see us out here…"

"Let Mrs. McBride say what she wants." He wiped a tear from her face. "Have I ever told you that I love you?"

"Once or twice. A thousand years ago." She took a step back and looked up at him. "What happens now?"

"I take you home, and we figure things out one day at a time. Things like a wedding and babies…" He ran his thumb down her cheek, his head still spinning. Like Jacob in the Bible, the seven years that had separated them suddenly didn't matter—because he was finally looking at a future with the only woman he'd ever loved.

POST CARD
CARTE POSTALE
Love Finds You

Want a peek into local American life—past and present?
The *Love Finds You*™ series published by Summerside Press
features real towns and combines travel, romance,
and faith in one irresistible package!

The novels in the series—uniquely titled after American towns with unusual but intriguing names—inspire romance and fun. Each fictional story draws on the compelling history or the unique character of a real place. Stories center on romances kindled in small towns, old loves lost and found again on the high plains, and new loves discovered at exciting vacation getaways. Summerside Press plans to publish at least one novel set in each of the 50 states. Be sure to catch them all!

NOW AVAILABLE IN STORES

Love Finds You in Miracle, Kentucky by Andrea Boeshaar
ISBN: 978-1-934770-37-5

Love Finds You in Snowball, Arkansas by Sandra D. Bricker
ISBN: 978-1-934770-45-0

Love Finds You in Romeo, Colorado by Gwen Ford Faulkenberry
ISBN: 978-1-934770-46-7

Love Finds You in Valentine, Nebraska by Irene Brand
ISBN: 978-1-934770-38-2

Love Finds You in Humble, Texas by Anita Higman
ISBN: 978-1-934770-61-0

Love Finds You in Last Chance, California by Miralee Ferrell
ISBN: 978-1-934770-39-9

Love Finds You in Maiden, North Carolina by Tamela Hancock Murray
ISBN: 978-1-934770-65-8

Love Finds You in Paradise, Pennsylvania by Loree Lough
ISBN: 978-1-934770-66-5

Love Finds You in Treasure Island, Florida by Debby Mayne
ISBN: 978-1-934770-80-1

Love Finds You in Liberty, Indiana, by Melanie Dobson
ISBN: 978-1-934770-74-0

Love Finds You in Poetry, Texas by Janice Hanna
ISBN: 978-1-935416-16-6

Coming Soon

Love Finds You in Sisters, Oregon by Melody Carlson
ISBN: 978-1-935416-18-0

Love Finds You in Charm, Ohio by Annalisa Daughety
ISBN: 978-1-935416-17-3

Love Finds You in Bethlehem, New Hampshire by Lauralee Bliss
ISBN: 978-1-935416-20-3

Love Finds You in North Pole, Alaska by Loree Lough
ISBN: 978-1-935416-19-7

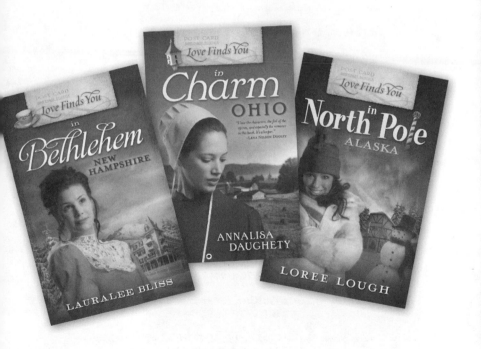

summerside
PRESS